T0113654

Praise for the novels of Tate Hallaway

Dead If I Do

"Abounds with magic, zombies, vampires, and ghosts so there is no shortage of fantasy action in the story to go along with the romance . . . A satisfying read and even though it is set in the dead of a Wisconsin winter (*brrrr*) it still ticks all the boxes for a fun summer read." —*LoveVampires*

"Bright, funny . . . Delivers all bridezilla's worst night-mares." —*Monsters and Critics*

"Quirky, different, and amusing . . . *Dead If I Do* is an interesting read full of twists, turns, and 'OMG what is going to happen to this poor couple next' anticipation. . . .You'll love it." —*Fang-tastic Books*

"The story line is fast paced from the moment Teréza curses the happy couple. Filled with angst yet amusing, *Dead If I Do* is a terrific bewitching tale." —*Genre Go Round Reviews*

"This paranormal romance overflows with danger, excitement, and mayhem; however, whenever things become too stressful a healthy dose of irony or comedy shows up to ease the way. Tate Hallaway has an amazing talent for storytelling." —*Huntress Book Reviews*

"This chapter in the first-person series is packed with humor, wackiness, and a touch of pathos. It's a genuinely heart-warming treat for fans!" —*Romantic Times*

continued . . .

Romancing the Dead

"A fun book with a nice whodunit, great characters, and the kind of detail that really brings a setting alive . . . a wonderfully fun read."   —*Errant Dreams Reviews*

"Ms. Hallaway provides another exciting adventure in her unique series."   —*Darque Reviews*

"This superb tale affirms the theory that 'life's a witch' worth reading about."   —*Genre Go Round Reviews*

"Lots of danger and comedy set within an extremely well-written plot."   —*Huntress Book Reviews*

"Fans of the Garnet Lacey series will certainly not be disappointed, and those new to this piece of paranormal escapism I'm sure will soon be fans as well."   —*Romance Reviews Today*

"One of the real pleasures of this series has been watching this spunky heroine come into her own . . . This is a genuinely funny, adventurous, and delightful read."   —*Romantic Times*

"Has lots of excitement and mystery to keep you guessing throughout. It's a fun reading treat."   —*Fresh Fiction*

"A truly enjoyable read if you like a jaunt into the paranormal . . . and enjoy humor as well as the more serious side of life!"   —WritersAreReaders.com

Dead Sexy

"Another wild adventure . . . Check out the highly entertaining *Dead Sexy* for a walk on the wild side."
                        —*Romance Reviews Today*

"The second Garnet gem is a delightful whodunit fantasy [with an] offbeat chick-lit style. Tate Hallaway combines romance, paranormal, and mystery into a fun read."
                        —*Midwest Book Review*

Tall, Dark & Dead

"What's not to adore . . . Tate Hallaway has a wonderful gift, Garnet is a gem of a heroine, and *Tall, Dark & Dead* is enthralling from the first page."
—MaryJanice Davidson, *New York Times* bestselling author of *Undead and Unwelcome*

"Tate Hallaway kept me on the edge of my seat . . . A thoroughly enjoyable read!"
—Julie Kenner, *USA Today* bestselling author of *Demon Ex Machina*

"Curl up on the couch and settle in—*Tall, Dark & Dead* is a great way to pass an evening."
—Lynsay Sands, *New York Times* bestselling author of *The Renegade Hunter*

"Will appeal to readers of Charlaine Harris's Sookie Stackhouse series."   —*Booklist*

"Unique, intriguing, and a sexy read . . . lively and fresh . . . and the ending will leave you clamoring for more."
—*Midwest Muse*

"Funny and captivating . . . in the style of the Sookie Stackhouse series [with] an intrepid and expressive heroine . . . Look out, fans of the paranormal, there's a new supernatural heroine in town . . . Tate Hallaway is an author to watch!"
—*Romance Reviews Today*

"I love how Garnet handled everything that came her way with grit, humor, and attitude as she kicked some serious butt! . . . Hallaway keeps you glued to the pages."   —*Romance Junkies*

"[Hallaway's] concise writing style, vivid descriptions, and innovative plot all blend together to provide the reader with a great new look into the love life of witches, vampires, and the undead."   —*Armchair Interviews*

Honeymoon of the Dead

TATE HALLAWAY

BERKLEY BOOKS, NEW YORK

THE BERKLEY PUBLISHING GROUP
Published by the Penguin Group
Penguin Group (USA) Inc.
375 Hudson Street, New York, New York 10014, USA

Penguin Group (Canada), 90 Eglinton Avenue East, Suite 700, Toronto, Ontario M4P 2Y3, Canada
(a division of Pearson Penguin Canada Inc.)
Penguin Books Ltd., 80 Strand, London WC2R 0RL, England
Penguin Group Ireland, 25 St. Stephen's Green, Dublin 2, Ireland (a division of Penguin Books Ltd.)
Penguin Group (Australia), 250 Camberwell Road, Camberwell, Victoria 3124, Australia
(a division of Pearson Australia Group Pty. Ltd.)
Penguin Books India Pvt. Ltd., 11 Community Centre, Panchsheel Park, New Delhi—110 017, India
Penguin Group (NZ), 67 Apollo Drive, Rosedale, North Shore 0632, New Zealand
(a division of Pearson New Zealand Ltd.)
Penguin Books (South Africa) (Pty.) Ltd., 24 Sturdee Avenue, Rosebank, Johannesburg 2196,
South Africa

Penguin Books Ltd., Registered Offices: 80 Strand, London WC2R 0RL, England

This book is an original publication of The Berkley Publishing Group.

This is a work of fiction. Names, characters, places, and incidents either are the product of the author's imagination or are used fictitiously, and any resemblance to actual persons, living or dead, business establishments, events, or locales is entirely coincidental. The publisher does not have any control over and does not assume any responsibility for author or third-party websites or their content.

Copyright © 2010 by Lyda Morehouse.
Cover illustration by Megan Berkheiser. Cover design by Diana Kolsky.
Interior text design by Kristin del Rosario.

All rights reserved.
No part of this book may be reproduced, scanned, or distributed in any printed or electronic form without permission. Please do not participate in or encourage piracy of copyrighted materials in violation of the author's rights. Purchase only authorized editions.
BERKLEY® is a registered trademark of Penguin Group (USA) Inc.
The "B" design is a trademark of Penguin Group (USA) Inc.

PRINTING HISTORY
Berkley trade paperback edition / May 2010

Library of Congress Cataloging-in-Publication Data

Hallaway, Tate.
    Honeymoon of the dead / Tate Hallaway. — Berkley trade pbk. ed.
        p. cm.
    ISBN 978-0-425-23412-9 (trade pbk.)
    1. Vampires—Fiction. 2. Honeymoons—Fiction. 3. Minneapolis (Minn.)—Fiction. 4. Occult fiction.
5. Chick lit. I. Title.
    PS3608.A54825H66 2010
    813'.6—dc22

                                                                    2010001851

147028622

For my beloveds: Shawn and Mason

Acknowledgments

First of all, I must take a bittersweet moment and say good-bye to all the characters found herein as this is the last of the Garnet Lacey series. "Gucci, Gucci, Garnet, you were a good series."

Despite that old adage about a writer's life being a solitary one, I find I've always been helped along in the process by a number of indispensable people. First, as always, the lovely and talented Anne Sowards, my editor, and the wise and indefatigable Martha Millard, the best agent anyone could ask for (seriously!).

Fellow writers who took the rough edges off this manuscript and smoothed them into the polished perfection you see before you now are Naomi Kritzer, who always sees the themes I intended and helps me exploit them, and Sean M. Murphy, who makes for an excellent plot monkey. The fine-grain sander on this work was brought to you by my incredibly supportive and infinitely patient partner, Shawn Rounds. Computer game breaks, silly fests, and very best parts of the story are thanks to my ever brilliant son, Mason.

Also a last-minute rescue was performed by Patrick Wood, computer god extraordinaire. I couldn't ask for better friends. Thank you. Your generosity astounds and touches me deeply.

Acknowledgments

The Minneapolis/Saint Paul in this book mostly exists, though it reflects the Cities as I see them in my own head. And, though last time I checked, there are no trolls on the city buses, my friend Nick Dykstra drives one and he's been a lot of things including an orc.

Lastly, thanks to you, faithful reader. I hope that after an appropriate period of mourning, you will continue to follow the strange meanderings of my imagination wherever it goes next.

Blessed be to you all and merry meet again.

1.

The Lovers

A honeymoon in Transylvania with her vampire hus-band. I ask you: What more could a witch ask for?

Well, for starters: How about everything going smoothly for a change and this plane leaving the tarmac sometime this year?

Minnesotans like to say "could be worse" or "can't complain" at times like this, but I've been living in Madison, Wisconsin, for several years now, so forget that. Besides, my wedding was nearly a nonstarter, what with the ex-wife zombie and all, so was it too much to ask that my honeymoon be just a touch better?

I could probably deal if the airline hadn't screwed up so that Sebastian and I not only didn't get first-class seats but also now sat two rows apart with me wedged between a sumo wrestler and a stringy-haired teen with his MP3 player so loud I could hear every word Slip Knot belted out.

And then there was the dinner with my Minneapolis cousins who couldn't make my wedding. My mother had insisted we see them before we left for our honeymoon, despite the fact that Sebastian and I had nothing in common with the ultraconservative, fundamentalist Christian, meat-loving side of my family. My stomach was still urpy after making polite attempts to ingest bacon-wrapped chicken drowned in beefy marinara sauce. I don't think they had a vegetable in the entire house! And the wedding present! Who wants to lug a heavy, antique porcelain figurine of two cherubic angels all the way to Europe? We would have shipped it home, but there just wasn't time, what with the storm and a plane to catch.

I didn't want that horrible thing in my possession at all. Sebastian privately joked about just leaving it on the side of the road, but it was Great-Aunt So-and-So's, so now it was taking up valuable space in my luggage.

My stomach roiled unhappily.

The heavy metal bass line beat in time to the pounding of my head.

Couldn't we at least get off the ground?

I adjusted my hips in the narrow seat and looked around the other passenger's girth at the gleaming expanse of the jet's wing through the window.

Admittedly, Sebastian and I couldn't have picked a nastier

time of year to go on honeymoon. At least the flights were cheap thanks to the New Year's holiday. Sleet rained from a dismally gray sky. It'd been an oppressive drive up from Madison to the Saint Paul/Minneapolis International Airport yesterday. If it wasn't for the oh-you'll-have-a-lovely-time-with-them-I-promise cousins, we'd have headed south to O'Hare and hopped a direct flight to Austria, but no . . . Instead, we braved ice slicks on the curvy stretches of Interstate 94 that had me holding on to the door handle with white knuckles. The snow really started hitting somewhere around Menomonee. The weather had only grown worse and worse the closer we got to the Cities. Honestly, I'd been surprised they'd let us board. I was sure the flight was going to be canceled.

In a way, I wished they *would* just call the whole thing off. At least then Sebastian and I could be laughing at our misfortune while snuggled under a scratchy blanket at a Days Inn.

I wished we could even just sit together.

I turned back to try to catch Sebastian's eye when the teen accidentally elbowed my breast. My stomach lurched in a you're-falling-catch-yourself sensation. I rubbed the injured part absently as I acknowledged the teen's mumbled apology. Laying my head back on the hard cushion of the seat, I waited for the dizziness to pass.

I'd been getting these strange touches of vertigo for a couple of weeks now.

In fact, I got them nearly any time someone touched

me. It was almost as if the nausea was some kind of magical feedback loop when my aura and someone else's collided unexpectedly.

Sometimes I experienced double vision too.

I should've probably told my new husband about all this before we booked a flight to Vienna, but I didn't want to worry him. Sebastian and I'd had a lot of adventures so far—crazy stuff involving zombies, shape-shifters, and ex-dead Gypsy ex-wives. And, you know, I just didn't want to burden us with what could just be some version of witch-aura flu.

Rubbing the space between my eyes, my frown deepened. In fact, because Sebastian and I had such a tendency toward trouble, before we left, I cast a just-let-it-all-be-normal spell. It wasn't much. Just a candle and some hurried visualization before rushing out the door to head to Minneapolis. I sure hoped Mátyás remembered to blow out the candle like I asked.

Mátyás was Sebastian's half-vampire, immortal son, now my stepson. There was something that was going to take some getting used to. Mátyás and I didn't always get along. Now we were family.

Over the intercom, the captain apologized for the continued delay. I snorted in disgust.

Had my "normal" spell even worked?

Given all the problems we'd had on this trip so far, I'd doubt my abilities as a successful witch if it weren't for the fact that where other people talked about being "goddesses,"

I really was one. Okay, really, it was more like this: I had this full-time resident Goddess, Lilith, whom I accidentally permanently bonded to me when I needed help fighting off an American Indian Trickster God.

The good news was that I could now call on Lilith when those zombies and whatnot attacked Sebastian and me, but the bad news was that She was the Queen of Hell and Mother of Demons.

And, worse, the more time we stayed together, the more inseparable we became. Yeah, I was becoming the original bitch. Nice, huh? I felt it today for sure. Carefully, I shifted in my seat, impatient for some movement. The snow outside continued to fall.

No offense to Sebastian, but I wished we were headed somewhere warmer—the Bahamas, Tahiti, or even Greece.

That reminded me, I was actually carrying two Goddesses around. Because of Lilith's darker side and tendency to destroy anything She touched, I called on another Goddess during the last big crisis that befell us—Athena. She could be hanging around because I kind of sort of promised to devote my life to Her worship in exchange for Her help.

In retrospect, that might have been a mistake.

I mean, I was beginning to think that maybe my body was overcrowded, and that was part of what was causing all these flashes of dizziness. Perhaps Lilith and the new Goddess in residence were duking it out for control over my spiritual real estate.

The speaker crackled to life overhead and the captain's

voice informed us that we'd be taking off as soon as the de-icer had a chance to work. Thank Goddess!—whichever one of my divine occupants answered my prayer!

The sumo wrestler's knee grazed mine and I felt that odd disorienting tingle, like the world just shifted under my feet. For a second, I thought maybe the plane was finally moving. I checked out the window. No such luck . . .

And it looked like we wouldn't be going anywhere for some time given that there was a Frost Giant on the wing.

Wait, what?

Doing a classic double take, I looked again. Yep, there she was crouching on the wing with a huge, black wolf-dog at her side. "Giant" might be a bit of a misnomer. She wasn't precisely a ginormous woman, but she had the build of a linebacker and enough magical energy to make her "feel" big. She crouched on the wing, her Prince Valiant cap of white gold hair barely shifting even as her fur cloak flapped furiously in the howling wind. Ice blue eyes met mine and she smiled wickedly.

Hey, this wasn't just any Frost Giant—I knew her!

It was Fonn, the ice-storm demon who tried to ruin Sebastian's birthday last Christmas.

Despite the nausea, I poked the sumo guy in the arm. "Hey," I asked him. "Do you see a woman out there?"

He dutifully pressed his face to the window and then gave me that you're-totally-doing-a-William-Shatner-in-that-*Twilight-Zone*-episode look. "There's no one out there, lady." I think if he could have, he would have edged away from me.

"Really?" Last time I interacted with Fonn she was very real to everyone else. In fact, she nearly sucked the life out of a snowplow driver.

I rubbed my eyes and looked again. Fonn was still there; this time, she waved.

"Seriously, you don't see her?" I asked the sumo wrestler.

Her dog's tail wagged happily. Like a Labrador on steroids, he bounded up to the window to look in at me, and stuck his big, black nose against the windowpane with a smack.

I started, nearly knocking the earbuds out of the teenager.

"Watch it, lady!"

"Sorry," I said, clutching at my spinning stomach. Unbuckling the seat belt, I stood up. The dog's snout left a wet smear on the glass.

"Nobody sees this?" I asked, pointing at the window. "You really don't see a black dog and a big, old Frost Giant with a personal vendetta against me on the wing?"

Because, you know, Sebastian and I did splash antifreeze into her face. She might still be a *little* mad about that.

A flight attendant tottered in high heels down the aisle, her face tense. "Ma'am?"

I glanced toward Sebastian and saw the other attendants looking at me nervously.

Outside of the window, Fonn grinned. She'd moved close enough to look in and she pointed a long, bony finger at me and then to the ground. I didn't need to hear the words her lips made when they moved. The implication was clear: *You're going down!*

"Sit down," groused the teen, as he jabbed the buds back into the hollow of his ear. "You're freaking everybody out."

"Are you all right, ma'am?" the flight attendant asked in a tone as crisp as her uniform and as tight as the bun of her bright blond hair.

Sebastian looked up from where he sat two rows back. He caught my eye and gave me the raise of the eyebrow that asked if everything was okay. I shook my head. Instantly, he started to unbuckle his own seat belt.

"Ma'am? If you could return to your seat . . ." The nervous flight attendant was starting to sound bossy in a very I'm-scared-of-you way. I noticed that another flight attendant seemed to have moved into position to guard the pilots' cabin door.

Nearly everyone was looking at me like I was planning to kill us all. How ironic that no one could see the real danger. Fonn giggled at me from the other side of the window.

"Um," I said, but didn't know where to start. "I'd like to, you know, maybe take the next flight. Please."

Sebastian came up the aisle to stand next to the blond attendant. Another attendant followed at his heels. Her arms pumped as she walked, and I thought she might be ready to tackle him.

Of the two of us, I could understand why the flight attendants might be afraid of Sebastian. Despite being able to walk around in the daylight, there was something preternatural about the silky, fluid way he moved. He'd removed his jacket in deference to the stuffiness of the canned air of the plane. The black T-shirt he wore stretched tight across taut muscles. Matching jeans showed off lean, long legs. Long black hair framed a vaguely aristocratic face and a chin scruffy with five o'clock shadow. He had a lot of the scary don't-mess-with-me-I-could-totally-eat-you vibe. The whole package just screamed *predator*.

And, well, yum. But that was my personal opinion.

By the way the attendants were staring at him, I didn't think they agreed.

"Sir!" The attendant who was trailing Sebastian nearly bowled him over when he came to an abrupt halt. Everyone was crowding around me now. The teen and the sumo wrestler were scowling bitterly up at me.

If Fonn weren't doing the happy Snoopy dance on the wing, I'd totally sink back into my seat and die from embarrassment.

"What's wrong, darling?" Sebastian asked, ignoring all the others.

Everyone was listening, so I couldn't exactly tell the truth. "We should get off the plane, I think," I jerked my head in the direction of the window.

Sebastian leaned down to peer through the small, oval opening. He gave me a quizzical look.

I spasmed my head at the window trying to suggest he look. Harder.

"She thinks there's a monster out there," the sumo wrestler said to be helpful.

I glared at him. Dude was *so* not from Minnesota. Here in the Scandinavian-populated upper Midwest we tend to keep our opinions to ourselves.

"Shut up," I said because I was starting to panic and I didn't know what else to say. I noticed that two or three people sitting next to the windows actually lifted their window shutters and checked. Alas, no one confirmed my vision.

Everyone stared at me like I was insane, except Sebastian, who mouthed, *Monster?*

I nodded.

"I strongly suggest you take your seat," said the feisty attendant who'd doggedly pursued Sebastian. She looked ready to grab his elbow and return him to his spot. She touched his sleeve urgently.

It was obvious he didn't like to be pawed at. Narrowing his eyes, Sebastian looked down at her from an intimidating height. "My wife and I will be disembarking," he said in a tone that wasn't to be trifled with. I smelled cinnamon and baking bread. He was using his vampire glamour. "Make it happen."

Someone—I think it was the teenager—groaned unhappily.

The flight attendants all bobbled their heads in disagreement and frustration. "It's impractical," said one. "We'll have to call security," said another. "I'll alert the captain," said the last, and she hurried off to do so.

Once the aisle was mostly cleared of attendants, Sebastian went back to fetch his bags from the overhead compartments. I stepped over the teen to get my own. I'd forgotten how heavy the statue was and nearly brained him. "Sorry," I said.

He shook his head at me. "You're crazy."

Fonn curled her fingers in a flirtatious wave.

"Yep," I said, hitching the bag over my shoulder. Sebastian retrieved his and came back to stand by me. Our every move was scrutinized by the other passengers. A toddler stood on his seat, his eyes following me as he slowly extracted boogers from his nose.

Cold, fresh air gusted into the cabin. Three National Guard soldiers armed with guns came in and looked around. One of the flight attendants pointed at us. They shouldered their weapons and moved toward Sebastian and me.

"You're sure about this?" Sebastian whispered to me.

I took a last glance at Fonn. Her face was plastered against the window. She seemed to be trying to figure out what was going on. She frowned at the sight of the soldiers. I resisted the urge to stick my tongue out and say, "Nyah-nyah!"

The guardsmen focused on Sebastian, sparing me only the barest notice. "Come with us, sir," said a serious young man with a sprinkling of freckles across his nose. His eyes flicked to me. "Ma'am."

It wasn't like we had a lot of choice. Turns out it was a guard for each of us, and one to carry our bags, which I guess would be searched and all that. I hoped they didn't mistake the cherubs for some kind of weapon.

They flanked us expertly. I didn't much like the look of the guns. I cringed closer against Sebastian and kept checking in with a glance. He gave me a brave smile that buoyed me during the long walk down the length of the plane.

As we were hustled out, I noticed someone else standing up and reaching for his overhead bags. He had short brown hair, big sad eyes, and an ordinary business suit. Everyone else on the plane looked nervous and ready to bolt.

The boarding ramp tube had been reattached and the wind howled and lashed against it like it was trying to get in. Given how mad Fonn probably was that I thwarted her plans, maybe it was.

"Bad weather," noted one of the guards.

I was about to engage in some small talk, when I was informed I'd be going one way, and Sebastian another. "Wait," I said. "I want to be with my husband!"

An arm restrained me, and I felt all swoony, like I might faint.

"It'll be okay," Sebastian said.

As we moved away, I craned my neck continuously until Sebastian disappeared from sight. Great, now I was on a honeymoon sans husband.

You know, for the record, I might not have chosen to wear my black leather jacket with all the chains and buckles and the gigantic white skull on the back if I'd known I'd be spending time in a Homeland Security holding cell.

The room I was in reminded me less of a prison than a run-down, outdated office cubicle, except with real walls. One of the security guards that had escorted us off the plane offered me a seat in a springy, wheeled chair opposite a large, scarred faux-wood desk. On the desk was a blotter complete with doodles, piles of papers, and a tiny American flag in a pencil holder. A picture of the president smiled beatifically at me from a small, framed print on the wall behind the desk.

In stark contrast, the security guard that stood at the door frowned sternly in my general direction much as he had for the last half hour.

I'm not a very patient person. I don't wait well. I fiddled. I twitched. I bounced the squeaky springs on the metal chair. I tried to engage grumpy guard in conversation about the weather several times and was rebuffed with a simple, "Just try to relax, ma'am."

Relax? What could they possibly be doing with my passport all this time? Why hadn't anyone come to let me out of here yet? Where was Sebastian? Had they found the hideous angel sculpture in my luggage? Did they think it was a weapon of massively bad taste? Or that I was some religious nut?

I tapped my toe and chewed my lip. My buckles clanked as I adjusted in my seat for the six thousandth time. Finally, the door opened.

I nearly leaped into the man's arms. "Dominguez!"

My first impression, as always with Gabriel Dominguez, was: cop. He was actually FBI, but there was just something about his walk, that steely-eyed gaze, the perpetually stern expression, the sharp, military haircut, and the dark, off-the-rack, yet well-fitting business suit that spelled c-o-p.

I felt myself smiling.

Though I first met Dominguez when he was trying to connect me to the murder of the Order of Eustace agents who killed my coven, we'd become friends . . . or good acquaintances . . . or, okay, maybe his kindness toward me might have been prompted by a little love spell that went awry, but still, I knew him. We mostly liked each other, I thought. Although he didn't exactly return my warm enthusiasm. In fact, he stood stiffly as I slowly unwrapped my arms from him.

"Oh, um." I straightened my jacket. "I mean, hi."

"Garnet," Dominguez nodded briskly in acknowledgment of our at least knowing each other.

An equally intense-looking black woman in a dark suit came into the room. Her hair was ironed straight, colored slightly reddish, and cut into a bob. She wore a skirt and fancy, Italian pumps that made me wonder if she ever dared step outside in the snow. She shot Dominguez a look that implied she didn't approve of his taste in acquaintances.

Taking a step away as though to distance himself from me, Dominguez gestured to his colleague, "Garnet Lacey, this is Special Agent Francine Peterson."

I quickly dropped my arms to my side and tried to act like I hadn't just been hugging an FBI agent.

She held out her hand for me to shake. When our palms touched, I got hit with vertigo. I nearly stumbled, but she caught my elbow. Looking up into her eyes, I saw bright emerald green irises, with cat-slit pupils staring back at me.

In surprise, I jumped back, breaking contact. The chair toppled with a bang.

For a second, I experienced a ripple of double vision, like the ghosts of bad TV reception. A Celtic faerie queen, with a porcelain white face and coal black curls and an African American FBI agent in navy blue wool power suit briefly occupied the same space before snapping back into . . . reality?

"Garnet!" Dominguez admonished, "What's wrong with you?"

That was the million-dollar question, wasn't it?

I glanced somewhat sheepishly at Special Agent Peterson, whose frown only deepened after my outburst. "Sorry," I said, and opting for the truth, added, "I've been getting these weird fainting spells lately."

"Have you had your blood pressure checked?" Peterson asked, and I swore I could hear the slight lilt of an Irish brogue in her voice.

"No," I said, eyeing her suspiciously. Was this faerie queen in league with Fonn? Righting the chair, I sank back into it too tired to fight even if she were.

It had never occurred to me that my dizzy spells might

have a mundane cause. Blood pressure? Wouldn't that be ironic?

Maybe I did just have the witch-aura flu!

"Can I get you a glass of water or something?" Dominguez offered kindly, putting a hand on my shoulder. At the contact, I steeled myself for another wave of vertigo, but it never came. Dominguez must have his psychic shields up. "Is this why you asked to leave the plane?"

"Not really," I said.

Dominguez settled on the edge of the desk, and his partner stood beside him with her hands resting lightly on her hips. The way he sat, his suit coat bulged open just so that the butt of Dominguez's gun showed plainly in its shoulder holster. He looked like one of those guys on cop shows, only I was the one sitting in the villain seat.

I tapped my toes nervously.

Since they seemed to be waiting for me to say something, I started talking. "Thing is," I said, "I have been feeling weird lately and I was *going* to go to the doctor after our big trip—you know, our honeymoon. I just . . . you know, I didn't want to ruin things." As I spoke I didn't look at Dominguez, because I was concerned about his reaction to the whole honeymoon bit. I mean, he did ask me to marry him once, even if it was under magical duress.

"That would be your trip to Austria?" Dominguez's voice betrayed no emotion.

"Yes," I said, hazarding a glance in his direction. His eyes stayed focused on the notes he was taking into a flip-top notepad he had balanced on his knee. I willed him to look at me, and his eyes flicked up momentarily. I tried to think "I'm sorry" in his general direction.

Dominguez *was* psychic, after all.

Seriously, he was.

I'd noticed his abilities in his aura when we first met. He even admitted that he suspected as much, but he tended to chalk those experiences up to a cop's intuition.

Thus, I continued to think things at him, like, "Really, I'm not crazy" and "You've got to believe me."

He shook his head at me. I wasn't sure if I should interpret that as a "No, I don't" or as "Sorry, the signal isn't getting through."

"Explain to us why you requested to disembark the plane, Ms. Lacey," Dominguez said.

"I suppose it's technically Mrs. Von Traum, but, well, I didn't take his name. That just seemed so old-fashioned to me," I said with a little laugh. No one else found it amusing, however. "Uh, well"—I looked between the psychic FBI agent and the Queen of the Faeries, and said truthfully—"there was a Frost Giant on the wing, and it just didn't seem safe."

Peterson laughed, or at least I thought I heard the echo of distant laughter, as Dominguez repeated incredulously, "You mean, you could see frost on the wing? And you felt it was unsafe?"

"Sure," I agreed, because that was kind of what I said, if you skipped over the whole supernatural part. I shifted in my seat, causing the buckles of my jacket to clatter against the metal. "I mean, do you trust that deicer stuff? All those chemicals and whatever?"

Peterson's brown eyes sparkled with a hint of green as she asked, "Are you aware that the plane you were on was forced to make an emergency landing shortly after take-off?"

"Bright Goddess!" I exclaimed. Though I was horrified to hear about the plane, strangely I also felt a brief hint of relief. I mean, maybe I wasn't entirely crazy. It was possible Fonn really *had* been out there, icing those wings. "Is everyone on the plane okay?"

"There were no injuries reported," Peterson said, matter-of-factly.

"But perhaps you can see why some might feel you had inside information," Dominguez added.

"Or," I said, looking him straight in the eye, "I might have been psychic."

"The FBI and Homeland Security don't believe in psychic powers," Dominguez informed me.

That's hilarious given your abilities and the fact that your partner is the Queen of the Faeries . . . or something, I thought at him. Out loud, I said, "How about a lucky guess? Does the FBI believe in coincidences?"

"Rarely," he said humorlessly.

"Well, then I'm screwed, aren't I?"

Except, it turns out the FBI *does* believe in rock-solid alibis and a complete lack of any kind of criminal activity.

I mean, I don't even have a speeding ticket on my record, thanks to the fact I'm an environmentally conscious "Green" witch and ride my bike (or the bus) all year round. But, while we waited for all that to check out, I spent a lot of time in the holding area observing Special Agent Francine Peterson.

The more I looked, the more I was absolutely convinced she was a faerie, and I don't mean the fabulous kind.

While she and Dominguez conferred over my astounding lack of connection to anything even vaguely illegal, I watched Peterson out of the corner of my eye. When I didn't look directly at her, but rather used my peripheral vision, I saw a woman with pointy ears, alabaster skin, and an impossible dress made of leaves, vines, and moss. If I shifted even the slightest—snap! She was primly suited Special Agent Peterson again.

What was going on? Was it possible Peterson was a witch and, like me, had accidentally caught and held on to a power she hadn't meant to? Yet, other than the one time when we'd first touched, I didn't get a sense when I looked at Peterson of two people sharing a single body. Plus, every once and a while, I'd catch her smiling this—I don't know quite how to describe it, but it was a kind of odd little "isn't it fun, pretending" childlike grin. Of course, that begged the question, why would the Queen of Faeries pretend to be an FBI agent?

And why could I suddenly see her?

I tapped my feet. Dominguez shot me a would-you-cut-that-out look. In exchange, I twiddled my thumbs.

Despite years of training as a witch, I'd never had any powers like this—at least not with the switch always flipped to "on." Sure, I could use magical senses to perceive the otherworldly beyond-the-veil bits, but I normally had to do a lot of mental prep before getting visions of sugar-plum FBI faeries dancing in my head.

Did my newfound touch-triggered nausea come with the second sight somehow?

If it did, did that mean I was going to start seeing things like this all the time?

Ugh, that prospect horrified me if for no other reason that I really wanted a lot fewer supernatural creatures in my life right now, not more.

When Dominguez flashed me another harsh look, I realized I was tapping my fingers *and* bouncing on my toes. With a chagrined look, I sat on my hands.

But my mind continued to race. I supposed I should also consider the possibility that I might be going crazy, but, well, it wasn't like I hadn't seen Frost Giants and Goddesses before. These sorts of creatures were all part of my everyday life.

I was married to a vampire, after all.

Speaking of him, I glanced at the clock. It had now been over four hours. I wondered how Sebastian was holding up.

It occurred to me that I didn't really know Sebastian's legal status. He was born into the Ottoman Empire or something like that. Did he even have legal papers current to this century? And, if he did, they had to be totally bogus. It's not like they issued birth certificates in the twelfth century, so he must have had someone forge his.

That didn't bode well.

I mean really, the more I thought about it, the more it occurred to me how much of Sebastian's legal life must be a total fraud.

As if on cue, Special Agent Queen of the Faeries asked me in a tone full of ice and suspicion, "How long have you known your husband, Mrs. Von Traum?"

Long enough to know I'm going to fail this quiz, I thought but didn't say. Instead, I replied, "A couple of years. And it's Lacey. Garnet Lacey."

"Is he an American citizen?" Dominguez asked.

"If he wasn't before, he is now," I pointed out, feeling rather smug. When they both shared a long look and then gave me that patented steely-eyed cop stare, I faltered a bit. "He is, isn't he? I mean, marriage makes Sebastian a U.S. citizen, right? I thought that's what that movie *Green Card* was all about. Did you see that one? It had that French guy in it . . . uh, what's his name? I think it started with a D. He was really popular for a while, like, in the eighties. It was a sweet story that movie, I mean. But, wait, that's not why Sebastian married me, of course."

Now they really looked at me like I was up to something sinister.

Maybe I should shut up now. I wasn't sure I was helping Sebastian's case.

* * *

In the end, they had to let me go. Other than being
married to a foreign national, I really hadn't done anything
wrong or associated with anyone who could be considered an
ice-wielding terrorist.

"I guess you *are* just lucky, Mrs. Von Traum," Dominguez
said as he showed me the way back to the ticketing area.

"I still say I was *psychic*," I teased him. "And, really, can't
you call me Garnet? I've been married all of a week. I'm not
used to sounding like I'm someone's mom." Even if I was
Mátyás's now, kind of.

Weird.

Dominguez gave a little chuckle. Instantly he covered
it with a cough and cast a guilty backward glance at his
partner.

"It's not that I'm not happily married, mind you," I said
quickly.

"Sure," Dominguez said softly, leaning close to my ear as
we walked along the back corridors of the airport. "Being
married to a bloodsucker must be all fun and games."

"Hey!" The walls were barren and steely and suddenly far
too close. "That's a little harsh, isn't it?"

Dominguez seemed unfazed by my admonishment.
"Speaking of which, I should tell you that Daniel Parrish
is back."

"Back from where?" I asked. I mean, I'd last seen Parrish in my living room. I hadn't known he'd left for anywhere.

"The dead," Dominguez said in a hushed, but firm tone. He gave a quick glance over his shoulder. But Peterson held back a short distance, like she knew Dominguez had some private business with me, and made small talk with the armed guard.

I nodded to Dominguez. I mean, yeah. No surprise to me. Daniel Parrish was an ex-boyfriend of mine who also happened to be a vampire. He was always kind of back from the dead. It was sort of his raison d'être.

And, anyway, I'd seen Parrish only last night because he was currently zombie-sitting Sebastian's kind of dead ex-wife. It was a long story, and not one I thought I should get into with Dominguez, so I tried to act surprised when I murmured, "Really?"

"The only reason I didn't prosecute you for the murders of those priests is because Parrish took the fall. I thought we had an agreement that he'd stay dead and buried."

Oh. We had? I'd kind of forgotten the arrangement that Parrish stay "dead" thanks to the ex-wife resurfacing. Literally.

"Uh, right," I said, and wondered exactly when my life had gotten so unmanageably weird. "But what are you going to say to the home office even if he is back? 'I thought I caught the guy but it turns out he's a vampire'?"

Dominguez stopped short of a door. His face flushed

red. "Look, if he . . ." Dominguez trailed off with a snarl. Then, after composing himself, he added, "Listen, it's like this: I'm not explaining to headquarters that I closed a case I shouldn't have because of a vampire who wouldn't stay dead and his . . . witch ex-girlfriend."

"I suppose the FBI doesn't believe in witches and vampires either, eh?" I couldn't resist asking.

"No, they don't."

I knew that was a bit of a lie, but I let it go. After all, when he was on my case, Dominguez had let slip that the government knew more than it was telling about the Order of Eustace and their operations in the United States. The order was a rogue offshoot of the Inquisition that took far too seriously the admonishment in Leviticus that one shouldn't suffer a witch to live. They tended to leave a lot of bodies in their wake. Hard for law enforcement not to notice, really.

"Well," I said, "for your sake, I wish they did." After all, it must be hard for Dominguez to be psychic and have to deny it to keep his job. Not to mention carrying the secret that vampires, witches, and a hidden order of witch hunters existed. "Still," I added, "I'm not sure what you expect me to do about Parrish."

"Figure something out." Dominguez just shook his head in warning and, without further ado, propelled me out into the fluorescent brightness of the cavernous main terminal. Sebastian, who had been waiting in one of the orange plastic chairs, stood up, his arms open.

Gratefully, I collapsed into his hug.

Honeymoon of the Dead

*   *   *

To make up for all the hassle, Sebastian booked us the Ordway Room at the posh Saint Paul Hotel. Apparently, this was the place visiting dignitaries stayed when they were in Minneapolis/Saint Paul. It wasn't just one room, it was a series of interconnecting spaces that made me feel a little like I was wandering into someone else's house. There was a living room with a working fireplace, a full bar, and bedroom with a four-poster bed and a fifty-inch plasma TV hidden in a mahogany cabinet.

Although, in all honesty, he could have gotten us a ratty room at the Flea Bag Express, for all I cared. And, given how much it cost per night to stay here, we probably could have hired a private jet to take us directly to Austria.

Still, I was just glad we were alive, together, and nowhere near the airport or Homeland Security or the FBI. All I wanted was to lie down and close my eyes. Especially since, after taking my bags from the bellboy, I got a flash of an image of a smiling monkey with wise, human eyes.

Maybe I needed to revisit the going-crazy possibility. Either that or Saint Paul was overrun with Gods.

While Sebastian tipped the Monkey King, I collapsed face first onto the fluffy king-sized bed. The sheets actually smelled good, like lavender soap.

The room—or rooms, really—was bigger than any I'd ever stayed in before. The hotel billed itself as historic, and it had definitely gone with an old-fashioned decor. All the furniture, including the bed, was fashioned of heavy, dark, ornately carved wood. The ceilings were high and had ornate plaster moldings. A glass chandelier had been fitted with flickering lights that mimicked gas flames. It was somehow both majestic and warm. A bank of windows presumably looked out over the elegant rooftops of downtown toward the Mississippi, though all I could see outside right now were bright streaks of white snow.

All in all, it made a nice sanctuary from everything that had happened so far. Maybe if I closed my eyes the whole day would reboot, like a great, big do-over.

I opened my eyes.

Nope, no luck.

The springs bounced slightly as Sebastian sat down on the other side of the bed. "He was a chatty fellow, wasn't he?"

I flopped my head over to squint up at Sebastian. "The Monkey King? What do you expect?"

Sebastian's eyebrows drew together, and he gave me a considering look. "Honestly, I thought he looked more like a young Jackie Chan. Isn't 'monkey' a little harsh? I'm not always up on current social custom, but I really don't think you're supposed to call anyone a monkey, darling."

"That's not what I meant," I said, propping myself up onto my elbows so I could better read Sebastian's expression. He'd been in a funny mood on the drive to the hotel, very introspective and quiet. We hadn't talked much. Now seemed like the perfect time to broach the subject of the visions and vertigo I'd been getting, but Sebastian's face seemed tight and tired. I'd wait. After all, we'd been through enough already thanks to my stupid, newfound sight. Slumping back against the bed, I pulled a pillow over my face.

"Oh, phooey," I muttered.

He patted my thigh lightly and got up. I could hear him moving around the room. Peeking over the edge of the pillow, I checked. Yep, he was brooding. His eyebrows knitted together tightly as he glanced around for the suitcases. Right now, we should be halfway to Amsterdam for a connecting flight to Vienna. Poor Sebastian. He'd been looking forward to this trip. He told me he hadn't been to his homeland in decades.

Pulling the pillow down to my nose, I peered over the edge at him. "I ruined our honeymoon before it even started, didn't I?"

"It's not over yet." Giving me a tender smile he added, "We'll find a way to salvage this, I'm sure."

I sat up, pulling my knees up. The pillow squashed my tummy and still hid part of my face. "Still. I'm so sorry," I said again. "There was ice, you know."

"My FBI goons informed me of that fact several times," Sebastian said glumly. "It made our departure that much more ominous, apparently."

His words confirmed my suspicion that things had been much more complicated for him, given that he wasn't born in America. I swallowed the urge to apologize again and asked, "Did they rough you up or something?"

He snorted. "Not hardly. I just didn't appreciate their line of questioning."

"Sorry," I said again, unable to hold it back this time.

He shrugged. "It's all right. Maybe if we'd stayed on the plane the—what was it, Frost Giant?—would have found a way to crash the plane."

"It wasn't just any Frost Giant. It was Fonn. Do you remember her?" I asked.

"My birthday present? How could I forget?" He grimaced at the memory. "I suppose it's too much to hope she's done now and will leave us in peace?"

"Given our luck? Doubtful," I mumbled into the pillow.

Sebastian grabbed his suitcase—we'd each only packed one, trying to keep our baggage light for the true European experience—and placed it on one of those luggage racks with the foldout metal legs. He started fussing with his things, unzipping his perfectly organized clothes. His socks were rolled and lined up, from dark brown to black. Shirts so sharply folded I swore they'd cut someone. He very carefully put everything away in the dresser drawers.

Mine, on the other hand, was a mess. I'd be lucky if I remembered to pack a toothbrush. I'd stuffed everything in willy-nilly, and now it was all wrapped around that horrible cherub gift.

I sighed. Look at him: so organized! I should really be more like that. Part of me always secretly wished I was the sort of person people could depend on, you know, the kind that always had a Band-Aid in her purse?

Honestly, I had to stop carrying any kind of handbag because I kept setting them down places and losing them. If it didn't fit in my pockets, I had to leave it at home. Thank Goddess they made slim cells these days. As it was, I lost my phone more than I'd like, and that was when I remembered to keep the battery charged.

Oh shit, I think I forgot the recharger at home.

I was about to say something to Sebastian, when he placed his—and mine—on the bed. He gave me a smile, which I returned, though inwardly I cringed. So much for being the lady with the magic purse o' plenty.

"Looks like you're planning on staying awhile," I noted.

"Didn't you hear the weather report? The cabbie had it on," he said, as he smoothed out his unrumpled shirts one by one. "I suspect we may be snowed in for a few days. But I suppose I should call my travel agent," he continued, sounding disheartened at the mere prospect. "There's certainly another flight tomorrow."

I made a face. Not only was I so, *so* done with airports, there was the real possibility that Fonn might sabotage the next plane as well. I swung my feet over the edge of the bed. "There's no real hurry. I like Minneapolis . . . or Saint Paul, which I guess is where we really are."

The temperature in the room was a bit on the chilly side and I considered snuggling under the blankets, only they seemed so fancy and nice. I didn't want to mess them up. I rubbed my shoulders instead.

"I've never spent much time here," Sebastian admitted. "Usually just passed through."

"You're a million years old and you've never been in the Twin Cities?" I was incredulous. After all, I'd lived here—well, over in the Seward neighborhood in Minneapolis—for nearly four years. I stood up, tossing the pillow back against the headboard.

"I'm only a thousand years old," Sebastian said a bit grumpily.

I resisted the urge to tell him that at his age it was only a matter of degree. After all, the fact that he kept correcting my exaggerations made me realize just how out of sorts he really felt. Nerds, apparently, have been the same since the dawn of time. As hard as it was to believe, my hottie vampire husband had a bit of geek in him. Back in his day, he had been an alchemist, which is a kind of mystical chemist. In other words, a nerdy science type, and when Sebastian got irritable he was possessed by an overwhelming yet completely unconscious desire to be right about everything no matter how insignificant. Most days I found it charming.

Today, when we were both cranky? Not so much.

"The point is," I said with a tight smile, "this is a pretty cool town. You should really see it."

"Maybe we'll have some time tomorrow. We could take a late flight." He seemed much less interested in the prospect than I was. "What about Fonn? Do you think she's still out there?"

"I do. You know what's odd? No one else could see her."

Sebastian, who had finished putting his clothes away, sat himself down on the office chair near the desk. He swiveled back and forth as he talked. "She must have been using magic. You can always see through that, thanks to Lilith." He paused for a moment. He gave me a long, measuring look. I felt like I was under a microscope, and not in a good way. "And our bellhop, what did you say he was?"

"The Monkey King," I said, trying not to sound too defensive.

Sebastian gave me a slow nod of his head. "Well, there are a lot of similarities between Jackie Chan and the Monkey King."

"Be serious," I said, perching myself on the edge of the desk. I folded my arms in front of my chest and gave him a mock serious pout.

"I'm sorry, darling," he said, gently putting a hand on my knee. "I thought I was."

I shrugged my knee out from under his touch, suddenly feeling frustrated. Despite my precaution, the protection spell clearly hadn't worked. In a matter of hours, our lives had spiraled into Bizzaro land. I twisted and untwisted the hems of my sleeves with my fingers. I wished he'd tell me what was on his mind, instead of brooding. "Why aren't you more grumpy with me? You should freak out more. Tell me

I'm acting like a crazy woman. Yell at me for ruining our honeymoon."

"How about I buy us dinner and drinks downstairs instead?"

Is it any wonder I married this man?

The dining room, dubbed the Saint Paul Grill, was a God-free zone at least. It made me feel a little bit better that Aphrodite didn't introduce herself as our waitress, and Anubis wasn't lounging near the fireplace.

In fact, the restaurant was mostly deserted, though that wasn't much of a surprise given the early hour. It was only just after five o'clock.

We took a seat near the window to watch the snow and the downtown rush hour. Despite the overcast and darkening sky, I could see lights of Rice Park across the street. The park was no larger than a couple of city blocks. The trees, bare of their leaves and snow covered, were festooned in bright Christmas bulbs.

Floodlights illuminated the red brick and green copper roof of the castlelike Landmark Center on one end of the park. Just behind it, I could see an eighty-foot pine tree bejeweled in a colorful array of decorations. Despite the slushy snow, people in heavy, Arctic-worthy parkas, hats, scarves, boots, and mittens bustled to cars and city bus stops.

Once we'd ordered drinks and they'd been set on the

white linen tablecloth within easy reach, Sebastian smiled. "Better?"

I took a long pull of the wine I'd ordered. "Much."

A waitress in a crisp white shirt and black tie appeared and asked if we were ready to order. We had to wave her away for the moment.

I glanced up at Sebastian. His eyes focused on something far away, and his jaw worked like he was thinking deeply about something. I wanted to ask him what it was that bothered him, but, in all honesty, I was afraid it might be disappointment about the disaster that was our honeymoon. Even though Dominguez confirmed that there was ice on the wings, I still felt kind of foolish for acting so quickly on my magical vision. Sebastian had been so looking forward to this trip, as had I.

Running my finger along the edge of the glass, I sighed. Sipping wine, I glanced through the menu. I peeped over the top of it at Sebastian, wondering if he was waiting for me to say something. He seemed engrossed making his own meal choice.

My eyes scanned over entrees, but my brain stumbled at the prices. Who pays sixty-eight dollars for anything, much less a hunk of steak?

"What are you thinking about?" he asked.

"Just how sorry I am that we're not in Vienna right now."

"Please stop apologizing. We'll work it out," he said.

"What is it you Minnesotans love to say? 'Could be worse.'"

"True." I laughed, imagining us sleeping in the airport waiting on a new plane or, worse, spattered on some highway.

The waitress came by again, so I absentmindedly ordered the walleye. Sebastian went for that sixty-some-dollar porterhouse. I gave him a little "Yikes!" glance as we returned the menus to the waiter. He seemed completely unfazed, however.

I was determined to try to turn this day around somehow, but my mind kept drawing blanks. The only safe subject that came into my mind was the weather, and I so did not want to be *that* married couple—you know the ones—staring at each other over dinner because they ran out of things to talk about twenty years ago. Yet we sat for a long time without a word. I started to fidget. Unrolling my linen napkin, I placed it in my lap expectantly. Then I moved my silverware around and thought about making a lame, joking reference to that scene in *Pretty Woman* when Julia Roberts learns to eat at a fancy restaurant. I decided that was too strained, too desperate to make a funny.

Sebastian, meanwhile, continued to stare out the window, lost in thoughts all his own.

"William is Pictish this week," I offered finally, referring to my dear friend and co-worker who was infamous among our set for changing the flavor of his religion like some people change clothes.

"Hmm," Sebastian murmured, seemingly more interested in watching the snowfall. "I thought that was an ethnicity."

Having gotten any kind of response, I pushed on valiantly. "It's also a kind of Scottish, nature-focused witchcraft. When we get back, he's off to some kind of retreat in the Boundary Waters."

"Cold," Sebastian said with a gruff smile.

"He's going with an experienced cold-weather camper. That ambulance driver he . . . I don't know . . . dates?" That was the other thing William wasn't entirely sure of. He mostly liked girls, but he lately had been having a sort of fling with a very fine-looking EMT named Jorge.

Our conversation had to be postponed when the waitress interrupted with food. She placed a steaming plate of pan-seared walleye with broccoli and garlic mashed potatoes in front of me. It was supposed to be the house specialty, and it smelled delicious.

Sebastian shrugged as he cut into a very bloody looking steak. "Shit."

"What?" I peered at his plate. Sebastian, unlike most vampires, could eat whatever and whenever he wanted with no ill effects. He'd been made by magic, not blood. The ultimate self-made man . . . well, vamp. Was there something wrong with his food?

But Sebastian was looking over my shoulder. "You see that guy over there by the window?"

I was almost afraid to look. Would it be Eriskegal or Loki? As casually as possible, I turned to glance in the direction Sebastian had indicated. The guy did look familiar, but not because he was leading some celestial double life. It was the man that I'd noticed leaving the plane the same time we had. He was an athletically trim white guy in his midforties with mouse brown hair, almost memorable for his unremarkableness. He sat alone, watching the snow drift from silver gray skies. "I think he got off the plane with us," I said. "Who is he?"

"My own personal stalker."

"Your own personal stalker? Since when? And how come I've never heard of him?" I asked through tight lips, trying to stay mindful of the echoing properties of a mostly empty restaurant.

"Trust me, you don't want to know," Sebastian said with a grimace.

Actually, I did.

"How long has this guy been stalking us, er, you? Are we talking days? Months? Why have I never seen him? What does he want? Is he some kind of peeping tom/vampire groupie? What has he seen, you know, between us?" Putting my elbows rather indelicately on the table, I leaned in and whispered, "Anyway, haven't you just, you know, eaten him?"

Sebastian laughed. "I haven't, as you say, 'eaten him,' because—as you of all people know—bodies rarely stay buried."

Unfortunately, I did have a bit of experience with skeletons in my closet resurfacing, as it were . . . uh, rather literally. Not terribly far from where we sat, in fact. In a lake inside a Minneapolis cemetery, Parrish and I had tried to hide the bodies of the Vatican assassins that Lilith killed in self-defense. A freak drought exposed them, and that was what had sent Special Agent Dominguez on my trail. I shivered at the memory.

This was really my first time back in the Cities since that night. I'd been so scared that I'd left in the middle of the night, abandoning everything but a few clothes and my cat. I wondered if that old apartment was still there and whatever happened to all my stuff.

With some effort, I shook my head to clear it. "Can we get back to talking about your stalker? What's he after? Is he dangerous?"

Considering, Sebastian turned back to his plate and sawed off another hunk of meat. "His name is James . . . uh, something. He's from the Illuminati Watchers; they follow me whenever I leave the country."

I poked my potatoes with my fork skeptically. "Did you just say, 'Illuminati'?"

2.

The Chariot

Sebastian nodded and took a bite of steamed cauli-flower. He frowned at his food for a moment, and then said, "Yes, Illuminati."

I raised my eyebrows but didn't say anything. Was Sebastian trying to lighten the mood after bringing up the whole dead-resurfacing thing? He had to be joking, right?

"It's not all that unreasonable, is it?" he asked, sounding somewhat hurt that I might not believe him. "I fit their profile. I have a ridiculous amount of money, a lot of overseas investments, property, gold, and, shall we say, a family history that extends over several centuries."

Only, the "family" would be just his—oops, *our*—son, Mátyás, and himself. Yeah, okay, I could kind of see how he ended up on a conspiracy theorist's list somewhere. "Can

I be honest? I don't really even know what the Illuminati is . . . or are, exactly. They have something to do with world domination, but after that . . . ?" I put my palms up and nearly flung a piece of winter squash on my fork across the room. "I thought they were . . . I don't know, made up?"

"Well, these days the term *Illuminati* has gotten kind of muddled." Sebastian returned his attention to cleaning up his plate. "Nowadays it can apply to any number of groups that people are convinced are attempting to control the political scene or establishing a certain world order. But it all started in Bavaria in the seventeen hundreds, the Age of Enlightenment."

There was something in that faraway look in Sebastian's eye that made me ask, "And you know this . . . because you read about it in a book?"

"No." Sebastian sighed, setting his fork down. "I might have been a founding member," he said almost so quickly I didn't catch all of it. "Look, at the time, it was the Austro-Bulgarian Empire, okay? I had a vested interest."

"Wait. Did you just say that the Illuminati started in Austria?"

"Really, it was Ingolstadt in Upper Bulgaria, but, for your purposes, yes, close enough."

"And you wonder why they've been following you? They've probably been trailing you since seventeen whatever." I couldn't help but laugh a little. Then I wagged my finger at him with mock accusation. "And did you also say you started it?"

"Good God, no. I try not to do anything worthy of an entry in Wikipedia—makes it much easier to live forever without people noticing. No, it was Adam. I mean, Professor Weishaupt from the university."

I scratched at the back of my neck. "Adam? I take it we were close?"

"You know my attraction to university and university types." It was true. Sebastian seemed to have spent most of his natural and unnatural life haunting various colleges and institutes of higher learning. He even taught a few extension courses in horticulture at the University of Wisconsin. And then there was the cute little comparative religion studies major in our coven I didn't even want to talk about he found alluring—intellectually, that is!

"Adam taught canon law," Sebastian continued. "I was on the science faculty. We had opportunity to talk. I thought he was brilliant."

My tone was all teasing: "Did you sleep with him?"

"No," Sebastian said, a tiny bit more forcefully than necessary.

He hated it when I teased him about that sort of thing. It was a big burden, apparently, to be the only straight vampire in the history of his kind. And what could I say? I found it utterly hilarious.

"You know I don't go that way without a lot of effort," he continued. "Adam wasn't that cute. It was more of an intellectual crush."

"Sure," I teased. "Your passions were inflamed by the desire to rule the world together. Oh! It was totally Anakin Skywalker at the end of that movie we both hated."

"One of the Star Wars ones, was it? Ugh, tell me again why you insisted we go?"

I was secretly kind of a fan girl, but I confessed the real reason to him: "Ewan McGregor is hot."

"Even in a bathrobe?"

I shrugged. "I like *you* in a bathrobe."

"Hmm. Good point. I thought he looked scruffy."

"I thought you didn't notice boys."

Sebastian flashed me a vaguely exasperated look and then rubbed his mouth with his hand. He let out a long breath before reaching for his wine. His eyes strayed to where his stalker sat sipping coffee. "I wish those conspiracy theory nuts would give up. It was several hundred years ago and, anyway, it's over. The whole Illuminati thing with Adam was a fad, a flash. We disbanded in less than a decade. And, for the record, we called ourselves Perfectibilitists, not Illuminati."

"It's no surprise that first one didn't stick. Illuminati is a lot easier to say." I smiled, taking a bite of my cooling fish. "Anyway, you don't have to convince me." I jerked my head in the direction of Sebastian's stalker. "This—is it James? He's the guy you need to convince."

"How likely is that?" Sebastian sighed, rubbing his forehead like he was developing a sudden headache.

"This guy, is he dangerous?" I asked, stealing another

glance at the very forgettable man in the ho-hum clothes, who seemed completely absorbed admiring the slow, soft drift of flakes outside the window. As I watched, he picked up a book and started reading. I could almost read the title, something about the secret architecture in America's capital.

"He could be," Sebastian said. "Larry, my accountant, is very good at keeping people like James from connecting any dots. But it wouldn't take much to blow my cover."

"No one would believe you're a vampire," I reminded Sebastian. "No way."

Most people didn't know vampires were real. Or, more accurately, they were in denial.

You see, there was a kind of veil that existed between the general populace and the truth about things that go bump in the night. If pushed, you might get a "rational" person to admit to having had an experience with a ghost or something else supernatural, but most of the time people just close their eyes and plug their ears, singing "la, la, la," to the things that make up the majority of my everyday experience.

It's my opinion that's why there is always a collective hunger for those cheesy, nonfiction exposés about haunted houses and reality shows featuring ghost hunters and psychics. It is because, on some level, everyone *knows*. They understand that this stuff is really out there just beyond their perceptions. All they really have to do is open their eyes.

I closed mine for a moment and pinched the bridge of my nose. "But what I want to know is this: This James guy," I said, "he's not going to jump out of the bushes with a knife or anything, right?"

"No," Sebastian muttered glumly. "He'll probably blog about me."

"Horrors," I snickered. "Maybe he's Twittering right now!"

"Laugh it up, but it's people like him that have kept me on the move my whole life and probably why the FBI put the screws to me."

"You think?" I'd mostly finished my fish and started in on the last of the veggies.

"Those guys knew more about me than I would have liked."

"Really? Like what?" My mind filled with visions of stake-wielding, garlic-waving G-men in matching suit coats and ties: Homeland Security of the Dead!

The waitress chose that moment to ask us if we found everything to our liking. We agreed that it was all lovely. She smiled pleasantly and after waiting another beat or two, finally moved to join a group of similarly dressed waiters loitering at the bar.

"So what did they ask you?" I kept my voice low, hyper-aware of the bored waitstaff and potential blogger/stalker who might be listening in.

"Well, they used the term *wealthy businessman,* which isn't really the persona I use in this country. Nothing in my visa suggests it either. In fact, my main occupation is listed as adjunct university professor, not usually a profession people consider terribly wealthy."

My brain sputtered at his use of the term *persona*. That made him sound very *Bourne Identity*. I wondered just how many personas he had. My mouth moved to ask, but the brain hadn't quite recovered enough to let me form anything coherent.

Sebastian didn't notice. His eyes had drifted to the condensation-steamed window. "It makes me wonder if I'm on their watch list as well. But why?" he asked mostly to himself. "That whole incident in Amsterdam is decades old. It was the 1970s, for God's sake. I was just a student; everyone was into that whole scene, you know? Anyway, I was using a completely different name at the time. How could they have connected me?"

I had no idea. In fact, I wasn't even born in the 1970s, had never been to Amsterdam, and was beginning to suspect I'd married a guy who'd been a part of every secret society since the dawn of time. "Did you bomb somebody or something?"

"No," he said. "It was just a building. No one was in it."

I choked on the wine I'd been swallowing.

Sebastian raised his hands, motioning me to relax. "It wasn't nearly as outlandish as it sounds. Or at least it made sense to me at the time. Look, it was cool back then to be a radical, antiestablishment, antigovernment. Everyone was into it. It was easy to get swept up. I fell in with the wrong crowd."

"What, again? Jeez, Sebastian, I never took you for such a joiner!"

"I'm social," he said with a sniff.

"Why don't you just join the Moose Lodge?"

"I have," he said, quite seriously.

"You have?"

"Sure, they have great dinners. I'll take you some time."

"Cripes, did you join the Illuminati for the food too?"

He laughed. "Come to think of it, they had some pretty excellent desserts!"

I shook my head in disbelief. "Honestly, you crack me up. But what I really want to know is who else you are when you're not with me. Who are all these other personas of yours?"

"Well," Sebastian said, a smile returning to his face. "I'm a real-estate magnate, but you knew that."

I did. Sebastian owned several business properties in Madison. In fact, we once had run-in with the Goddess Hel in one of his office buildings, but that was another story.

"I'm a car mechanic, botanist, alchemist, mountain climber, and a father."

"Tell me about someone I don't know."

"I raised goats in France."

I smiled at the image. "What century was that?"

"The twentieth. It was actually right before the whole Amsterdam thing, in the sixties. My lover ran a commune near the Côte d'Azur. It was really gorgeous countryside, but, for your information, goats stink—both literally and figuratively. And I really never got a taste for their milk."

"Was your lover a boy or a girl?" I asked precisely because I knew it would tweak him a little.

"Hmmm." He smirked in a way that for a moment made me think he wasn't going to tell me out of mischievous spite. "Free love, baby. Everyone at the commune was, uh, experimenting, but it was Estelle that brought me into it."

"Estelle. She sounds pretty." I couldn't believe I was jealous of a woman that had to be dead by now.

"No one holds a candle to you, my love," Sebastian said, reaching across the table to stroke my cheek. Despite the nearby fireplace, shivers ran down my spine.

"I want to continue this conversation upstairs," I said, feeling the sudden, irrational desire to assert my wifehood all over him and his Estelle memories.

"Indeed." Sebastian smiled wickedly. "So do I."

Getting up from the table, I took his hand: "Let's go make this honeymoon official."

Knowing that Sebastian was now my husband made me strangely shy. It wasn't like we hadn't made love on our wedding night, but, honestly, that whole wonderful day was kind of a happy blur. Then afterward, we'd been so busy making plans and getting ready for the honeymoon that we'd . . . well, neglected certain things.

I'd packed a special, lacy outfit just for this moment and now wondered if it was too trashy or too silly.

The suite was dark. Outside, the gray wind yowled restlessly and spattered angry splotches of snow against the pane. Sebastian, who could see perfectly, of course, led me through the rooms. It was so quiet that I could hear his breathing, shallow and anticipatory.

I doubted he needed the lace.

Despite his obvious interest, a stab of self-doubt raced through me. Would I still be sexy as a wife?

Wife was such a loaded word, and, tripping clumsily through the lavish and expensive honeymoon suite, I felt all its weight settle on my shoulders. What if this moment disappointed? Would he question his commitment?

At dinner Sebastian had said that people like James were the reason he'd kept on the move. Now that we were married, picking up and leaving would be more complicated to say the least. I'd settled him. Is that what he'd been brooding about?

We reached the bedroom. Sebastian took both my hands in his and held me at arm's length. "Let me look at you, my wife."

Eek, there was that word sounding so foreign and fraught on Sebastian's lips. I tried not to flinch.

I should have known the dark wouldn't hide my reaction from a vampire. "What's wrong?"

"I'm having a little performance anxiety," I admitted with a ghost of an embarrassed smile. "This is it. The big night."

He shook his head, but I couldn't read his expression in the muted light that filtered in through the window. "Every night is special with you," he said.

Aw.

His words helped, but I still felt an enormous pressure to live up to the expectations of this night, the label "wife," and, well, everything.

"Just relax," he coaxed, drawing me closer.

I tipped my head back, ready for his kiss and for everything to be all better. Lilith chose that moment to rouse from Her usual slumber. Every time I thought too much about marriage, She bristled. I felt a white-hot surge of power encircling my wedding ring. It burned.

"Ow!" I shook my hand, breaking the moment with Sebastian. Clenching my teeth to suppress the desire to pull the ring off and throw it to the floor, I hopped around uselessly. My fingers pinched hard on the gold, keeping it on my finger. "Ow! Ow! Ow!"

Something nudged inside me, and Lilith relented. Her sudden release made my limbs feel like wet, limp noodles. Luckily, before I hit the floor, Sebastian caught my elbows.

"Lilith?" he asked.

I nodded mutely, still trying to shake the phantom burning sensation.

"What was She objecting to now?" Sebastian sounded really angry. "Is She planning on joining us, perhaps?"

Except She was always between us.

I didn't want to make things worse by reminding him of

that fact, though. "Forget about Her. Let's get back to where we were, shall we?"

Reaching up, I stroked the planes of his face. Stubble scratched my palms pleasantly. I made a noise of appreciation of his manliness, and shifted my hips to press closer to him.

My ploy worked. I could sense his mood shifting, softening.

He ran his fingers through the spikes of my hair, pausing, as he always did, to tousle the shortest hairs at the back of my neck, as though he liked the prickly feel of them.

I closed my eyes, heightening the sense of blindness, and let my hands slowly trace the outline of Sebastian's body. I felt the strong lines of his long, aristocratic neck. Then I let them trail the lean muscular frame of his broad shoulders. A sigh escaped my lips, only to be caught up in his mouth.

Sebastian kissed me with a similar tentative exploration. It was as though we kissed for the first time. His tongue gently, slowly probed my mouth. We played, back and forth, controlling the kiss. When it was my turn, I was careful of his fangs, though I let the tender skin of my tongue glide past their sharp edges. I let them cut just enough to give him a small taste of blood.

His whole body quivered slightly, as though instantly more alert.

My hands had come to a rest on the firm muscles of his

chest. At his response to the blood, I let my hand drift down to the growing bulge beneath his belt.

My attention spurred Sebastian to reach his arms around my back. He felt for the clasp of my bra under the thin fabric of my shirt. Finding it, he expertly undid the hook without even lifting my shirt, releasing the heaviness of my breasts. Taut with excitement, my tender skin felt exposed under the loosened bra. My nipples brushed lightly against the fabric with every quickened breath.

As though in retaliation, I pulled at his buckle until I had it free in my hands. I stripped the leather from his waist so fast it made a hissing sound.

Lilith murmured a warm approval along my nerves, increasing my already intense sensitivity. I ached. With a moan I returned to the kiss we'd momentarily forgotten with renewed passion.

Eagerly, I pressed harder into him, letting Sebastian know exactly how much I wanted him with a firm stroke of encouragement.

We broke from our kiss so he could hurry me out of my shirt. The cold air prickled along my exposed flesh. I shivered, but not from the temperature. Even in the dark, I could see the glitter of Sebastian's brown eyes.

Quickly, I wriggled out of my jeans to stand completely naked under that sexy, predatory gaze. My eyes had grown accustomed to the dark and I enjoyed the sensation of being observed. Half seductive, half self-consciously, I rubbed and caressed my own goose-pimpled flesh.

A slow, secretive smile spread across Sebastian's handsome face. "What if I put on a show for you?" he asked. "Shall we play a little role reversal?"

Why not? It sounded fun.

At my assent, he looked downright pleased with himself, though he muttered, "What I could really use is some music."

We'd brought along an MP3 player for the trip. It had a speaker it slipped into, but both were somewhere in my jumble of a bag. "I could try to find it," I offered.

"No, no, I'll improvise," he said. "You can imagine that song 'Take Your Hat Off.'"

"Are you going to do a striptease for me?"

"Watch," he said with a waggle of his eyebrows.

So I did, as he popped the buttons on his shirt. At each one, he jutted his hip out. It was meant to be sexy, but I couldn't hold back a little laugh. My reaction only encouraged him. His movements became even more exaggerated, and he did a little shoulder shimmy with his completely open shirt. When he did the classic twirl and toss, I squealed with joy. His shirt landed on a lamp, nearly knocking it over.

"You are so awesome," I told him between laughs.

"The best is yet to come," he promised as he ran his hands down his now bare chest to his pants. Despite the silliness, I found myself anticipating this part. He played coy, and turned his back to me to look over his shoulder. Wiggling his butt at me, he slid his hands into his jeans.

"Take it off!" I shouted, egging him on.

The pants came down a bit, revealing a taste of his fine behind, but then slid back up. He waggled his hips as if to say, "Not yet!" He did a series of peek-a-boos that got progressively more revealing. He started turning a bit so I got a hint of the front. I was busting a gut, but tantalized too. I couldn't remember having this much fun in the dark with my clothes off. If I wasn't already in love with Sebastian, I'd have fallen for him all over again at this moment.

At last he let his jeans fall to the floor. With a "Ta-da!" he turned around for me to see him in all his glory. What a fine sight it was. Worth the wait and the hype! I applauded with all my might. After sketching a quick bow, he came up and wrapped me in his arms.

The mood shifted to serious the second our skin touched. We stumbled backward until I was pressed against the wall. Sebastian took my breast into his mouth. My fingers grasped his head as his tongue tore breath from my lungs.

When his fangs pierced the sensitive skin of my areola, a hot rush coursed through me, electrifying every nerve end. My knees wobbled, but I impressed myself by staying upright and not collapsing in a spaghetti-muscle heap.

From his growling grunt, I knew he'd nicked the skin enough to draw blood. He suckled the blood from my breast with slow laps of his tongue. The sound of his feast stirred heat in my thighs again, and I moaned.

Still sucking on my breast, Sebastian's hand found the space between my legs. His fingers slid easily into me, given how wet I already was. I roughly twisted his hair in my fists as he explored deeply, rhythmically. I felt my heat rising, but I desperately wanted his cock inside me.

Sensing my need, he lifted his bloodied lips from my breast. He kissed me, and I tasted a coppery tang.

Sebastian removed his fingers so quickly I nearly wept. Scooping my buttocks up in one arm, he lifted me off my feet. Instinctively, I spread my legs to receive him. His hard, thick shaft drove deep inside me.

My cell phone buzzed. Tinny strains of Rob Zombie's "Dragula" sounded somewhere on the bed.

My body jerked in surprise and an impulse to answer it, but Sebastian continued pounding into me so hard I forgot everything until the phone rang through into voice mail with a loud, shrill tone. Despite the shocking interruption, it took no time to work ourselves back into a frenzy. He came in a wave that I followed shortly after.

Though I could tell he was spent, I clung limply to him as he carried me hot and panting to the bed. Exhausted, I dropped off to a deep sleep with a satisfied smile on my lips.

I woke up half a minute later when the caller tried again, and that horrible voice mail alert twittered noisily. It was so dark out that I thought it must be past midnight, but the clock read eight. My hand flapped blindly on the bed until I found the phone.

I'd intended to switch it off, but the caller ID showed the number for my pagan bookstore back home in Madison, Wisconsin. My eyes snapped open in a shot of adrenaline. I untangled myself from Sebastian's arms and quickly hit "connect." My mind raced with fear of fire, burst frozen pipes, theft, or worse. William answered after the second ring. "Mercury Crossing, your friendly neighborhood source for all things New Age!"

Well, he sounded too cheerful for a complete disaster. "William, what's wrong? Is everything okay?"

"Oh, Garnet, thank God it's you."

"Why? What's going on?"

Sebastian must have heard the frantic sound in my voice, and he cracked open one eye to watch me warily. I pointed to the phone and whispered, "The store."

"Mátyás woke me up from a very pleasant nap, I might add, screaming about some plane crash dream. Then I heard on the radio about all the trouble the Minneapolis airport is having with ice. I was worried sick."

I rubbed my face with my hand, the fading excitement making my entire body feel heavy with a desire to sleep. "Great Goddess, William, I thought the store had burned down or something."

"That kind of crazy stuff happens only when you're here," he reminded me. "No, everything's fine. In fact, it's been a bit quiet. Are you in Austria yet?"

"The plane had to make an emergency landing. We're still in Saint Paul."

"Oh, man," William said. "You know, Mátyás is always right about these things."

Mátyás could dream-walk—though he mostly dream-*stalked*. He was also aging so slowly he'd been a teenager for the last century and a half, or so, which might explain why he was such a pain in the ass most of the time.

My sexed-up-and-sleep-deprived fuzzy brain returned to the part of the conversation where Mátyás woke William up. Mátyás normally didn't sleep anywhere near William. In fact, last I heard Mátyás was dating my best gal pal, Izzy. "Are you and Mátyás . . . ?" Oh, this was awkward. Maybe I misheard him. "Uh, how did you say you found out the dream?"

"Mátyás is sleeping on my couch. He and Izzy are on the outs again."

Again? I had no idea there was any trouble between them, but William made it sound like an everyday thing. Boy, maybe I needed to call Izzy to get the scoop. But I didn't want to sound out of the loop to William so I just said, "Huh."

"So, when are you leaving?" William asked.

Sebastian and I hadn't really talked about our plans yet other than that we needed to make some, but I had my own ideas. I poked Sebastian lightly on his arm. He blinked an eye at me, like an annoyed cat. "I don't know, but I was thinking about talking Sebastian into hanging around up here. You know I went to school in Minneapolis, and I'd kind of like to take him on a tour of my old stomping grounds."

"Hmm, sounds nice," William agreed absently, like his

mind was elsewhere. I could hear the ding of the cash register faintly in the background.

Sebastian's eyes opened, and he sat up slowly. He frowned, but not deeply. "What about Europe?" he asked.

"We could go to Austria when the weather is nicer, like summer or something, don't you think?"

Sebastian seemed to be considering that, when William said, "I'd love to see Vienna in the spring myself."

"You don't get to come on our honeymoon, William, sorry," I said with a teasing laugh. "But yeah," I said, meeting Sebastian's eyes and nodding, "spring does sound even better."

Sebastian twitched his lips and echoed my nod, like he thought that might be all right as well. I smiled at him and he returned it warmly.

"Since I have you on the phone, where do we keep the Dittany of Crete?"

I told him to look in the storeroom on our herbal shelf and reminded him of possible substitutions to offer the customer if we were out of it.

"Well, I should go," William said. "Things are picking up here. After Yule rush, you know."

"Glad to hear it," I said. "Bye!"

William signed off with a good-bye and hung up. I snapped the phone shut and looked again at Sebastian. "Is that really okay? About us staying here this time?"

Sebastian shrugged. "I haven't booked new tickets yet. We could wait. Vienna is beautiful in the spring."

"I can't wait to see your home," I said, suddenly regretting my selfish impulse. "We could go now, if you really want to, honestly. It was just a spur of the moment thought."

"Well, given that Homeland Security and the Illuminati have us on their watch lists, we could probably stand to lay low for a while," he said.

Sebastian and I agreed to do a little nighttime sight-seeing. After a brief nap and a shower that involved mutual soaping up—I was loving the naked parts of the honeymoon so far!—I called for a cab to take us to Uptown in Minneapolis.

It should be noted that cabs in the Twin Cities are nothing like they are in other major metropolitan areas, except that the driver usually speaks little English. Here, they're likely to be immigrants from Somalia or other parts of Africa and observant Muslims, to the point that they may refuse to carry the case of wine you've brought back on the airplane with you from your recent visit to the Napa Valley. You also cannot catch one by waving, no matter how frantically. They rarely stop for people on the street. Most times, you have to call and book one, though they will wait in queues at the airport and some hotels.

This is why, when I lived in Minneapolis, I actually owned a car. I still tried to take the bus when I could, but there are actually many places in the nearby suburbs that are unreachable by Twin Cities public transportation.

As we stood in the blustering snow under the awning of the hotel, I muttered beneath my fluffy scarf, "Maybe we should just take our own car."

Sebastian brightened up. "Can we?"

I'd explained this earlier. "We could, but parking is horrific in Uptown. Not to mention all the weird snow-emergency rules. I can't remember anymore which side of the street is the one you're allowed to park on."

"So you said," he said, clearly disappointed. Though watching eddies of snow swirl in the street, I was just as happy to have someone else navigate unfamiliar streets in these conditions.

"We can drive around tomorrow. I promise. Especially if it clears up." I smiled and gave him a playful poke in the arm.

Despite the nearly freezing temperatures, Sebastian wore a thin, tweed black coat and a paisley silk muffler and matching necktie I'd bought him from the Smithsonian catalog. He looked pretty styling, and I'm sure I looked like I had my arm wrapped around a truly fabulous gay man. Especially since I never pulled off fashion quite the way he could, what with his vampire glamour and all.

I'd decided to go with warmth over fashion and so had on my black jeans and knee-high, faux-fur-trimmed boots. Over that I wore the coat I found at a rummage sale, which I called my babushka coat, because it looked like something a grandma in Russia might wear. It was sort of shapeless, red and black checkered, with big black buttons, and a black trimmed, wide collar. It could pass as retro chic, on a good day, I supposed, but next to my fab guy I felt a bit frumpy.

Sebastian scanned the snow for any sign of our cab. He checked his watch. "Why can't we just wander around downtown Saint Paul?"

"Because," I said. "It's after six. In fact, it's nearly ten. The streets are rolled up. Nothing will be open."

"You can't be serious," he said.

When I shrugged, a tuft of snow slid off my shoulder. "Saint Paul likes to think of itself as an old-fashioned small town. The neighborhoods are strong and the downtown is dull. Well, okay, maybe that last part isn't fair, but, trust me, there's a lot more happening on the other side of the river."

Sebastian looked to the east, where, through the buildings, you could see the frozen expanse of the Mississippi and the cliffs on the other bank. "I thought that was still Saint Paul over there."

I nodded. It was "the Eastside," which was largely settled by Spanish-speaking immigrants. I was hoping to take Sebastian to a bakery there tomorrow. "The river actually bends around. We'll cross it on the way to Minneapolis. You'll see."

Sebastian shook his head. "What did Jesse Ventura say about this place and its streets? Something about being planned by drunken Irishmen?"

I raised my gloved hand to shake a finger at him in warning. "Oh, honey, you haven't even seen the worst of it. Wait until you see Tangletown."

The taxi finally came into sight as it turned into the driveway in front of the Saint Paul Hotel.

I had the cab driver take us to the Uptown Theatre on the corner of Lagoon and Hennepin. It's an old-fashioned movie theater. Attached to the Art Deco exterior is a tall, oblong-shaped marquee lined with bright, round bulbs proclaiming its name. Snow clung in the crevasses between the lights, giving it a frosted look.

The cab let us out on the corner. Sebastian paid quickly, as the cabbie had double-parked and blocked a lane of traffic, though everyone in Minnesota was too polite to honk.

There was some foreign film playing at ten thirty, so we bought tickets. I tugged Sebastian's arm in the direction of the bookstore down the street. "Come on," I said. "You'll love Orr Books. Oh, and Magers & Quinn."

Uptown is the closest Minneapolis has to bustle. Although none of the buildings in Uptown are more than three or four stories high, the area compensated for its lack of height with a multitude of neon and bright twinklies. Cars hissed by on slushy streets. Small white Christmas lights entwined nearly every branch of the scrawny gingko trees lining the sidewalks.

When I lived here, Uptown was artsy in that best-kept-secret kind of way, as in artists could actually afford to live there. After years of the successful Uptown Art Fair, the neighborhood had gotten "noticed" and, as a consequence, was much more commercial and high priced. Now the Gap and Aveda and McDonald's beckoned customers to enter their brightly lit interiors. But here and there, in the shadows of the chain stores, lingered cute, trendy, independently owned stores selling cards, jewelry, and various must-have curios. Remnants of the Uptown I used to know.

I'd been hoping to share old memories, but instead I found myself showing Sebastian a lot of ghosts.

"The Rainbow bar used to be here," I said as we passed a place that now seemed to serve sushi. "It was really cool," I said rather wistfully.

Sebastian nodded.

I suppose, of anyone in the world, a thousand-year-old vampire understood that things change.

Me, I wasn't ready for it.

Orr Books was gone too replaced by a Barnes & Noble. Most of my favorite funky shops had disappeared or seemed to me to be trying too hard to be what Uptown used to be. Their attempts struck me as a little too much intentional hipness, the way window dressing was ever so artfully placed. It wasn't a complete loss, however. For every snarky, self-referential, modern-too-cool-for-you bit of sparkly consumerism, there were genuine bits of whimsy—a funny bird made from used garden tools or stationery so bright and textured I just had to pull Sebastian into the store to fondle it.

Sebastian and I strolled slowly, holding hands, as picture-perfect snowflakes slowly shifted colors as they drifted down through the lights of the city.

My nose was chilled by the time we entered Magers & Quinn bookstore. The comforting smell of old books greeted me along with a rush of overheated air from a nearby vent. Sebastian and I stomped our boots on the soggy rug and went our separate ways. I knew he'd head first for the philosophy section, and I'd scour the nearby occult and astrology shelves. We'd probably meet where alchemy and New Age joined.

Poetic, huh?

After stuffing my gloves in the pocket of my coat, I rubbed my hands together briskly with delight and, as a bonus, to warm them. Despite managing a bookstore back home, I loved browsing for books, especially used ones. Mercury Crossing mostly carried only the newest titles. We didn't have room for much else, especially since we also stocked incense, tarot cards, candles, jewelry, and pretty much everything else a modern witch might need. But when I shopped for myself, I particularly loved looking for old astrology books that were published before—or just at—the discovery of Pluto in 1930. Though, honestly, I loved leafing through any book on my favorite subject.

As I was glancing through the titles—many of which, sadly, I recognized as remainders—I suddenly had that feeling of being watched. I turned, half expecting Sebastian, only to glimpse a hulking figure ducking quickly behind the stacks.

"Hello?" I asked, because part of me is a bit like Pooh—I always invited the strange noise inside, even when it could be an Animal of Hostile Intent. I walked over to where I thought I saw the person disappear and peered around the edge of the tall, wooden bookshelf.

No one was there.

I stood for a moment, chewing the fingernail of my thumb. I stared at the empty aisle and doubted my sanity. I had seen somebody, hadn't I?

"Sports section? That's not really you, is it, Garnet?" Sebastian's hand on my shoulder made me jump about three feet straight in the air.

"You scared the crap out of me," I accused, once I found my voice.

"Obviously." Sebastian smiled lightly. "Do I dare say you look like you've seen a ghost?"

I laughed a bit breathily. Given our life, it wouldn't be totally implausible that I had, but I shook my head. "I don't think so. It was probably just some kid playing tricks."

Sebastian gave me a disbelieving look. "A kid? Garnet, when is it ever a kid?"

"I just had that feeling of being watched, and—" I spread my hands to indicate the expanse of the empty aisle. Then I frowned and put my gloved hands on my hips. "Why couldn't it be a kid? I mean, just once. Why couldn't something in our life be completely nonmagical and ordinary? Other people get spied on by kids. Why can't I?"

Sebastian gave me a patient grimace and hugged me to his

chest. "You're babbling, darling." I might have felt patronized, but it felt good to be wrapped up in his strong arms for the moment. Besides, pressed as I was into his chest, I could smell the scent of him: cinnamon and musky maleness.

"Why couldn't it be something normal?" I muttered into the silk of his tie, trying to keep the whine out of my voice.

"It could be," he acquiesced, nudging me upright so he could look me in the eye. "But you're some kind of a vortex all your own, my love. Magical things are attracted to you like a magnet. Hell, my life was more mundane before I met you. Where you are, excitement follows."

"You make it sound much cooler than it is," I said. And what did it mean for our marriage? Would we always be plagued by things that go bump in the night?

"You wouldn't know what to do with a normal life," he teased.

That was it! Of course my life had been going to hell; I'd cast a spell for everything to be normal. As soon as we got back to the hotel, I was going to reverse it.

I gave Sebastian a deep, passionate kiss. "Thank you," I said.

He looked a little baffled, but he returned my smile. "Let me know if I can do it again—whatever it was."

The movie was some kind of period piece in Croatian. The popcorn was perfectly salted and went well with the four-dollar Milk Duds I gobbled greedily. Sebastian put his arm around me as we sat in the balcony of the majestic theater, with its funky Art Deco reliefs and velvet seats. I may have drifted off to sleep near the end, but I had a great time.

I didn't see any Gods or ghosts until we headed home on the bus. We could have taken a taxi, I suppose, but just as we stepped out of the theater the No. 4 into downtown seemed to arrive like a coach. When the doors whooshed open, Sebastian and I gave each other a "Why not?" look and hopped on.

At this hour the bus was completely deserted. An old guy with frizzy white hair whose features were almost completely obscured by an olive military parka seemed to be asleep at the rear, his head bobbing to the jostling rhythm of the bus's lurching gait. Sebastian and I took seats near the middle.

"This is a grand adventure, isn't it?" Sebastian said with a smile. He offered me the bag of books we'd bought, and I fished out my copy of *Murder by the Stars,* a sensational look at the astrological charts of famous serial killers, and he settled in with some esoteric book about Plato.

I tried, but I couldn't really focus on reading. I kept seeing familiar landmarks—oh, look, Kinhdo Restaurant; I love that place!—surrounded by entirely new buildings and businesses. Where was the old bike shop? That ice-cream shop used to be around the corner, didn't it? When did Minneapolis put up so many slick-looking condos?

Plus, occasionally, I'd see things that brought a whole

different kind of memory back. As we passed the huge synagogue, I remembered turning down that side street often to visit an old friend who lived in one of those huge historic apartment buildings near Lake of the Isles. She had the coolest pocket doors in that place, and that cute, narrow little pantry. I must have visited three times a week for walks around the lake and gossip sessions about the pagan community. Oh, I almost laughed out loud with memory of that time the Canada geese chased us! She was so kicky and fun to hang with.

Of course, that all ended when she found out I was sleeping with her boyfriend.

Then I became the one gossiped about, since that little misadventure of mine sent huge ripples among my friends, especially when it came out about that stupid love spell. Why do I never seem to learn how dumb-ass those things are?

I shook my head. I'd lost a lot of friends over that little kerfuffle.

Hey, look, Rudolph Valentino's rib place survived! As the bus moved into downtown, I noted to Sebastian that he was now turning from Hennepin on to Hennepin. He just shook his head and muttered about drunken city planners.

I didn't even rise to the bait. My brain was still elsewhere. "How do you live with it all? All the memories. All the history," I asked. We crossed over a light-rail line with a bump, and I had to ask, "It's weird enough to see trains in this town for me. How was it to see trains, well, invented?"

He laughed, and put his finger in his book to mark his place. "I don't know that you ever really cope. It's harder here in America. You people never sit still. Nothing ever stays the same." He sounded reflective and a bit melancholy. Giving me a sad smile, he added, "But that has its upside too."

I thought about my ex-friend. I wouldn't have remembered her if that neighborhood had changed more, and so I nodded my head. "I think I understand that part."

With a nod, he went back to his book, and I returned to staring out the window.

It was only after we made the switch downtown to the Washington Avenue/University bus line that I noticed the new driver was a troll.

Our fingers touched when he handed me the transfer ticket back, and suddenly I saw that the irises of his eyes were the color of stone as was, honestly, much of his skin. Bushy moss hung in place of brows, and his hair seemed to be an odd assortment of twigs and fern.

I blinked, rubbed my eyes. The image wavered, but held. The vegetation-topped bus driver started to pull away from the curb, and Sebastian had already taken a seat in the middle. I stumbled my way to my seat.

Holding on to the back of the metal handrail of the seat in front of me, I continued to stare at the bus driver. We moved along Washington Avenue, going under the pedestrian bridge connecting the two halves of the university's campus, which was divided by the Mississippi.

I noticed the troll looking back at me in the rearview mirror. I nudged Sebastian. Sebastian looked up from his book sleepily.

"Does our bus driver look like a troll?" I asked him.

The bus had stopped to let on two black women in heavy parkas and brightly decorated silk *hijab*. They chatted in a mix of English and Somali as they flowed past us in their snow boots and long, swirling skirts.

As we started up again, Sebastian cocked his head thoughtfully and squinted, as though taking a long, serious look at the bus driver. "I suppose he does look like a troll a bit, particularly around the shoulders. He has a rather heavy forehead. For myself, I'd have to say more Cro-Magnon."

"Really? The moss hair doesn't seem more trollish?"

Sebastian glanced at me, and then slid his gaze to the driver. Returning his attention to me, he said, "I don't really see moss, though it is thin in places and yet somehow wiry." After a moment of consideration, it occurred to him: "This is like Fonn, isn't it? You're seeing something magical. You know, trolls and Frost Giants are from the same pantheon. He could be working with her. Should we get off?"

I didn't know. Even though the troll kept glancing surreptitiously in our general direction, he didn't seem terribly threatening. All the same, I didn't really want to die in a fiery bus accident either. I was about to tell Sebastian the same when I noticed: "Hey, isn't that James Something?"

Sebastian's eyes flicked toward the front of the bus.

Nondescript in his brown coat and forest green knit

stocking hat, the guy dropping coins one by one into the meter looked a lot like Sebastian's personal stalker to me. Though he did have the kind of face that, well, didn't really remind you of anyone in particular, but you'd thought you'd maybe seen somewhere before. He was handsome enough not to be noticeably unattractive, and I could see him making a living playing that extra in the movies who gets a line in the credits as "guy number two on the street." He never looked up at us, however, and took a seat on the bench at the front that faced inward.

Sebastian squinted at him. "Are you sure?"

"No. I mean, how can I be? He's the definition of forgettable."

Sebastian nodded slowly, like I'd said something profound. "Then it's him for certain."

"Have the Illuminati invented a cloaking device or something?"

The look Sebastian gave me was a combination of amusement and confusion. "What are you on about? You're starting to sound far too much like William sometimes, you know that?"

My co-worker William had a tendency to quote Monty Python out of context or make references to the more fringe areas of New Age, like Area 51, without a lot of buildup or explanation. It's why we loved him, so I didn't take Sebastian's comment as a dis. "I just wondered why you were suddenly convinced. I mean, what about being uninteresting makes you so confident that's James Something?"

"Because they're all like that. I swear it's a job requirement for being a watchdog: 'Required to look like no one in particular. Blending skills a must.' "

I laughed. "That'd be a great classified." I continued to play with the idea. " 'Experience tracking vampire billionaires preferred.' "

" 'Up-to-date passport a plus,' " Sebastian continued. " 'Applicants should have knowledge of latest conspiracy theories.' "

"Yeah," I said, growing a bit more serious. "But aren't they partially right? Rich people do exert a lot of influence on things like foreign policy, don't they?"

"I'm sure some do, but you know what? I've never been invited to a single secret cabal meeting." Sebastian put on a tone of mock hurt. "I've never gotten a piece of the world domination agenda."

"What, you never attended a Skull and Bones meeting at Yale with former presidents?" I teased. "Sheesh, and I thought you were 'connected.' "

"Sorry, darling. If you wanted a mover and a shaker, I am not him."

Running a finger along the line from his shoulder to his bicep, I flashed Sebastian my best bedroom eyes. "You always move me, baby."

"Growl," he purred, and then smiled at me fondly. "You make me wish we were somewhere more private."

"Ever wanted to have public sex?"

It was hard to believe, but Sebastian—my thousand-year-old lover, who had probably seen everything under the sun, *twice*—blushed.

Which just aroused me all the more.

I slowly, provocatively, ran the toe of my boot up his pant leg. Leaning over, I took the soft lobe of his ear in my teeth and gave him a nibble.

"We can't—uh, can we?" His smile was huge with hope.

Well, I wasn't sure how much I was really willing to do for an audience, but I'd go pretty far for the fun of it. Whispering in the ear I'd just been munching on, I said, "There are things I'd be up for, if you are." My tongue darted into his ear.

"I don't know," he admitted honestly, huskily.

It was kind of fun to have Sebastian so antsy. "Oh? It'd make a good video on the Illuminati site, don't you think?" I slid my hand into his lap. My fingers traced the creases of his pants, but skirting the, shall we say, main attraction.

He laughed lowly. "I think this is our stop. Thank God."

Like newlyweds, we raced through the lobby holding hands and giggling. The mere idea of the possibility of public sex totally ramped up our whole experience. We talked through several scenarios. It was kind of like phone sex, but with benefits of . . . well, being actual instead of entirely imagined.

The biggest perk of all, in my opinion, was that we had

so much fun that I completely forgot about all our troubles, at least until Special Agent Dominguez called the hotel the next morning.

"I need to speak to Sebastian," he said when I picked up the phone and mumbled something vaguely like hello. "There's a problem with your husband's papers."

3

Strength

ASTROLOGICAL CORRESPONDENCE:
Leo

My heart pounded in my ears. Lilith stirred in antici-pation of danger. I glanced over at Sebastian, who still slumbered peacefully—or, at least, as peacefully as he could given that when he slept his body always returned to the position he was in the moment he died.

"Uh," I said to Dominguez, wanting to stall this whole conversation. "He's asleep."

"This is a courtesy call, Garnet. I want you to know that Immigration is on its way."

I clutched the sheet to my naked chest. "What? Why?"

"Seems his birth certificate has been forged—at least once," Dominguez said businesslike, and then he broke. "Christ, Garnet. How many vampires are in your life, anyway?"

"Two . . . oh, three, really, if you count Teréza, and a half: Mátyás is a dhamypr."

Dominguez muttered some expletives and a string of Spanish I couldn't quite catch. After his short rant, he added, "The people from Immigration are really serious. They may deport him."

"How can they? We're married." When Sebastian stirred, I struggled to keep the shrieking panic out of my tone, but my whisper was a little strained. "He's an American citizen now."

"Not if he committed fraud. In fact, if it's true, your marriage license isn't worth the paper it's printed on."

"We're on our honeymoon. You can't do this to us."

"I'm not. Immigration is. And, honestly, I sympathize, Garnet, I really do. That's why I called to warn you. I've got to go. Good luck."

He hung up before I could voice a response. Lilith's strength pulverized the phone's receiver. Sebastian groaned but didn't wake. There was a time when Lilith's show of power would have snapped him into alertness. But the blood bond he had with Her got diluted every time he drank someone else's blood. Even though I let him bite me on a regular basis, he needed more than I could possibly provide. I'd be jealous, but I had bigger things to worry about, like the Immigration goons showing up to deport him.

I shook his shoulder. "Wake up," I shouted. "We have to go."

Jumping out of bed, I immediately started packing our

suitcases. We could drive to Canada. It was relatively close. Plus, it had to be easy to cross the border; it's not like they had a fence.

As I packed, I consciously calmed my breathing. We could not afford to have Lilith rise up at a moment as delicate as this. When Lilith surfaced She had a tendency to, shall we say, overreact. She made no distinction between friend or foe, right or wrong. Her motto could be summed up as "Kill. Kill them all."

Sebastian sat up and blinked at me sleepily. "What are you doing?"

"Packing," I explained, tossing his shirts into his open suitcase. His jaw tightened as they formed a jumbled pile. "Immigration is going to be showing up any minute asking questions you can't answer about your birth certificates. I guess you have more than one?"

"Why were they looking into my birth certificate? My passport is valid."

I stopped my frantic tossing for a moment. "I don't know."

"My country of origin isn't going to dispute my birth certificate," he said, emphasizing the singular nature of the last word. "Of which there is only one, officially."

Without anything more to do, I started shifting from one foot to another, which must have looked pretty silly given that I was stark naked. Suddenly, I was feeling not only at a loss as to what to do next but kind of chilly too. I hugged my chest. "I don't understand."

"I have an arrangement with certain people in the Austrian government," Sebastian said. Reaching to the floor of his side of the bed, he picked up his underwear and jeans. "My money stays in Austrian banks and I invest in Austrian interests as long as my identity is protected and supported. They will not, if they want to keep my money—and believe me, they do—deny the validity of my birth certificate."

"So . . . what do you suppose the problem is?"

He stood up to stomp into his clothes. Out of his jeans pocket, he grabbed his iPhone. Sliding his finger over the surface expertly, he flicked through some screen then put it to his ear. "I don't know, but I'm going to call the Austrian embassy in D.C. right now." Smiling at me with a wolfish grin, he added. "You should probably get dressed. You look, uh, cold."

Blushing, I covered my nipples and hunted around for my clothes. We'd been a little exuberant last night. My panties were on the lamp shade. "I still want to run away and hide."

"Let's find out if we have to," he said. Someone on the other end must have connected, because he said, "Hello? This is Sebastian Von Traum. I need to speak to Ambassador Nowotny. Tell her it's an emergency."

I pulled my panties off the shade and tossed them onto the "dirty" pile I'd started to one side of the dresser. Out of my suitcase I grabbed a new pair. Of course, because this was meant to be our honeymoon, all the panties I'd packed fell squarely into the "sexy" camp rather than on the practical side. After wedging myself into a thong, I resolved to buy some new underwear at Target if we stayed here much longer.

"Eva? Good to hear from you too. Yes, it's been far too long. Uh-huh. Yes, definitely. We loved your wedding gift," Sebastian said, giving me the munching-fingers gesture that implied she was far too chatty.

What gift? I mouthed to Sebastian.

He waved me away with a "Later," and then turned toward the wall.

"I'm sorry, but I may not have a lot of time," he said, which reminded me to quick get into my jeans and throw on a bra. "Let me cut to the chase." After that came a flood of Austrian, which I guess is basically German, but it was all Greek to me, if you know what I mean.

I was just slipping my favorite pink and sequined Hello, Kitty sweater over my head when there was a knock—really, more of a pounding—at the door.

"Immigration," someone announced, like they were going to ram the door in if I didn't voluntarily unlock it. "Open up!"

I glanced at Sebastian, who spoke even more furiously into the phone. Then he jabbed his finger onto the touch pad angrily. He slammed down the iPhone onto the end table so hard I thought they both might shatter.

"Should I answer the door?" I squeaked, almost too petrified to move. Lilith sent waves of heat along my body just to let me know that She'd be more than happy to dismember these guys.

If Sebastian didn't do it first.

Another presence bubbled at the edges of my consciousness, momentarily disorienting me. Though the feeling this Goddess brought with Her was quiet calm and strength. If I needed a little divine help, it seemed Athena offered something not quite so destructive.

My lips curled in a snarl as Lilith asserted Herself.

Ignorant of my inner war, Sebastian marched over to the door and flung it open. "Apparently," he shouted quite angrily into the stunned faces of a bunch of men in yellow vests with Homeland Security emblazoned on them, "I need to let you assholes arrest me so the embassy has 'reasonable cause' to get involved." He threw his arms out as though offering his wrists for handcuffs, but which looked, in practice, a lot more like a rude suggestion. "I surrender," he snarled, though that also sounded more like a challenge.

Nobody moved. Despite the fact that some of them had guns at the ready, they all seemed confused as to how this was supposed to go down now that Sebastian had rather belligerently capitulated.

One really brave guy holstered his gun and stepped forward with handcuffs. He stood in front of Sebastian for a moment, as apparently he didn't quite have the guts to actually snap them on Sebastian's wrists. Sebastian grabbed them and started putting them on. My heart ached at the sound of the metal teeth slipping into place. As he finished he said to me, "Garnet, go to the consulate of Austria." My mouth opened uselessly, and he said, "There's one here in

Minnesota. Eva said it's on Highway 55 or something. Anyway, you sit on the consul general until he tells you I'm a free man. Understood?"

"Yeah," I said. Athena's calm had settled around me like a protective cloak, muffling my desire to slaughter the enemy. Taking in a deep breath, I filled my lungs with a cool, dispassionate collectedness. "Of course."

"Also," he said, "I would like a shirt."

I suddenly realized he hadn't put one on yet. I hurried and grabbed one from his suitcase. It was a white button-down . . . and a bit wrinkled. I handed it to the brave Homeland Security officer. He started to put it over Sebastian's shoulders, but Sebastian shook his head. "I'll carry it," he said. When the man handed it to him, Sebastian looped it over the cuffs on his wrists. "Thank you. Now, gentlemen, if you would escort me out." He gestured toward the elevators.

Sebastian's voice was still clipped with anger, but he sounded a lot calmer than I felt watching them take him away.

In fact, it took all my effort not to loosen Lilith on all their asses. My hands shook as I carefully closed the door with a click.

Turning the lock, I couldn't hold back anymore. I let Her go.

I woke up in the middle of the floor in a room that looked like a rock band from the seventies had partied there.

Chairs were smashed. Splinters from the bed frame littered the floor. Wallpaper hung in strips. The bedsheets and curtains had been shredded. Shattered pieces of tabletop decor spread out from where I knelt, like blast marks from the epicenter of a bomb.

And there, at my feet, lay the smashed remains of the cherubs. Like a sadist with a fly, Lilith had plucked their little wings off, one by one.

I guessed Lilith didn't like the statue much either.

At least two of my fingernails had broken, and my knuckles felt bruised. I was still breathing like a racehorse.

This was the part I hated.

Any time Lilith emerged there was always some kind of horrible cleanup involved. Picking up a shard of a once-beautiful pottery bowl, I sighed. I supposed I should be grateful this time didn't involve burying bodies.

The memory made me sick. In fact, a little flutter of nausea burbled up, and my stomach dropped, like I was suddenly falling. Dipping my head, I put my palms on the floor to steady myself until the feeling passed. I breathed through it and managed not to add a puke stain to our mounting property-damage bill.

Jesus, the Ordway Room! Given that it cost us a couple thousand a night just to sleep here, I couldn't even imagine what it would take to replace it.

Sebastian was going to be hopping mad about that. Despite having a lot of money, he usually hated spending it—especially to take care of Lilith's problems—but he'd be more ticked if I didn't get my butt to the consulate like I'd promised. I found the alarm clock half under the bed. Its case was a bit cracked, but, miraculously, it was still plugged in and working. Lilith's tantrum had only taken five minutes. Okay, I had time to find a mind-clearing cup of coffee before I headed out. I picked myself up off the floor, brushed the plaster dust from my hair, and hung the Do Not Disturb sign on the knob on the way out.

I'd grabbed Sebastian's keys and his iPhone from the pile of debris that had once been the nightstand. I was really grateful Lilith hadn't smashed the phone. If I was going to find the consulate, I needed a Google map, bad.

My thick winter boots shuffled on the soft carpeting of the hotel hallway. Passing a cleaning lady, I looked away guiltily. Lilith always wrecked everything. She had almost literally come between Sebastian and me during sex. Now there was the room. Was our marriage always going to involve Lilith and Her disasters? Sebastian thought I was the vortex of some bad juju that always invited creatures of the night into our lives. What if it wasn't me so much as Lilith? My life had been crazy before Lilith, but rarely did it involve Gods or elves or zombies. How much easier would my marriage be without all these complications?

Hardly noticing my surroundings, I made my way down to the parking garage. It took me a few seconds after getting off the elevator to remember where we'd parked the car, and then a couple minutes more to remember what it looked like. I'd have asked the valet upstairs to fetch it for me, but that always made me feel weird, plus I didn't really want an audience while I tried to remember how to drive. Thank Goddess the loaner car was an automatic or I'd be completely screwed.

Sebastian favored classic cars built in the twenties and thirties, but they didn't tend to come with things like heaters. So in the winter, we borrowed whatever junker Hal had laying around at Jensen's, the auto shop where Sebastian worked whenever he wasn't teaching at UW.

Finally recognizing the beat-up Toyota with Wisconsin plates as the one we'd driven up from Madison, I stood beside the driver's-side car door for a moment in order to puzzle out Sebastian's phone for directions. I'd just managed to figure out how to turn it on when three guys in shapeless black parkas rushed up, shouting, "Down with the Illuminati!"

It all happened in kind of a blur. My brain registered kids in parkas brandishing their fists. One was tall, the other two medium. If the police asked me their description, all I'd have been able to come up with in that moment was: Yikes!

Apparently, Lilith decided She finally found the fight She'd been looking for. I squeezed my eyes shut. Oh, Great Goddess, my mind screamed, these poor kids are going to die! But instead of losing consciousness as was typical with Lilith, suddenly, and with hardly a thought from me, my hand that wasn't holding the phone snapped up in a classic traffic cop gesture of "Stop!"

The boys, who were running at full speed, bounced back, like they'd hit an invisible wall . . . which, I guess, technically, they kind of had.

With my magical vision, I could see it sparkling silver, like a giant circular shield. My inner ear heard the sound of a thousand hissing snakes—wait a minute, snakes? That wasn't a sound I usually associated with Lilith, no, it seemed a lot more like a certain classic Greek Goddess.

Athena!

My knees trembled as if with the effort of supporting something heavy, and I thought that they might buckle any moment. My eyes blurred, but I saw the boys standing still as stone.

They seemed uncertain what to do next. Meanwhile, I showed them Sebastian's phone. "I'm calling the cops!"

That made them exchange nervous glances, but they didn't move. Maybe they could tell I had no idea how to use Sebastian's phone. Or perhaps they sensed that Lilith's fire had started competing with Athena's cool control over my body. My knees knocked in earnest, and sweat steamed from my forehead. I had no doubt that if the boys attacked again it would be Lilith they'd face.

And this time, when I awoke, there'd be blood on my hands.

My arm started to droop from the fatigue of holding Athena's mighty shield. One of the boys in a ratty parka took a daring step forward.

"Don't," I said weakly. "You wouldn't like me when I'm angry."

Just then, from out of the shadows of the parked cars, someone approached. "You there!" he shouted, carrying a baseball bat. "Get away from her!"

I blinked. The menacing figure approaching almost looked like James Something, except, you know, I couldn't be sure. Which I guess meant it was him.

"Get out of here," he yelled again, this time waving the bat around threateningly. Taking one look at James and his manly command of the Louisville Slugger, the boys bolted. But not before one of them—the brains behind the operation?—spit on the ground and snarled, "Eat the Rich."

Wait, was I just assaulted by a roving gang of social progressives? Ack, those were supposed to be *my* people!

Light-headed, I held on to consciousness by tightly gripping the car door. Lilith seemed equally unsettled. She shifted and scattered under my skin, giving me hot and cold flashes. I thought I might actually throw up this time.

James Something cautiously came up beside the car, holding the bat loosely at his side. "Are you all right?"

"You know, I used to have a shirt that said that," I muttered. "I stopped wearing it because, you know, with Sebastian the connotation seemed kind of kinky."

"Sorry?" He asked again. This time I noticed the slight British accent.

"James Something!" I said in happy acknowledgment, even though my world spun as I turned to face him. "Am I ever grateful you've been stalking us!"

He put his arm out to steady me, but I stumbled away from it. "Sorry, but if you touch me I'll probably puke."

His hand retreated guiltily.

Lilith finally settled with a low, uncertain groan, deep inside my belly. It felt wrong, somehow, like She retreated in pain or fear. Despite the unease of it, I was just happy to feel the floor solidify under my feet. Plus, without Athena's intercession those kids would be dead, I was sure of it.

James Something continued to hover nearby protectively. I looked him over measuringly, keeping a careful watch on that baseball bat. "You know," I told him, "I really would have thought you were on their side."

"Not hardly. The Order of the Green Garter is ever at your service, madam."

Oh, well, if it was like that . . . "Great. Do you know how to work an iPhone?"

Turns out my main problem was a lack of signal. James Something suggested we go upstairs, but the restaurant wasn't open and I wanted a cup of coffee. It was actually quite unreasonable how much I'd done this morning before imbibing a single drop of caffeine.

I still didn't trust James Something, but since he was going to stalk me anyway, I took him along in my search for a cup of joe. Since I needed to get to the consulate as soon as humanly possible, I decided if I didn't find something in a block or two I'd give up and go cold. Meanwhile, James ditched the baseball bat in back of a beat-up Outback station wagon parked not far from Sebastian's car. The brief view I had of the various weaponry in his trunk did little to make his case that he was friendly, especially since he seemed to have a good supply of garlic and sharpened wooden stakes.

Of course, I'd be more worried if either of those really worked on Sebastian. Sebastian is really quite fond of garlic, and a stake to the heart only immobilizes him. And pisses him off, but I figured that was a detail James Something could figure out on his own, if he was stupid enough to go after Sebastian, which supposedly he wasn't going to since he claimed to be some kind of knight and on our side and everything.

When he noticed my eyes on the weapons, James quickly shut the hatch and flashed a nervous smile. "It's good to be prepared."

"Hmmm-hmm," I murmured, though it was a skeptical affirmative. "Sure, so the Green Garters are Britain's answer to the Boy Scouts?"

"What?" He laughed. "No, no, nothing like that."

Yet somehow he didn't manage to answer the question either. Why was I not surprised?

We found a place in the Landmark Center across the street where I could get a pastry as well as a nice, strong cup of coffee.

With my hands wrapped around the paper cup for warmth, I stared up at the reddish marble columns of the four stories that loomed majestically over the wide, empty space below. The coffee shop huddled against one end of the atrium, like a mouse in the shadow of a cathedral.

Noticing my glance, James Something said, "John Dillinger was held here when it was the courthouse, did you know?"

"Really? That's kind of cool." I took a sip of the black, deliciously bitter coffee, and headed for the door. When I was at home at my favorite coffee shop in Madison, Holy Grounds, I always had a honeyed latte, but I found when I traveled I preferred hard-core coffee. Plus, there was something about Minnesota—a nod to its spartan Norwegian heritage, perhaps—that made me take my coffee unadorned here. "Did you figure out the phone?"

"Oh, some time ago. I've got you all set to get to the Austrian consulate." He handed me Sebastian's iPhone with a polite smile.

Up close, James Something radiated a bit more personality. His eyes, I noticed now, were a delicate shade of pale blue, which actually seemed capable of flashes of intensity. The boring mousey color of his hair occasionally had streaks of gold blond that could, in the right light, shine. "So, what's this organization you're part of again?" I asked, checking the time on Sebastian's phone. Great Goddess! It'd been nearly a half hour. I needed to get a move on, especially since, according to the phone, the consulate was all the way out in North Minneapolis or something.

"Order of the Green Garter," he said in a reverent whisper.

The guy seemed normal enough, except he got the vaguely intense gleam when he mentioned his order. Frankly, I was always a bit leery of people who belonged to orders, given my experience with the Order of Eustace, the Vatican witch hunters. Plus, anyone who carried weapons in his car made me more than a little nervous. "Well," I said, with what I hoped was an okay-this-is-your-cue-to-exit tone, "thanks again for the rescue."

He touched his hand to his heart and gave me a slight bow. "At your service, as always, lady."

James's show of chivalry tickled me almost as much as being called a lady. I wondered why Sebastian was convinced that this guy was with those Illuminati Watch thugs. He seemed sincere, but honestly, I'm not the best judge of people. I shrugged.

"Well, I really have to take care of this," I said, lifting the phone.

Like some old-fashioned guy, James held the door for me. I stepped out into the cold air. Aches had settled into my body. I could feel the bruises Lilith had left after Her tantrum in the hotel room and the muscle strain from holding Athena's shield. I was getting too old for this; it kind of made me miss trolls and Frost Giants.

James Something was still at my heels after crossing the busy intersection to Rice Park. "Are you coming with me all the way to the consulate?" I asked, a bit irritated.

After last night's snow, the ground was dusted with fluffs of white that sparkled blue and yellow in the sun. Pigeons milled around near a broad, circular fountain that had been closed for the season. They cooed noisily and scattered in a flurry of wings as we passed a bronze statue of F. Scott Fitzgerald holding an open book.

"I'll follow in my own car, of course."

Right, I'd forgotten he had nothing else to do but stalk Sebastian and me all day. I chewed on my lip at that thought. I wondered how Sebastian was holding up. He was so mad when he left. And who knew we'd gotten a wedding present from the Austrian ambassador?

Sebastian certainly had his share of secrets.

I was anxious to get to the car and get a move on.

"We should really cross at the light," James said as I stood between two parked cars trying to gauge the best time to make a dash for it.

"Why? Did you take a vow not to jaywalk?"

"A knight is required to be as law abiding as possible."

"I'm not a knight!" I said with a snort. A break in the flow of cars came, so I darted through the exhaust-smudged slush to the other side. James shook his head and pointed to the crosswalk. "I'll see you at the consulate."

I rolled my eyes. I probably would.

The trip out to North Minneapolis was relatively pleas-ant, especially considering how much I hate to drive. I only got a little lost on the highway interchanges, and I got to listen to the radio stations I liked.

The meeting with the honorary consul general was uneventful, other than having the disconcerting experience of being treated like royalty. The "embassy" wasn't much more than a modern office in one of those ubiquitous brick and glass, five-story buildings in the suburbs that seemed to always house a tax consultant, chiropractor, and three law offices.

At first, I couldn't believe I was at the right place. Then I saw the consulate listed on one of those cloth building directories with the push-in letters near the elevator bank. The consul general himself was a nice, older man with a noticeable comb-over and a bushy gray mustache. He invited me into his office, which smelled faintly of pipe smoke, and plied me with coffee and treats and assurances that D.C. had everything under control and that Sebastian would be released later this afternoon.

Some honeymoon this was turning out to be.

Still, there didn't seem to be much I could do about it. At least nothing sitting here . . . I still had a "normal" spell to undo. Though I got the sense that the consul general would be happy to pull out a game of checkers or some other grandfatherly pastime while we waited.

No offense, but I could find better places to hang out. I knew that Sebastian wanted me to stay on this guy, but he seemed so competent that I really didn't know what relentlessly harassing him would really get us.

Thus, I stood up with a smile. I thanked the consul general for his help and made sure that I'd left my contact information so as soon as he had news he'd let me know.

In complete opposition to my mood, the sun shone cheerily as I stepped outside. Chickadees twittered argumentatively in the tall white pines that lined the parking lot. The glare from the sun reflecting off the snow made my eyes water.

After waving hello to James Something, who was sitting in his brown Outback reading the *Star Tribune*, I drove aimlessly in the direction of Saint Paul and the hotel.

Somehow I found myself headed for my old neighborhood. Having exited the highway, I tooled along River Road heading from the Saint Paul side toward Franklin Avenue and Minneapolis. There were several open spots on the Mississippi despite the cold, and an enterprising bald eagle swooped in lazy circles above the wooded banks.

I hardly needed the sign to let me know I'd crossed over into Minneapolis proper. All of a sudden there was an almost palatable switch of . . . attitude. Square gave way to hip. Reserved became "artsy." It wasn't that the Minneapolis mansions were any more elaborate—no, in fact, if anything, the Saint Paul houses had more dignity and poise with their long stretches of snow-covered lawns and perfectly trimmed box hedges. On the Minneapolis side, in comparison, gardens got more plentiful, more showy, and much, much more whimsical. Boulevard arrangements became the norm. Tall, fluffy spikes of pompous grass stuck up above the snow along with dried seed heads of purple coneflower and withered black-eyed Susans, with pink flamingos or salvaged-metal sculptures thrown into the mix.

I smiled. Ah, home.

Crossing the bridge, I passed an art gallery that featured various, odd, brass Humpty Dumpty–type eggs smiling or grimacing at passersby from their perches atop a small fence.

Despite all the treats I'd been offered at the consulate, I pulled into the parking lot of the Seward Cafe. The parking lot of the Seward was cobblestone, and the tires hissed and sang as they bounced to a stop in front of the garden. Seward Cafe was across the street from a Holiday gas station and was wedged among a brick apartment building, an asphalt parking lot, and the co-op grocery, and yet it managed to provide a wild oasis of greenery in the summer. Even in the winter, I could sense its lingering glory. I got out of the car and wandered among the handmade trellises overflowing with the remains of last season's beans, tomatoes, and yellow squash. Yet, despite these careful plantings, mullein and scrub mulberries grew freely, poking above a thick carpet of leaf-littered snow. An icy cedar-chip path wound between the bare trees, leading to a weathered wood structure that looked a little bit like a house with the roof blown off.

I ducked under a canopy of Boston ivy and Virginia creeper vines into the roofless bricked patio. I stopped for a moment and let the magic of the place soothe me. The chaotic combination of carefully placed stones, random weeds, and odd bits of pottery gave the impression of something primal. It was intentional and fated, planned and wild, organized yet free.

Magic.

The cafe building itself was not impressive. A single story with a flat roof, and nearly windowless, it looked like an overgrown box in desperate need of fresh paint. The screen door sagged on rusty hinges.

The interior was like a sauna. The smell of coffee was so strong that a person could get a contact buzz from breathing too hard. I inhaled deeply and wished Sebastian was here with me. This was one of the places I really wanted to show him.

The space was divided in two. There was a front area where you ordered, and the other side was devoted to seating. Old-fashioned wooden booths lined a slightly raised platform near the wall, and tables made of thick planks of wood were scattered on the linoleum floor. Over one table hung a wire sculpture of a bird with black feathers; its eyes stared rather menacing out at all the dreadlocks and body piercings that sat at various tables eating dishes with names like Whole Earth and Vegan Fluffy.

Ordering food was a little like taking part in some kind of art installation as well and wasn't easy for the uninitiated. Luckily, I felt I was among my own kind here. I knew customers were expected to make their selections from a shared menu that had a permanent spot near the front, write down their choices on a slip of paper complete with prices and totals, and hand it to the cashier. The guy behind the counter wore a T-shirt that expressed hopefulness for the eventual release of Leonard Peltier. I smiled at him as I handed over a request for my old favorite, Super Green Earth, and a cup of regular, plain coffee.

With a grunt that I took as flirtation, he handed me a mug, which I filled myself from a big, silver urn. Beside it sat a glass mason jar with a handwritten label announcing that refills were fifty cents. Bills and coins nearly spilled out of the top. The honor system seemed alive and well, but, no surprise, given that this place always seemed to me like a throwback to a more trusting era of idealism, like the sixties or seventies.

While I waited for my name to be announced when my food was ready, I took my graying, chipped porcelain cup and found myself a booth under a slightly less disturbing piece of wire sculpture. This one seemed to be a hand break-ing through a canvas. The artist's description merely said, "Peace on Earth," which didn't really illuminate what she'd been going for, in my opinion.

Shrugging out of my coat, I leafed through a copy of the *Phoenix* someone had left at the table. It was a newspaper devoted to the substantial population in the Twin Cities of people recovering from drugs and alcohol or other addic-tions. As my eyes scanned articles about twelve-stepping, my mind wandered.

Seward Cafe was one of the first places I'd been drawn to when I moved to Minneapolis from the small farming community of Finlayson, Minnesota, where I'd grown up. The people this restaurant attracted shared my values of recycling, renewable resources, and general respect for the earth. I'd mellowed in the intervening years and felt a bit conspicuous in my leather boots.

The younger me would be horrified to know what I sometimes fed my cat, much less myself, some days. Of course, in those days I didn't harbor a vengeance Goddess and wasn't married to a vampire.

My life certainly had taken quite a turn for the odd, hadn't it?

I looked over at a couple seated at a nearby table. She had a nose ring and multicolored hair, and he had dreads that roped nearly to the small of his back. They were laughing about something, and I found myself kind of jealous. Sure, they might be outside of the mainstream with their fashion and, most likely, their politics, but they were probably able to walk home without being accosted by Illuminati Watch thugs or werewolves.

Even without the faerie queens and trolls, my life wasn't very "average," was it?

Oh, nuts! That reminded me, I should find someplace to do the "normal" reversal spell.

I had half hauled myself to my feet when I heard a voice call my name.

"Garnet?"

I looked up into a face straight from the past I'd been lamenting. "Larkin?"

Oh, this was awkward. Larkin was the guy I'd had the scandalous fling with. Worse, I sort of forgot to dump him. Instead, I stopped answering his calls.

I remembered Larkin as a sweet guy. In fact, I had a tendency to go for two types of men: alpha males and what used to be referred to somewhat derogatorily among my friends as SNAGs—sensitive New Age guys. Larkin was a SNAG.

And was standing there wearing tie-dye no less.

His short blond hair was stylishly unstyled, and he had a scruffy, oh-despite-myself-I-couldn't-help-but-find-it-kind-of-cute goatee. It struck me how much he looked like William, my co-worker at Mercury Crossing. That thought made me blush. I had once told William I would have dated him in another life; apparently, I had.

"Wow, you look different. I almost didn't recognize you," Larkin was saying. He shouldn't have recognized me at all. When Lilith had entered me on that fateful night, my blue eyes turned purple. I used to have blond hair—I guess I still did; it was just hidden under black dye.

But bits of the love spell lingered between us. I could feel it stirring my own heart.

"I thought you were dead," he said. Again, he was supposed to have. After the witch hunters killed my coven, they burned the covenstead to the ground. I let the authorities and everyone else presume I'd died alongside of them. It was part of my clever plan to keep the witch hunters off my scent, which would have worked much better in retrospect if I hadn't continued to use my real name and Social Security number when I moved to Madison. Master criminal, I was not.

"Yeah, I know," I said apologetically. "Hey, how've you been?"

"You mean after you disappeared on me?"

"Uh," I said, hiding my guilty face as I took a sip of my coffee. I cleared my throat. "Yeah."

"Liza and I got back together for a while, kind of for show and because everyone sort of expected us to. But we could never rekindle the flame. It didn't last."

"I'm sorry," I said, because well, Liza had been a good friend and I totally messed up her life for this guy I thought I wanted so damn much. Turns out, I needed less talking and more alpha in bed. I snuck out on Larkin after only one night. I found it hard to look him in the eye now. The wood grain on the table seemed infinitely more fascinating at the moment.

"Nothing has really worked out in the romance department, honestly."

I looked up at the quaver in his voice. Was he going to cry?

In an uncharacteristically bold move, he grabbed my hand. My sense of balance shifted, but I didn't get double vision at least. I resisted the urge to pull away with clenched teeth.

"I've only ever loved you, Garnet," he said. He brought my knuckles to his lips and kissed them.

"Uh . . ." There was so much wrong here, including the

strange desire I had to grab his lapels and smash my lips into his. So I blurted out, "I'm married now. Didn't I mention it?"

His eyes widened and he stared at the ring on my hand, and then let go like it was hot. "Oh. Uh. Congratulations."

"Thanks," I said, feeling more than a little awkward and cruel. Here I was hurting this guy over and over again.

Larkin sat back in the seat and his shoulders slumped, defeated. My heart did a little thump in my chest. He looked so cute. I just wanted to take him home and take care of him. Of course, it had been that feeling that had gotten us in trouble in the first place.

He let out a long, slow breath, as if coming back to himself. He put on a brave smile that made my heart ache. "You know what's weird?" Larkin asked. "I swear I had a dream about you a couple of months ago. It was about you getting married, I think."

"How funny," I mumbled. That had been yet another magical goof-up of mine. When Sebastian and I were sending out invitations to our wedding, I'd been disappointed that so many of my friends in Minneapolis thought I was dead, so I'd conjured up a spell that sent out a "dream invitation." Except I kind of forgot to put a friends' filter on it. Everyone I ever knew got it, even sworn enemies.

I think I'm lucky Larkin never owned a car, or he might have spoiled that whole "any objections" moment at the wedding.

"So . . . what have you been up to, anyway?" he asked tentatively, clearly trying to make nice and be all adult with his see-we-can-be-friends tone. "I thought of you the other day. I saw your old tarot deck on the used shelf at Present Moment."

"What? You did? How did you know it was mine?"

"It was still in that case you made. Your name was on it. I almost bought it as a memory of you."

I tugged my ear. "Ah."

It was weird to think of my stuff out there, but the moony look in Larkin's eye was even stranger.

Luckily, the cook called my name and order, so I had to excuse myself for a moment to go fetch my food. After grabbing a tray and silverware, I stopped to dig two quarters from my pocket and refill my coffee.

Finally, I couldn't delay any longer. I returned to Larkin's expectant face.

"So, you never said what you've been up to," he said the second I sat.

What was I going to tell Larkin? Well, let's see, after killing the witch hunters with the help of the Queen of Hell, I moved to Madison, fell in love with a vampire, fought off zombies, shape-shifters, and a crazy ex-girlfriend of Sebastian's who was now dead, sort of. Oh, and I formed a new coven and got married to the vampire, who has a kind-of-teenage-mostly-immortal son.

Maybe I should just lie.

I set my tray down. "Yeah," I said, stuffing broccoli and eggs into my mouth quickly, "I've been okay. Living in Madison now. Sebastian and I have a farm. Well, really, it's

Sebastian's, but . . ." Larkin looked pretty crushed. Maybe the less talking about the new guy, the better.

"So where is this husband of yours? I mean, are you here alone?"

Okay, so it was stupid, but I started to cry. Maybe it was all the stress of seeing Larkin again, nothing being the way I remembered it. I don't know, but I found myself blubbering a bit.

"Oh," he said, helpfully. A little glimmer of something akin to hope flashed in his eye. "Oh. I'm so sorry."

He sounded like he really was sorry for me, but which part would he feel the worst about if he knew—the Frost Giant that ruined our trip or the anti-Illuminati creeps who probably sicced Homeland Security after Sebastian? I wiped my nose on a paper napkin.

"Can I ask? What's happened?" Larkin's voice was soft and soothing. He really was a sweet guy, and he reminded me so much of William just then I forgot how crazy I'd sound if I said:

"It's all the damn trolls and the monkeys and Homeland Security."

"Monkeys?" Larkin's mouth opened and closed a few times as he chewed on my response. Slowly, a smile spread across his thin face. Whiskers disappeared into dimples. "You know, conversations with you were always so . . . challenging. I miss that."

"Uh, thanks," I said with a final sniff, though I wasn't entirely sure how to take that. Minnesotans were notorious for their veiled insults. To describe something as "interesting" meant you found it vaguely inappropriate or offensive. To be "unique" was to be downright certifiable. So who knew how I should take "challenging"?

"You know," Larkin said after a few moments of smiling broadly at me, "if you're in town for a while, some of us are getting together for the full moon over at Courtney's place tonight."

"Oh, I don't know . . ." I mean, all the people who remembered me and Liza and Larkin would be there, wouldn't they?

"I'm sure everyone would be glad to see you," Larkin assured me. "Time heals all wounds, you know."

Did it? Or would I just leave that many more screwups in my wake after a thousand years?

"You've got to come for Courtney's food, at any rate. Don't you remember her scones?"

I did. Despite all the food I'd ingested, my stomach made happy noises.

"Courtney's is the house with the fire pit in the backyard?" I asked, mentally dredging an image from my memories.

"Yeah," he said, standing up. He gave me the rest of the details and added, "Dress warmly, if you come. And, you know, bring your husband . . . if he's the sort. Either way, I'm sure everyone would like to meet him."

"'K," I said, waving good-bye as he headed for the door. "It was nice running into you."

He gave me a long stare, like he was trying to decide if I was being sarcastic or not.

"Seriously," I said, because I felt I had to.

Larkin's eyes dropped. "What is it we always say? Merry meet, merry part, and merry meet again."

That was a strange thing to leave me with. It was usually said after magic was performed in a group, and I dunno, I didn't exactly "merry part" with Larkin. It was more like "badly part."

The cowbells on the door clanged as Larkin stepped out. Wind from outside brushed me coldly.

I brooded over Larkin until I started to feel genuinely depressed and my butt got sore from sitting for so long. Besides, the reversal spell was way overdue. I needed to find a place to do my magic, and the cafe was too crowded. I could go back to the hotel, except Lilith had trashed the room. As cold as it was, I felt certain I could find a quiet spot somewhere outside.

In fact, River Road had a number of secluded spots that would do the trick. Though I could easily walk the six or seven blocks from the Seward Cafe to the Mississippi, I decided to go in the car. That way, if Sebastian or the consulate called, I could get to them quickly.

Franklin Avenue and its odd collection of art galleries, co-op groceries, and trashy apartment buildings led directly to the river. In practically no time, I found myself snaking along the curvy road looking for a likely, out-of-the-way spot. Despite the subzero temperatures, plenty of runners and bicyclists frequented the sidewalks and street. From my previous knowledge of this area, I knew that it would get just more populated the closer I got to Lake Street and the Longfellow neighborhood. As soon as I could, I made a tight U-turn and headed back toward Franklin and the University of Minnesota's West Bank campus.

The road dipped closer to the river proper, and a sandstone cliff rose sharply on the left side, blocking my view of the city. Bare, gnarled trees clung precariously to crannies in the hillside, some growing almost horizontal to the ground, giving the whole area a much wilder, untamed, magical feel.

Plus, the instant I crossed back over Franklin, the atmosphere of River Road grew quiet and still. It was almost as if I'd passed some unseen barrier between the worlds . . . or that the faeries guarded this section of the riverbank.

Now we were talking.

This was *just* what I was looking for.

The only problem was that between the natural barriers of the cliff and the river, the road became quite a bit narrower and there was no real place to park the car.

When I finally found a spot, it was marked Permit Parking Only, but, as the place was deserted, I paid it no mind.

Crossing the street, I headed into the woods. I didn't have to be outside to do this spell, but it was always easier for me to get in the mood when surrounded by wildlife. The cliff had become more hill-like here, and I scrambled up the slippery, icy slope. I pulled myself upward by grabbing onto the rough bark of nearby tree shrubs. The flora was pretty sparse and I could still see the road, but all I really needed was a nice spot to sit for a second. A fallen tree provided just the place.

Wedging myself between some remaining branches, I sat. The Mississippi was almost completely covered in ice, though a small, slender spot near the center remained open water. A black crow cawed loudly as it passed overhead, chased by a gang of sparrows.

Seemed like a sign to me—a natural metaphor for my beleaguered life—so I got ready to cast the reversal. I closed my eyes and took in a deep, grounding breath. Once I felt myself relax, I reached out a gloved hand and traced a circle around myself. I didn't need to call any elements, as I was surrounded by them. I breathed in air, the sun heated my face with a soft fire, I felt water in the ice melting through my jeans onto my butt, and the earth lay under my feet.

My previous spell had been kind of a meditation on what I'd wanted. I'd burned a candle and tried to visualize a honeymoon without hiccups. Since it was all mental, perhaps the easiest way to dissolve my intention was to write it out, in the snow, and simply erase it.

I took my finger and wrote *a normal life*. With the soft snow, it wasn't entirely legible, but I knew what it said and that was the point.

Taking a moment, I meditated a little about what normal meant in my life.

Although perhaps *meditate* was really too strong a word, as I tended to focus on something—this time the ice-covered Mississippi—and let my mind ramble a bit around the subject. Running into Larkin had brought back memories of my life before Lilith. Bright Goddess, it was a sad day when demolishing a hotel room was considered a success because at least no one ended up dead.

Athena seemed to offer a more peaceful form of protection. I wished there was a way to trade. Maybe I could trade in the Mother of Demons for the Goddess of Wisdom?

Goodness knows I could stand to be wiser. Wisecracking I had a good handle on; making smart decisions about magic or people, not so much.

Above, I heard a strange sound, like a hoot. I glanced toward the sky and saw a snowy owl perched on a barren cottonwood limb, preening its feathers. When it caught me looking, it blinked once slowly, and then took off on silent wing.

Lilith's bird was an owl, but wasn't the owl one of Athena's symbols too? How strange that both Lilith and Athena shared that.

Looking at my markings melting in the sun, I tried to focus a bit more on my spell's intent. Out loud, I said somewhat ruefully, "Normal for me is messed up. I don't need any more of that, thank you very much."

With that, I rubbed it out from right to left.

"So mote it be," I said.

Lilith stirred, as though weakly trying to add Her

strength to the spell casting. At the same time, I felt a different presence settle over me for a moment. A shadow fell over me that seemed to be in the shape of a woman warrior, with muscles of steel, a shield, and a toga like the one Russell Crowe wore in *Gladiator*.

I scanned for the source, but it was only a cloud passing in front of the sun. My stomach dropped strangely. A sudden dizzy spell nearly toppled me from my log.

Then the feeling was gone. Had I raised power to end the spell? Something certainly happened. I could only hope it was what I needed. It wasn't much of a spell, but all it had to do was release whatever forces might be in play.

Then I wiped out the circle I'd cast around myself, only in the opposite direction. With a shiver of released energy as well as cold, I got up and headed back to my car.

Somehow, I'd gotten a traffic ticket. I grabbed it off the window with a silent curse, which I doubled when I noticed that a message was flashing on Sebastian's phone. Still, I took it as a good sign. Sebastian had been freed. I just needed to go pick him up.

Sebastian had the look of the proverbial bird whose feathers had been ruffled when I picked him up in front of the immigration office.

And he looked cold.

Even though I knew he was impervious to the weather,

my muscles gave a sympathetic shiver to see him standing on the snowy corner without a coat.

"I am going to kill someone," he said firmly, as he slid into the driver's seat I'd vacated as soon as I found a nearby parking spot.

"Oh?" He might be serious. He was a vampire, after all.

Sebastian pulled out into traffic. Downtown office buildings cast long, dark shadows on the narrow, busy streets. The growl of rumbling engines and the ding of the light-rail train penetrated the closed windows.

"Yes, and I think I'm going to start with that James Someone and then drain the life from all those Illuminati Watchers."

"Why?" Not that I didn't agree, I was just curious, you know.

"Because I'm sure someone tipped off Homeland Security to all sort of 'irregularities' in my history, and currently he's my only stalker. Besides, when I pushed Homeland Security guys on their sources they got all huffy, like they were embarrassed to have fallen for that conspiracy theory stuff. I'm sure it was James."

"James is in the Green Order of Garters or something like that, not the Illuminati Watch," I corrected, turning up the heater a notch. Ice clung to the hairs of Sebastian's arm.

Sebastian was so distracted by the news that he nearly turned the wrong direction down a one-way street. Of course, in downtown Minneapolis that was easy to do. It seemed every other one had a Do Not Enter sign. He sputtered, "The Order of the Green Garter?"

"That's what he said. Why? Is that bad?" I asked.

"No, just strange."

I hated that I always ended up having to ask questions like this, but I really was not up on my conspiracy nut-jobs. Monsters and magic, sure, but who shot JFK or where Atlantis went, not so much. "What's the Order of the Green Garter, anyway? Do I even want to know?"

"That's the odd thing. They're just, you know, knights."

"You mean, like, King Arthur knights?"

"Well, Arthur was the king, but yes."

"Okay, thanks for the technicality, nerd-boy." I sighed inwardly, but gave him a smile to soften my words. "So riddle me this: Why would a knight be sworn to protect you?"

"That would be silly. No one is."

"Well, James said he was," I noted, though I was suddenly less sure those were quite the words he'd used.

"Then he's just crazy."

I didn't know what to say in response to that, especially since it was very likely true. In a way, it would be a relief. Having a crazy guy stalking you seemed pretty normal compared to everything else in our lives. Maybe the reversal spell was already doing its magic.

Sun glittered on gray steel and glass office buildings. Interspersed were older, brick facades, and those with ornate stone carvings, their beauty lost among the taller shadows.

I wanted to tell Sebastian the good news about the spell

reversal, but I'd never quite gotten around to explaining the problem in the first place. Well, I thought, with a little internal shrug, what he doesn't know won't hurt him. Now that all the strangeness of faeries and monkeys and trolls was sure to fade, I should concentrate on salvaging what was left of this honeymoon. As long as Lilith doesn't interrupt us again, that is.

Glancing over at Sebastian, who squinted into the bright sunlight, I wondered what regular people talked about. Oh! I could ask about his day. "So I guess everything worked out with Immigration?"

"Oh yes," Sebastian said in a clipped tone that implied he was still quite angry about the whole situation. "There will be a formal apology issued by the U.S. government if I have anything to say about it."

"Wow," I said.

"There is one thing I've learned that has stayed true in every century: Money talks."

I mumbled my agreement. Sometimes it was hard to believe I'd married such a staunch capitalist, though his comment got me thinking about those "Eat the Rich" guys who attacked me. Hmmm, was that another need-to-know-basis thing Sebastian didn't need to know?

It all depended, of course, if they were part of the not-normal normal of our life. On the surface, they seemed pretty mundane and not at all magical, which would put a big check in the "I should tell him" column. Plus, if he somehow found out I neglected to mention an attack, he might get pretty cranky. Like any good alpha male, Sebastian wants to be my protector, even if he knows I'm carrying a pretty high-powered Goddess and can mostly take care of myself.

Mostly.

Frowning, I placed my hand over my stomach where I always imagined Lilith slumbering, coiled up like a snake. I could sense Her presence, but it seemed somehow muted, distant. Maybe She was feeling as off me as I was of Her.

It struck me as a little odd, but maybe Her detachment was a good thing. I mean, Lilith was all about vengeful passions. And why I got stuck with Her of all Goddesses when I put out an open call for help that night when the witch hunters attacked, I never really have understood. I mean, maybe She was on my mind because my coven had been studying the Sumerian pantheon, but I've often wondered why me, why Her?

Athena's wisdom could be a nice change. Fierce and smart! Yeah, that's more who I'd like to be.

We turned down Sixth Avenue and drove past the Metrodome, a covered stadium, which always looked to me like a supersized version of one of those old Jiffy Pop popcorn pans all filled up, except white instead of silver. Or maybe like a blimp had gotten stuck inside a round building. Anyway, it was one of the weirdest-looking downtown landmarks, in my opinion.

The speeds on the highway weren't much better. We were in stop-and-go traffic. Behind us, the sun set bright orange, complementing the endless line of deep red brake lights that stretched ahead.

"You realize you stopped talking, right, darling? It's not like you. Are you okay?"

"Sorry, lost in thought," I said, staring out at the steep bank along the shoulder. Barren lilac bushes, scrub trees, and tangled weeds grew wild along the upper edges to form a natural sound barrier for the neighborhoods that flanked the highway.

"I can't wait to get back to the hotel and just relax," Sebastian said.

Oh no, the hotel room! "Uh, oh . . . about that . . ." I started.

Sebastian's face instantly crumpled into a deep scowl of suspicion. In the moment he took his eyes off the road, we nearly rear-ended the car stopped in front of us. Sebastian angrily laid on the horn.

I seriously didn't want to tell him about the trashed room in the mood he was in, so instead I said cheerily, "We've been invited to a party."

"A party?" Sebastian's face lightened, but he still sounded very incredulous. "How . . . we've been here less than day; you work fast."

"I happened to run into a friend at the Seward Cafe. It's a full-moon ritual, but, trust me, it's more like a party." Or maybe everyone there will point at me when I walk in and shout, "Jezebel!" Though that still seemed slightly better than dealing with how Sebastian was going to freak when he saw the state I left the room in.

"Oh, well, sounds fun. We should stop back, anyhow. I still need to change."

"Let's go shopping!"

"What?"

"Seriously, we could go to the Mall of America, grab something to eat, and head over to my friend's house in time for the party. I mean, the sun is already setting." I checked the dashboard clock. "They'll be starting in an hour. Perfect!"

Apparently, acting like things were decided made it so. As soon as he could, Sebastian turned us toward the Mall of America.

When I lived in the Cities I was never a huge fan of the place my friends called "the Sprawl." But Sebastian had earlier confessed to secretly wanting to see the place that had been originally built to be the largest shopping center in the United States, so I knew it would be an easy sell. As an environmentalist, I tended to be ambivalent about the concept that bigger was better, and though I liked to shop as much as the next girl, there was something about the fluorescent lights and polished, slick surfaces of the mall that always made me bone tired after too long.

Still, I seemed to have postponed the whole hotel disaster. I could put up with the mall for that.

The building didn't seem all that huge upon approach. It wasn't any taller than four stories, and the empty, underdeveloped land all around confused my sense of proportion.

"Is that really it?" Sebastian asked, sounding a bit disappointed.

"Afraid so," I agreed, as we pulled into the parking area of the mall and found a spot near the doors of the very top ramp, named after the state of Pennsylvania.

Once inside, the volume of stores was much more apparent. We found a coat for Sebastian, a fun winter hat for me, and, miracle of miracles, something half decent to eat at the food court that fit my vegetarian diet. Only briefly did I think I saw the bulky image of a troll or some otherworldly creature staring at us from behind the cash register at Long John Silver's.

By the time we were back in the car headed for Courtney's backyard full-moon ritual, Sebastian and I were smiling and laughing again.

It was amazing what a little retail therapy could do for a body.

Finding Courtney's house from memory, however, proved slightly more difficult. Luckily, Seward isn't all that big, and it hadn't changed much in the years I'd been away. In fact, the neighborhood probably hadn't been substantially altered in decades given the size of the cottonwoods, silver maples, and other trees on the boulevard.

The area was largely residential. A lot of the houses were bungalows, mingled with two-story working class Victorians. The streetlights were on, casting pale yellow light on neatly shoveled sidewalks. Nearly every yard sported a campaign sign for a city council race, though there didn't seem to be much contention, except to see which candidate was the most liberal. I even saw several Green and Socialist party supporters.

"This was your old neighborhood, wasn't it?" Sebastian said. The dash lights illuminated a crooked, appreciative smile.

"You can tell, huh?"

He nodded.

As we turned the corner, I spotted my old apartment. The lights were on, and the shadows of people moved around inside. "Slow down," I told Sebastian.

He pressed the brake. "Did you spot it?"

"Not exactly. That's my old place," I pointed at the brick house with the wraparound porch. "I lived downstairs." Where there were new curtains and new tenants and no trace of anything to connect me, but I could almost still smell the basil herbs from my garden drying in bundles over the porcelain kitchen sink and hear Barney sharpening her claws on the eight-foot tall "kitty condo."

"Looks nice," Sebastian said, his foot tapping the accelerator. "Any sign of this place we're looking for?"

I glanced behind me one last time, and wondered if old Mister Pete, the landlord, ever fixed the downspout so the basement didn't flood every time it rained.

We drove around the block one more time, and, this time, as we scanned the narrow spaces between the houses, I spotted the flicker of firelight. We pulled into the first open spot we found.

Having seen my old place, I wasn't in a hurry to get out, however. A sense of foreboding, almost like a Spidey-sense, tingled at the back of my neck. Courtney's house looked both familiar and very different. Had she painted the trim or was it always that deep shade of purple and I had never noticed when I lived here? "Are you sure about this?" I asked.

"I thought you wanted to go," Sebastian said, his hand hovering over the key.

"I do, but I haven't seen any of these people in years." And there was the whole scandal, but I didn't mention that.

Sebastian nodded, waiting. "Honestly, I'm just as happy to go back to the hotel, myself."

The hotel. That cinched it. I reached for the door. "Yeah, well, the ritual won't last longer than an hour or so. I suppose it'll be fun." Pretty much anything would be more fun than the moment Sebastian saw the mess Lilith made of the room.

As we made our way down the block, Sebastian grabbed my hand. "Is everything okay?"

What to say here?

I mean, I hated to lie, but if I'd wanted to get into this before we'd already be on our way back to Saint Paul. "Uh, well, I suppose you'll find out if I don't tell you," I started.

Before I could go on, Sebastian took me by the arm and spun me so we faced each other. His face was shadowed with concern under the streetlight, and his breath came in a white cloud, "What? *What?*"

"I used to be lovers with one of the guys in Courtney's coven. I kind of broke up his relationship with my friend Liza, and, uh, people might remember because of the whole love spell deal. Bad witch. Dark magic. I feel terrible."

The tension evaporated from his posture, and he gave me a vaguely quizzical look. "Oh, is that all? The way you've been acting I was convinced it was something much more serious."

You mean like the hotel? But I just shrugged. "It was a pretty big deal at the time. The coven ended up hiving off over me!"

"Trust me, no one remembers."

"How can you be so sure?" I tucked my arm into his and we continued making our careful way toward Courtney's house on slippery sidewalk.

"Because. There's always a new 'it' scandal. Most people's memories for that sort of thing are mercifully short. If everyone remembered every inappropriate sexual encounter I ever had . . ." He shrugged. "Please. It's yesterday's news."

Now I was wondering what constituted "inappropriate" to a vampire. I resolved to ask him about it later. We'd come to the door. Courtney or one of her housemates had made an ivy wreath in the shape of a pentacle. Sprigs of mistletoe were scattered among the dark, spiky leaves.

It was totally the sort of thing I would have done in my craftier days.

"I hope you're right. I hope they've forgotten everything."

The moonlight suited Sebastian, of course. Somehow the darkness glowed on his skin, and deepened the color of his hair. Such a beautiful creature of the night, my husband.

"I could use my glamour and distract them," he said.

"Not necessary. They'll like you," I said. I rang the bell and hopped anxiously up and down on my toes. Sebastian put an arm around me to quell my nervousness. He was just kissing the top of my head, when the door swung open. It was Courtney. She squinted at me in that do-I-know-you? look, until I remembered how much I'd changed, what with the dyed-black pixie cut, Goth outfit, and purple eyes.

"It's Garnet," I said, untangling myself briefly from Sebastian to point to my chest. I tried to look like the blond, natural-fiber-wearing Green witch I used to be. "Garnet Lacey."

Her nose wrinkled for a moment, and then she clapped her hands excitedly.

"Garnet! Oh! I'm so happy to see you! Larkin said you might come!"

Much about Courtney was an exclamation point. She had big auburn curls, a large smile, and a brilliant green gown. Dimples punctuated a pleasantly round face, and she had an ample, though not overly large figure.

"This is my husband, Sebastian," I said.

"Oh, my, my!" Courtney nearly drooled as she scooped an arm under Sebastian's and all but dragged him inside. "Oh, do come in, darling."

The door would have slammed in my face had I not caught

the jamb with my toe. I rolled my eyes: Courtney hadn't changed much, it seemed. Sebastian twisted in Courtney's grip to give me a help-me glance.

Meanwhile Courtney was busily introducing Sebastian around as if he were the returning prodigal, not me. After leaving my coat in the pile on the built-in parson's bench, I trailed about two steps behind, mostly because the circle of friends seemed to close around them before I could squeeze in.

Like Courtney herself, the house was cheerful and exuberantly homey. The walls were painted bold colors, deep maroons and dark gold, which were probably historically accurate as the woodwork had been painted glossy white. Eleven-foot ceilings held tulip-shaded chandeliers. Likewise, her furniture was large, overstuffed, and comfortable looking. She had a collection of witchy-related knickknacks tucked into wall alcoves and on shelves of glass-fronted built-in buffets. She had glass unicorns and statues of delicately winged fairies that held tiny magic wands. An ammonite fossil was propped next to a reproduction of the squat, lumpy form of the Venus of Willendorf.

The house was crowded in more ways than one. People milled about, and I expended a lot of energy trying not to get jostled.

I was also sort of grateful that my complete change in appearance made me somewhat less recognizable. A few people squinted in my direction, when Courtney gestured, but their gaze never quite landed on me, like they couldn't discern the old me under my new look. My overtly Goth attire was catching a few disapproving stares, though, and I tugged at the lace on my shirt trying to hold back the desire to explain in a very loud voice that it was just a disguise, honest! Smoothing the cap of my short, dark locks self-consciously, I fell further behind Courtney's procession as I avoided the press of people.

Though there was no music, there was plenty of noise. Everyone chattered excitedly and now and again laughter would erupt from some corner.

I felt very left out. I'd been expecting a grand reaction, and all I got was indifference and blank stares. Sebastian was right. My old crowd had moved on, forgotten me. Much like Minneapolis and its changed landscape, it made me feel disoriented and lost.

Sebastian kept bending around, trying to find me in the crowd. I'd drifted farther away than I'd meant to, sort of hoping to see a familiar face of my own, some kind of sign that this world wasn't completely lost to me.

Lilith rumbled protectively.

As though prompted by jealousy, Athena's strength settled around my shoulders. The combination made my stomach unsettle even more, and I sat down on the edge of a sofa. Hard.

"Well, if it isn't Garnet Lacey. I hardly recognized you under all that tarty makeup, although I guess I should have. Showing your true colors finally, girl?"

It was, of course, Liza. My old, good friend from whom

I'd stolen Larkin. I guessed I was going to get that big reaction I'd wanted, after all.

I wished Larkin had told me *she'd* be here. If I'd known, I never would have come, wrecked hotel or not. Where was that weasel Larkin, anyway? I needed to give him a piece of my mind.

"Uh, hi, Liza," I said, cringing as I awaited the firestorm of her fury.

She hadn't changed all that much in the years I'd been away. Though still quite slender, Liza was a little plumper in the hips, like maybe all the trauma of the breakup had led to a lot of late-night, desperate ice-cream pints. She'd changed her hair; it was longer now. Plus, her dark brown locks were now shoulder length with highlighted stripes of auburn and burnt gold. It was a good look on her, honestly. I wished her face wasn't all blotchy and scrunched with anger, so I could tell her so.

"Surprised to see me?"

"I should never have come here," I admitted. "I'm really sorry."

Liza's grumpy expression crumbled deeper. "What? No 'It was a long time ago,' or 'He was never right for you anyway,' or 'Fuck you'?"

Was that what I used to say in situations like this? I didn't remember ever being quite such a bitch.

Lilith stirred warmly in my belly, almost like a deep, happy sigh.

Was *that* why Lilith chose me?

"No," I said, shaking my head violently, as if to reject the mere idea of myself as so hateful, so spiteful. "No, I'm not like that." And then to Liza's quizzical eyebrow arch, I added, "Anymore? Anyway, it was a long time ago, but I am still sorry. I never meant to hurt you. I never meant to hurt anyone."

She put her fists on her hips. "Well, maybe you should have thought of that before you screwed up my life."

Maybe I should think a lot more generally before I act. Perhaps I needed a shirt that read: What Would Athena Do?

"You're right," I said, stifling the urge to cower. What else could I say? Liza seemed baffled by my response and stood there staring at me like she'd just discovered me under a rock.

"Damn straight," she muttered, her anger seeming to dissipate.

Twiddling my thumbs in my lap, I found myself wanting to ask after old friends or find out what was new in her life. Knowing that the happy-chatter avenue was permanently closed made me feel even more awkward about the whole situation. Staring at her was no fun.

Though Liza blocked the most direct exit, I opted to scramble clumsily off the side of the couch in order to make my escape. "I've got to check in with Sebastian, make sure he's okay. Maybe we can talk more later. Bye!"

And then, despite the queasiness of all the human contact, I pushed my way deeper into the crowd, making my way toward the kitchen. I left Liza in my wake, her mouth moving in some response I couldn't hear. I didn't really want to know what more she might have to say; I just wanted to hide.

I knew, however, I couldn't escape for long. Now that Liza had recognized me, the word would spread through the crowd. I found the bathroom, which was surprisingly unoccupied. Stepping inside, I closed and locked the door behind me.

Oh, this sucked.

Most people did seem to have forgotten all the drama, but the two injured parties hadn't, and somehow that was worse.

Courtney's bathroom was a riot of color. Though it was a small room, the walls were painted a soft blue and she'd stenciled happy little cartoon fish everywhere. There were fish on the shower curtain, fish-shaped toothbrush holders, and a night-light in the shape of an angler fish whose bulb glowed when you turned the light off.

I sat down on the fuzzy, yellow toilet-seat cover, and stared blankly at the pink yarn rug with . . . yes, more fish. I couldn't help but smile a little at it all, even as I continued to fret. When I saw Larkin again, I was really going to give him a piece of my mind for setting me up like this, especially since, as far as I could tell, he hadn't bothered to show. It had been kind of shocking, though, to hear what Liza thought I'd say when I saw her. Had I really been that mean and unthinking when I lived here?

My own image of my past self had more to do with natural fibers and living simply, than with all these scandals and dramas. But when I really considered who I used to be, there was always Parrish . . . and Larkin . . . and I could easily think of a dozen or more other dubious choices that had brought chaos swirling into my life.

Maybe Sebastian was right. Perhaps there was something about me that engendered this particular kind of crisis. I mean, there was that time I accidentally conjured a djinn and it took the coven two months to track it down and send it back to the other side. Oh yeah, and those faeries I thought would be so cute? Turns out Irish Tuatha de Dannan are actually Gods and not something to be trifled with. Who knew?

Is it really any wonder that when I called for help, it was answered by a Goddess known for death and destruction?

Lilith warmed my skin with a soft tingle, as though She were saying, "There, there."

I ignored Her. How could I be so wrong about who I thought I was? I always thought I was more of a do-no-harm sort, and it turns out I'd been blithely causing damage at every turn!

With my hands clasped between my knees, I hung my head. Lilith didn't help. She was always making things worse, drawing bigger, nastier consequences to my innate stupidity.

I frowned thoughtfully at the *Finding Nemo* toothbrush holder. In my mind's eye, I saw an image of Athena: upright, steady, and calm. I felt myself standing up, as though ready to rise to any challenge.

Yeah, this is more like it, I thought, stopping for a moment to encourage the pathetic-looking woman in the mirror. You can be who you want to be, I told myself that classic affirmation. The past is gone. The future is ahead.

With those brave words and the sense of Athena striding boldly alongside me, I went back into the party in search of Sebastian.

Though I was ready for a battle, everyone seemed to be heading outside for the ritual. I grabbed my coat from the quickly dwindling pile in the front hall and I made my way through the kitchen and followed the flow of the crowd into the backyard. Even in the dead of winter, you could tell that Courtney had an enviable garden. The back door led to a cedar-plank patio. A path to the stairs had been shoveled. On either side of the steps, dozens of solar lamps in the shape of dragonflies cast a soft, purple glow on snow-covered strands of ornamental grasses. Along the edges of her property were artistic, nonlinear mounds of what were probably bushes or hedgerows. Here and there seed heads of some kind or other poked through the deep snow. Snow clung to the curves of a concrete statue of the Nile goddess, her crescent-shaped arms raised in a circle over her slender, serpentine head.

We followed a paving stone path someone had brushed clean. A fire had been started in a simple stone pit on the far end of the lot under the wide branches of a huge, gnarled red oak. Sebastian waved frantically at the spot next to him. I scurried to join him.

"I thought I'd lost you for sure," he said, tucking an arm around me.

"No chance of that," I said, standing on my tiptoes to give him a peck on the cheek. Courtney, who was standing on Sebastian's other side, gave me a jealous, yet mischievous smile.

"You two look nice together," Courtney said with a broad smile. "I sense a long, happy relationship."

Sebastian and I shared a goofy grin. Courtney's pronouncement seemed like a good omen. "Thanks," I told her.

"Hey, honey, I just call 'em like I see 'em," she said.

The thick oak logs on the fire snapped and popped. Someone tossed on a dry pine branch, and the flames leaped dramatically. Briefly, a welcome wave of heat warmed the front of my body. The firelight threw an amber flickering light on the faces gathered around the circle. Voices stilled. The dance of flames mesmerized us into a natural hush.

We all watched the bonfire quietly. Despite the chill, my shoulders relaxed. Something drew my eyes upward, maybe it was the sound of a passing jet. In a clear, dark sky hung the moon, full and yellow, shining through the twisted, gnarled branches of the neighbor's catalpa tree. My breath caught.

Following my gaze, Sebastian looked up as well. After we shared a moment of awe, he gave my hand a quick squeeze as if to say he could feel the magic too.

"I'm glad we came," he whispered into my ear.

I was, too, until, of course, Fonn dropped out of the tree and smothered the fire with a *whomp* of snow.

4.

The Hermit

ASTROLOGICAL CORRESPONDENCE:
Virgo

With the fire gone, the backyard plunged into a sud-den darkness. Someone gasped. The ambient light from the alley streetlamp illuminated the form of the Frost Giant. Fonn stood in the middle of the circle. Her eyes slowly swept the group, glittering menacingly. Icicles dripped from every part of her body, almost like the fringe on a leather jacket. Her short hair was white as the snow, and a tiny ice droplet hung from her hawkish nose. Wind swirled at her feet and billowed her brown fur cape around her.

There was no mistaking her otherworldliness, especially when, with a whistle of wind, her hound materialized out of thin air at her heel and let loose a soul-piercing howl.

Most people had been too stunned to react at first. But with the appearance of the dog and his hellish wail, everyone burst into activity—most of which could be summed up with, "Run, run away fast!"

Some people leaped toward the house. Others jumped to hide in the bushes. With shouts and screams, bodies scattered in every conceivable direction.

Sebastian grabbed my hand and started hauling ass to our car.

"I knew she'd be back," he snarled. I could see his fangs dropping with frustration.

He, of course, could run at inhuman speed. Meanwhile, I was stuck at mortal pace. The ground seemed uneven, and, though he was trying to help, Sebastian's grip jerked me forward clumsily. I concentrated on not tripping us up like some bad horror-movie heroine. It was difficult because I swore I could feel the breath of Fonn's hound at my back.

Somehow we made it to the car. I started to let go of Sebastian's hand to dash over to the passenger side, but Sebastian took me by the waist. He tore open his door and heaved me ungraciously over the driver's seat. My leg knocked into the stick shift, and my face slammed the upholstery. At the same time, I heard a dog whine. I'd just gotten myself into a more traditional arrangement on the seat when the car door slammed shut. An ice-covered Sebastian jammed the key into the ignition and fired up the engine. I hardly got the belt buckled as he peeled out of the parking space.

"Well," Sebastian said a few minutes later as we turned onto the highway at full speed, "that went pretty much the way I expected."

"What do you mean? Five minutes ago you said you were happy we'd gone."

"I was. I should remember it never lasts," he said. A shake of his head sent a shower of ice crystals everywhere.

I swiped white, melty flakes off my sleeves. Was that fair? Probably, but that didn't make me feel any better about it. "Not *every* time," I mumbled.

"Pretty much." Running fingers through his long hair, Sebastian combed out more snowy bits. He glanced in the rearview mirror and took a little pressure off the gas. "At least I think we lost her this time."

I double-checked. No rampaging ice hellhounds or demons. "That's weird," I said, turning back to face the front. "Seems kind of easy, doesn't it? We just drove away."

"Actually, I wrestled a giant dog first, but yes. And frankly, I think we should roll with this. I just want to go back to the hotel and shower."

Ooooh, he was cranky.

So I sat quietly and stared out the window at the moon we didn't get to worship as it seemed to skip like a stone over the rooftops of the buildings near the highway.

"Were you serious before?" I asked, coming back to something that had been niggling at the back of my mind since Sebastian had said it at the bookstore last night. "Was your life really more normal before I came into it?"

"Oh, definitely," he said without a moment's hesitation.

"Really? But you're a vampire," I pointed out.

"Thank you for noticing, but, really, outside of the being dead and drinking blood bits, I'm really pretty average when you think about it."

"Not to me, darling," I reminded him with a fond smile.

Without taking his eyes off the road, he returned my smile softly. "You know what I mean, though. I mostly fix cars and teach the occasional class."

"Nothing blog-worthy," I said.

"Exactly."

And not at all like me. The moon's face looked like a woman with her mouth open in a scream. "Is there something about me that attracts darkness, do you think?"

Truthfully, and despite his mood, I'd been hoping for a quick denial from Sebastian. Something along the lines of "Don't be foolish, of course not," but instead he gave an unconcerned lift of his shoulder and said, "Maybe it's karma from a past life. Some people just have more drama in their life."

What kind of person must I have been in the past to end up with the Queen of Hell as a body-mate? I shook my head. "Drama?" I repeated. "That seems more like the stuff I used to do. Stealing people's boyfriends and causing mischief."

Sebastian's lip twitched into a faint smile as if to say, "And this is different, how?"

"I don't cause all this stuff, do I?"

"Well, maybe if you stopped casting love spells your life would become a lot less complicated."

Because that felt far too true, I got mad. "You think I'm an irresponsible witch."

"That's not what I said," Sebastian shot back quickly. "I hate that you always jump to conclusions."

This fight had clearly been brewing under the surface. "Well, you always have to be right."

Sebastian's eyes narrowed to angry slits, and I had to resist the urge to stick my tongue out at him like a petulant child. We drove the rest of the way back to the hotel in stony silence.

I was so upset about our fight that I had nearly forgot-ten about the state I left the hotel room in. Sebastian stood staring at the ragged carpet and torn curtains, his face slowly turning purple with rage.

"Uh," I said. "Lilith was really upset when you left."

"Of all the stupid, irresponsible things . . ." There was that word again, the one I'd been brooding on. The blush on my face deepened in shame as he continued. "How could you let Her out?"

Irresponsible was becoming one of my least favorite words in the English language. Especially since, in this one case, I thought it was undeserved. "You have no idea how hard it was to keep Her from killing those Homeland Security guys."

"Oh, well, thanks for that."

His snotty tone had me seeing red, and I got the distinct impression that Lilith would be more than happy to explain Her actions to him directly. I gritted my teeth. Despite what Sebastian might think, unleashing Lilith was a responsibility I took incredibly seriously. So seriously, in fact, that I wasn't about to let Her at him, no matter how satisfying it might seem in theory.

When I spied my swimsuit hanging on the closet-door handle, I grabbed it and stomped off in the direction of the hotel's pool. "We can talk about this later," I said through clenched teeth. "I'm going away. Swimming. Or something."

"Typical," I heard him mutter as I jabbed my finger on the elevator button. Over his shoulder, he said louder, "I'll just take care of everything, shall I?"

The elevator doors swooshed open. "You do that," I shouted, stepping in.

"Fine," he said.

"Fine," I agreed as the doors closed with a ding.

Our first fight as a married couple had put me in a foul mood. I figured after a good soak in the whirlpool, I could head back upstairs and see if Sebastian had calmed down enough that we could have a reasonable discussion. In the public changing room near the pool, I slipped into my swimsuit.

Since I didn't have a lock for the locker, I decided to bundle everything under my arm and carry it with me, except my sparkly underwear kept slipping out and falling on the floor. And when I went to pick those up, I dropped my shoes.

Worse, when I accidentally brushed against someone's extended foot, I discovered the Sun God Apollo seemed to be lounging poolside with me. As I got up to head to the Jacuzzi for a long soak, feeling rather exasperated, I said to him, "Don't you have a golden chariot to ride or something?"

He glanced at me over the rim of his glasses with a look of pure arrogance. With a strong Italian accent, he said, "Listen, sister, sun's down, if you haven't noticed."

I stopped in my tracks. I hadn't expected a response, and certainly not one that seemed to confirm that my visions weren't just the hallucinations of a crazy lady. I probably should have taken the opportunity to ask him how it was that I could perceive his holy presence, but instead I blurted out, "You speak English? What are you doing in Minnesota, anyway?"

"I am everywhere and nowhere," he said in a voice that sounded like a thousand people speaking at once. "Part of everyone and everything, and yet not."

Surprised by the voice, I stepped back. The image of the gorgeous, golden-haired God shimmered, like heat coming off asphalt in the summer. Then he vaporized. A portly guy with wiry black hair and blue and white striped swim trunks sat blinking at me in confusion. He said in a harsh Boston accent, "Can I help you, lady?"

"Sorry," I murmured, scurrying to the Jacuzzi. The former God's eyes followed my progress into the foamy water. Then, with a shake of his head, he returned to the book he'd been reading, some spy thriller from the look of the cover.

I sank into the superheated water and tried not to keep looking over at the guy who once was Apollo. I had a very sick feeling in the pit of my stomach because, thanks to the God's words, I was beginning to understand my second sight. The answer lay deep inside my religious beliefs. I was seeing the "divine spark" that existed in everyone.

There was a story that was told about how the Goddess, desiring to experience and merge with the world, broke Herself into a million pieces and fell to earth. Everything living contained a bit of that divine spark, which, in turn, longed to be reunited to the Goddess.

I'd always believed that story because I liked the empowering idea of being one with the Goddess, but I'd always thought of it as, well, a metaphor. Maybe it still was, I told myself. I mean, just because when I touched someone I could see the God or Goddess within them, it didn't mean that image wasn't just their ideal core manifesting itself as a vision to me.

Of course, that whole they're-just-metaphors idea might be easier to buy if the God hadn't just spoken right to me.

I sank deeper into the bubbly water, trying to hide from the truth.

Despite living every day with a Goddess, I tended to mentally distance myself from the idea that, well, you know, all that was really real. It was, I suppose, another veil my mind just wasn't quite ready to cross. Vampires and ghosts and zombies seemed easier to accept, I think, because they were part of the darker side of nature.

It's like that personality test. It's always far easier to list the things about yourself that you hate. You can come up with five without even batting an eye. But when the tables turn and you have to list a similar number of positive attributes, the brain seizes up. You sputter. You realize this is hard, and it shouldn't be.

That's how I felt about acknowledging the divine presence.

It shouldn't be so difficult. I was on a first-name basis with at least one Goddess who, quite literally, was within me. But, see, that was the crux of the problem.

What if Lilith came to me that night when the witch hunters attacked and I called to any Goddess in desperation because like attracts like?

What if She, the Mother of Demons, was my personal inner reflection of the divine spark?

What did that say about who I was at the core of my being?

A few days ago I would have replied nothing and made the case that Lilith and I were like dark and light, polar opposites. But I was beginning to suspect that I didn't really know myself as well as I thought.

I'd certainly come face to face with a past I wasn't entirely comfortable with.

As if on cue, I saw Larkin waving at me from across the pool.

What was he doing here? I wondered, lifting my hand in a halfhearted return wave. Larkin took my response as an invitation, and he came over to the whirlpool. He wore a sporty red and blue ski jacket, like he'd just come to the pool from outside.

"I heard about the ritual. Are you okay?" he asked, crouching down on the concrete edge of the pool.

"Uh, yeah, fine. Although thanks for nothing. You didn't tell me Liza would be there," I said.

"Yeah, you know, it never occurred to me. She's been kind of out of the pagan community since everything went down. Talk about bad luck." He stared at the bubbles of the Jacuzzi's water for a moment, and I sensed he had something more serious on his mind. Finally, he looked up and asked, "Can I buy you a drink? I'd really like to talk."

"About what?"

"Some closure?" he sounded doubtful that it was even possible. "That whole thing between you and me was so long ago. I thought maybe it might be time to bury it."

Bury? That sounded ominous, but he seemed to be struggling for the right words. I saw a range of emotions play across his face. It would be nice to put the past behind us. I'd like to show Larkin the kind of woman I could be, given a chance.

I was about to agree when he added, "Or I bet that new

husband of yours would love to hear about your casual infidelities."

My mouth hung open. "You can't threaten me with exposure. I already told him about you and me and Liza."

"But does he know you had a boyfriend at the time?"

Was that true?

"Sebastian wouldn't care," I said, even as I pulled myself up out of the superheated water. Goose pimples rose on my skin from the temperature difference, and I grabbed my nearby towel.

"Are you sure about that? Because I'd be happy to fill him in on every little detail." Larkin stepped closer to me. I thought I caught a whiff of cheap beer.

"Are you drunk? I thought you came here to make amends."

He seemed to find the idea amusing. "I came here because I have some things I want to say to you that you need to hear."

The guy-who-was-also-Apollo watched us with a nosy, annoyed expression. We must have looked quite the sight with me in my yellow one-piece and Larkin in his puffy ski jacket. He had the look of a guy who might call security on Larkin and me. I didn't want to cause any more trouble with the hotel. Sebastian and I were already in it deep thanks to Lilith.

"I'll meet you in the bar. Just give me a minute to change."

"You're not ditching me that easily. I'm coming with you."

"Not into the women's locker room you aren't."

"Just put your clothes on here—over your suit."

I snuck a peek at the Apollo guy, who seemed to be hunting around for his cell phone. "Okay, okay!"

I quickly pulled my shirt over my head and shimmied into my jeans. They stuck to my wet hips and I had to tug at them, all the time Larkin stood there. That left me holding my lacy bra and my thong underwear. Larkin seemed ready to smirk, so I wadded them into a ball and hid them under my towel.

"Let's go," I said, sliding my bare feet into my tennis shoes. The insoles squished uncomfortably as I walked, and water instantly soaked through my shirt at my breasts.

When we came to the bar, the waiter took one look at my damp breasts and sneered at me like I was the tramp who wandered in off the streets instead of Larkin. He had the kind of darkly handsome, haughty look of someone who might be a waiter but really an actor. I thought he might actually turn us away, so I showed him my key card and said, "We'll start a tab. Put it on my room."

The waiter's attitude changed the instant he realized exactly what room I was staying in. He showed us to a very private booth with a view of the park and all but bowed and scraped his way back to the bar.

"This place sure is fancy," Larkin said, looking a bit wonderstruck. For a moment he reminded me of the guy I used to like.

That made me irritated. I didn't want to like the guy who had basically blackmailed me into having a drink with him—for what? Closure? Yeah, could we get on with getting to the end of this? "What did you want?"

"To buy you a drink," he said, standing up. "I'll get something from the bar."

I was about to explain we could just sit tight because the waiter would pretty much bring us anything we asked for short of the Taj Mahal. But Larkin was already halfway across the room. Hopefully he would make a complete fool of himself as well as forget to charge it to my room.

I drummed my fingers on the linen tablecloth while my swimsuit soaked through the seat of my pants, probably staining the satin seat cover. I couldn't believe I'd forgotten that I was dating someone during the whole Larkin/Liza scandal. But I couldn't have told you his name right now if my life depended on it.

I guess that just proved what a heel I used to be.

Across the street in the park, ice-skaters swished and swirled under a brilliant floodlight. My eyes tracked their graceful movements, but my mind whirled. What would Sebastian say about it all? I'd like to think he'd laugh it off and tell Larkin where to stick it because he knew he had nothing to worry about.

But if I was honest with myself, I'd have to admit monogamy wasn't my strong suit. I like men. I'm a shameless flirt. And I tended to have trouble with "good-bye." My relationships always had some residual entanglements. Even though we broke up, Parrish kept showing up in my living room, declaring his undying affection. Though I shattered the love spell with Dominguez, he claimed to still love me. Much like Larkin, actually.

Sebastian might make that connection too and see a pattern. It would not be a favorable one either. What if between this disastrous honeymoon, the hotel, and what Larkin might say about my past behavior, Sebastian decided I wasn't worth the hassle?

Here I'd been worrying about what Lilith was doing to my marriage. Perhaps I should have been worrying about my own contributions.

Larkin returned to the table with two crystal glasses full of amber-colored liquid. He must have been able to persuade the waiters to let him bring over the drinks himself.

"I'm usually more of a beer girl," I noted unhappily. The lights in the restaurant were dimmed, and a candle in a cut-glass holder flickered softly as Larkin slid into the seat opposite me. A few men in business suits sat at the bar, but otherwise the place was quiet.

"It's the happy hour special." Larkin shrugged.

I noticed the others at the bar seemed to be drinking something similar, so I nodded and took an experimental sip. The alcohol was smooth, rich, and warmed my throat. "Good stuff," I said. I wasn't much of a hard liquor connoisseur, so I asked, "Brandy?"

Larkin nodded. His head was bowed and his fingers

wrapped tightly around the glass, as though he were praying to it.

Larkin took a long swallow and then began. "It's like this," he said. "When I found out that you were supposed to be dead, I thought you'd gotten off lightly."

"Oh, well, that's mighty big of you," I said, because, well, what did you say to an opener like that? I took a long drink, letting the alcohol burn my throat.

"See the thing is," he continued, ignoring my comment, "you got a lot of sympathy dead. People were very forgiving when they thought you'd gone down with the rest of the coven. No one had a lot of sympathy for my—and Liza's—plight."

I had the feeling if I said "sorry," even if I meant it sincerely, Larkin would take it the wrong way. So I just nodded. The brandy got smoother with every sip. I was beginning to think I was getting a taste for the harder stuff. Or maybe I just wanted to get blind drunk and forget everything.

"Everyone said 'Poor Garnet' and 'She was so great' when they talked about you. Do you have any idea how maddening that was? If I pointed out what you did to me and Liza everyone acted like I was some kind of a heel for speaking ill of the dead."

Yeah, that would kind of suck. But there wasn't much I could do about it now, so I let him rant without interruption. Every so often, he'd look at my drink and check my eyes and smile a strange grin.

"There are a lot of things I wish I could do over," I admitted. I was surprised to hear my words slurring. I hadn't drunk that much, had I?

A slow smile spread across his face, and, I have to say, it wasn't an attractive one. "Got you." He sneered.

"Got me?" I asked, perplexed. A curtain formed at the top of my vision. I felt myself starting to pass out. Had he slipped something into my drink?

The smug, self-satisfied look on Larkin's face said it all. He'd totally slipped me a Mickey.

Well, he'd be in for a surprise.

"Ha," I said, full of something akin to drunken bravado. "You're going to be the one that's going to get it, pal."

Willfully, I surrendered to the feeling of falling and let my consciousness start to drift away. After all, if I passed out, I was more than certain Lilith or Athena or some inner Goddess would hand this jerk his ass on a plate.

5.

The Devil

Thus I was completely floored when I woke up to di-scover myself in someone's basement.

My head pounded so fiercely, tears streamed from my eyes. The inside of my mouth felt dry and cottony. Blearily, I tried to take stock of my surroundings.

I lay on my side on a cracked, dust-caked concrete floor. My arms twisted behind me, bound with something that felt a bit like duct tape and stuck to my wrists painfully. Someone had thrown a blanket over me, which was good because I wore only my chilled, moist swimsuit.

That bastard stole my clothes!

A bare bulb harshly glared down on an uneven stone floor. Tangled spiderwebs gathered dust between exposed copper pipes near the cracked ceiling tiles. A water stain on crumbled concrete made a patchy pattern on the nearby wall.

Eclipsing much of my view of the rest of the basement was one of those huge octopus-armed furnaces that a lot of older houses still had. Nearby, a rusty bicycle was propped against wooden shelves filled with cans of paint, half-used containers of wood stain, spray paint, and tubes of caulk. Somewhere close by I could smell the sour, rancid odor of a litter box overdue for a change.

I didn't remember Larkin having a cat.

Lifting my head even the slightest made my stomach lurch, so I wisely determined to move as little as possible. The whole of my body continued to ache in tune with my heartbeat. I closed my eyes and felt around for any inner Goddess. I thought I caught a whisper of Lilith's—or maybe Athena's—presence humming deep inside, but it seemed as impossible to catch as quicksilver. Every time I thought I had a hold of it, it slipped away.

Damn drugs. Whatever Larkin gave me must be making it impossible to connect to Lilith. Or Athena, for that matter.

I heard the creak of rusty hinges followed by the sound of heavy footfalls on a wooden stairway. Screwing my eyes shut, I tried to continue breathing normally, despite a spike of fear that sent shooting pains behind my eyelids.

"Jesus, dude, you totally overdosed her."

"So?"

Without opening my eyes, I strained to distinguish Larkin's voice. I thought the gruff response might be him, but it was hard to tell. Who were these other guys?

"So she could die, man. Don't you ever watch *House*? We don't get the ransom if she's dead."

Ransom! I was being held for a ransom!? What was going on? All I could figure was that Larkin set me up again. This time, however, it was much more serious.

"How long has she been out, anyway?"

There were some fumbling noises. I thought maybe I heard the sound of a cell phone being flipped open or a watch being pulled from a pocket. It was hard to keep my eyes from twitching open to check which one it was. "Twenty minutes. That's bad."

"Let's give her another five. If she doesn't wake up, we'll have to call the master."

The master? They couldn't be serious about that, could they? I mean, it sounded like a line out of a bad made-for-TV horror movie. Something about the other voices sounded familiar. Had these guys been the ones that jumped me in the parking lot? The "Eat the Rich" guys?

Feet padded up the stairs, and I heard the fading bits of their conversation—"That sucks, dude" and "It won't come to that" and a final "Let's hope not, anyway"—before a door swung shut with a bang.

Though they'd clearly gone, I still had the sensation of someone watching me. They might have left someone behind to guard me, so I kept my eyes squeezed tight and tried to think. What was I going to do? I was in such rough shape, I could hardly sit up, much less form a plan of escape. Besides, what if I was overdosed or something like that guy said? I didn't want to die. Not on my honeymoon, damn it. Not when the last words I exchanged with Sebastian were in anger.

That last thought made my heart constrict and my skull thud dully. My brain might be swimming, but I was pretty sure my heart was breaking.

I had to live long enough to tell Sebastian I was sorry. He was kind of a know-it-all, but I loved him for it, not in spite of it.

Pulling desperately on my tape cuffs, I managed to gum up my wrists and not much else. I needed some divine help here. Maybe my inner Goddesses just needed a little coaxing. I mean, perhaps if I could concentrate on one thought long enough, I could break through the drug haze and reach one of them.

So I did something I hadn't done in a long, long time. I prayed. Having not one, but two Goddesses at your beck and call tended to make a girl complacent, I guess. Before the incident with the Vatican witch hunters, I used to have a practice of daily devotion that included saying a short, informal "good morning" to the higher powers Wiccans called the Lord and Lady. My life had grown so complicated after that, with a new Goddess inside my body, I neglected that sort of thing in favor of spells and big, showy rituals.

I really wasn't the witch I wanted to be at all, was I?

That thought made me sad, so I prayed for help with all my heart. I sobbed a little in desperation, but crying actually made my head hurt worse so I settled for trying just to remain open to the presence of the God and Goddess.

I'm sorry I've been so absent, Lord and Lady. Please help me in my desperate hour.

I lay there in that dark, dank basement, and I waited for a sign.

Nothing.

I'm not sure what I was expecting, maybe a feeling of oneness with the universe or something else deeply profound. But I didn't even feel a glimmer from Athena or even Lilith.

I sighed. I guess I was on my own after all. At least until the drugs wore off.

Lying there, I felt dejected. Finally, despite the fact that the feeling of being observed remained, I carefully cracked one eye open.

A rail-thin, short-haired black cat sat back on its haunches regarding me with yellow eyes as though I might make a delectable lunch if I would just hurry up and die. Apparently noticing my conscious state, it stood, yawned, and arched its back, as if to say, "Oh, never mind."

The cat stretched its front paws out until claws popped out inches from my nose. Then, with a soft, plaintive mew, it bonked its forehead against mine.

Soft as it was, I still expected shooting pains again. Instead, it felt warm and almost pleasant. "Good kitty," I murmured appreciatively. After licking its lips, the cat seemed to give me a smile in return.

It hopped over me, with a brief bounce off my shoulder, and seemed to be nudging around by my wrists. It was acting a bit like it might settle down for a nap. I tried to wiggle my fingers, hoping to shoo it away. Like any good cat, it completely ignored me. Suddenly, I heard the crunch of teeth and felt warm cat drool on my palm.

Holy Bast! The cat was chewing through my bonds.

"Thank you," I whispered. I half expected an answer, but instead I felt a sharp nip near my wrist. Giving the bonds an experimental tug, the tape gave way with a tearing sound.

Pins and needles raced down the nerves in my arms. Awkwardly, I flopped an arm over to slap on the floor in front of my face. Given the scream of my muscles, I wasn't entirely sure that was such a good idea.

The next thing I tried was even more stupid. I sat up. The contents of my stomach roiled to the surface. Standing on shaky legs, I made a stumbling dash for a nearby concrete laundry sink. I mostly made it. The cat twined itself around my legs as I hurled.

"What was that?" I heard someone say above.

I gripped the edges of the sink and tried to think of where to run. Out of my line of sight, the door at the top of the stairs started to creak open. My hands shook. The cat bounded past me to a root cellar door and scratched at it. I stumbled after the cat.

I had just pulled the door closed behind me when feet pounded down the stairs.

"Shit!"

"Look at the cuffs, man. She's gone! How the hell did she do that?"

"I told you she was a witch." Yep. That definitely sounded like Larkin.

"Check it, dude. She totally barfed in your mom's sink."

My ear pressed against the door. Ostensibly, I was trying to hear what was said, but really I was hanging on for dear life and trying not to spew all over my bare feet. The room spun. I gritted my teeth in an effort not to whimper.

The door I was leaning on suddenly sprang open, swinging inward. By some miracle, I stumbled back between the wall and the door without exposing myself, upchucking, or making any noise. I held my breath, convinced I'd be noticed any moment. When the light flashed on I might have squeaked, but it didn't matter for all the screeching from the cat, who sounded like it had gotten its tail stepped on.

"Jesus, Snot. You scared the bejesus out of me," one of my kidnappers said.

The cat shot out the door and banged into a number of paint cans, yowling up a fuss the entire time. There was a lot more cursing and some chasing of the cat. Then, finally, mercifully, the light shut off and the door to the root cellar closed. I sagged back against it gratefully.

"She got away," I heard a guy say. "We've got to find her."

"No shit," the-one-I-was-now-fairly-certain-was-Larkin said. "But it's subzero out there and she's in a bathing suit. That's why we took her clothes in the first place."

"Right," another said with that kind of we're-so-clever snort of a laugh. "She won't get far. C'mon."

Goddess knows how long I slumped dizzily against the door until I finally responded to the cat's plaintive scratching to be let in. "Snot is a terrible name for you," I told the cat as I cracked the door open for it. I gingerly leaned down to give its back a long pat. "If you came home with me, I'd name you Hero."

It chirped happily at that idea.

"Okay, my Hero, let's find me some clothes and a way out."

Slowly, with my head still heavy and cloudy, I made my way up the staircase, cringing at every squeak of loose boards.

At the top of the stairs, I paused to listen. Whatever lay on the other side was silent, and so I gave the door an experimental push. To my surprise, it opened easily. The protesting hinges wouldn't win me any stealth awards, however. Grimacing, I stood stock-still for a moment, waiting for my kidnappers to swoop in and knock me back down the stairs or something worse.

Hero sat by my feet on the top step, looking up at me. He meowed encouragingly and then slid through the narrow opening. "I guess that means the coast is clear, eh, kitty?"

I got a sharp "meow" that seemed to say, "Yes, but hurry."

The door opened into a narrow kitchen with gleaming oak floors. Decoratively carved, glass-fronted cabinets showed off a surprising array of china patterns.

"What, are these guys the Martha Stewarts of kidnappers?"

At the cat's continued insistence, I dragged myself jealously past a shining, dish-free porcelain sink with a silver gooseneck faucet.

Was this Larkin's house? What had that guy said: "Your mom's sink"? Did my old lover still live with his mom?

Sadly, I couldn't remember very much about our sexual rendezvous. Had I taken him back to my place? Or . . . good Goddess, tell me we hadn't done it in his mother's house, had we?

Hero nudged my leg, reminding me I needed to get a move on. It was just as well, the thought that I'd somehow messed around with Larkin with his mom in another room made me feel barfy all over again.

An archway led into a huge dining room with a beautiful built-in buffet. A Persian rug covered more polished hardwood. As I made my way into an equally large living room full of comfy-looking couches, my fingers traced the dust-free surfaces, admiring the Victorian-era spindle work.

"I think I would have remembered this," I told Hero, though he cocked his head at me like he didn't believe a word. Instead, he stood waiting by a coat-tree full of parkas, and, to my great delight, a pair of snow pants that almost fit me—they were a little long in the legs. Boots were a little more difficult to fit since my feet are so tiny, but I figured a couple of blisters would be a small price to pay if I actually managed to get out of here and not freeze to death.

The worst part was that I got the distinct impression I was running off with things that belonged to the lady of the house, Larkin's mom? I felt bad about that.

"Here I thought you were living in a dump," I told the cat, kneeling down to give my Hero a scratch behind the ear. He bumped happily against my fingers. "I was hoping to return the favor and rescue you. But, you're probably doing all right, eh?"

He sat back and regarded me in that enigmatic way cats have. I couldn't tell if he agreed or not.

"Well, if you're ever in Madison, I'll introduce you to Barney. You'll like her. She's a mouser, and very fluffy and fat. Not like you. You big, handsome man." I gave him a final pat and stood up with a lot of help from the arm of a bench. My head thudded at the effort, reminding me I needed to get a move on.

Boy, how much did Larkin slip me, anyway?

After grabbing a scarf and a purple stocking hat with the Vikings' logo on it from a basket by the coat-tree, I fumbled my way out the front door. The second the door was open, Hero darted out.

"Are you supposed to be an outdoor cat?" I asked him.

The cat didn't seem at all bothered by the packed snow

on the unshoveled walk, so I figured he must be. Before Barney became a barn cat at Sebastian's, she used to try to run outside now and again. Whenever her paws felt snow, she'd desperately try to shake off the cold, like it was some goo stuck on her pads.

"So, you're coming with me?"

He sauntered down the sidewalk with his tail held high, so I followed.

I had no idea where I was.

The sky was pitch black. Despite the city lights, a bright star—or maybe a planet—twinkled just below the moon. An airplane's lights streaked across the sky. Nearby, the loud razzing thump of a car stereo's bass line reverberated down the street.

I thought I might be in Central neighborhood in Minneapolis because the house I'd left was a three-story Victorian, much like its neighbor. Both were grand old Painted Ladies in need of a bit of care. Remains of bright paint peeled on dormers and missing shingles dotted sloped roofs. The snow-covered yards were small and close together. I ran my hand along the top of an industrial-strength chain-link fence that surrounded another Victorian in slightly better condition. A rainbow flag glowed in the soft yellow of a porch light.

Hero scampered quickly ahead on four feet; my lurching pace couldn't match his and I fell behind. Every time I thought I'd lost track of him, I'd see him flopped down on someone's walkway, his thin, black stomach stretched out as though he were a prince waiting for someone to tend to his every need. He seemed to expect me to stop and pat his tummy, so I took a breather to do as he wished.

I listened for the sound of the guys out looking for me, but everything was quiet. Well, "city quiet," that is. Not far away, I thought I could hear the hum of vehicles on a highway. A car with a failing muffler sputtered noisily.

Tall trees lined the boulevard, their branches casting crisscross, skeletal shadows on the pavement. Parked cars lined the street. A few of the houses had open curtains and I could see inside to big-screen TVs and bookshelves and pictures on the walls.

The cold numbed my head a bit. It didn't seem quite as heavy as it had, but movement made the world pitch and sway in a way that made me think I must look drunk as I tried to stay upright and moving forward. "I don't know," I told Hero as I crouched there unsteadily. "I don't think I can make it much farther. I hope you're taking me to a hospital."

He licked his paw and looked past me to the street.

I turned in time to see the corner streetlight illuminate the white and black of a police patrol car slowing down to inspect me. I waved him over. Her, actually, I realized when the window powered down. "Are you okay, ma'am?" she asked.

I shook my head no, which sent my world tumbling

again. "I think I'm going to pass out," I managed to explain before I did exactly that.

The sad truth is that there have been a lot of moments of unconsciousness in my life.

Whenever Lilith takes over, I'm out like a light. But when that happens I experience nothing. It's a big, old blank. From my perspective, it's like no time has elapsed from conscious moment to conscious moment.

It was unsettling to find myself dreaming. At least, I assumed that's what was happening, given the unreality of the setting.

A Greek temple surrounded me. In fact, where I stood reminded me of pictures I'd seen of the Parthenon in Athens, except not so crumbly. This place could pass for new. Gleaming white marble columns surrounded a cool, flagstone floor. Orange blossoms and sea salt scented a warm breeze that rustled my hair and tugged at the edges of my simple, wrapped toga. Somehow I'd lost my bra, underwear, and shoes. Whoa. The last time I was dressed like this, it was at some pagan-festival ritual.

When I turned around, I discovered a huge statue of Athena. She looked majestic holding Her ever-present shield and a wicked-looking spear. Ringlets of hair fell out of Her crested helmet, and Her face was smooth and polished marble that had been painted an olive flesh color. Athena's eyes gazed unseeingly over everything with pupils colored a perfect stormy gray. It looked odd, but then I recalled my history professor in college explaining that most of the marble in Greek and Roman times had actually been painted quite garishly.

A voice in my head said, "The Old Ones demand sacrifices."

I had no idea what that meant. Was She the Goddess who had answered my hurried, hopeful prayers in the basement? Was I to assume it was Athena who had sent Hero? The police officer to my rescue? I mean, someone's magic had clearly been at work, and Lilith had never been exactly subtle.

"Uh. Thanks?" I said.

Athena's eyes flashed unkindly. I shrank back a bit. After all, the last time I had any kind of direct communication with Athena, She'd implied that what She wanted from me was devotion, worship. I *had* been neglecting that aspect of my craft, and in all the post-wedding excitement, I never really made good on that promise. So I knelt down before the terrible beauty of Athena, perhaps my new patroness, and asked, "What can I do for my Goddess?"

The smile She flashed was cold. "Sever all ties to that Other."

She didn't need to tell me who She meant. It was clear She wanted me to jettison Lilith.

But we were bonded, Lilith and I. Was that even possible? I looked and saw a vision of myself standing beside Athena. Only, the me that stood there was strong and confident. I wasn't hiding behind my Goth gear anymore either. My hair was blond again but really cute—kind of still in a pixie but more spiky. I was wearing my skinny jeans and a white T-shirt and looked like I had a seriously healthy glow about me that was kind of sexy in an I-could-see-myself-on-the-cover-of-*Women's-Health*-magazine kind of way.

Wow. Was that the person I could be if Athena were my patron?

It looked like all I stood to lose was a few pounds and the Queen of Hell, so I said simply, "Thy will be done."

Before I even opened my eyes, I knew I was in a hospital because I could smell the antiseptic. Then someone shone a light in my eye. "Oh, you're awake. Do you know your name?" the man with a trim salt-and-pepper beard asked.

"Garnet Lacey," I said somewhat uncertainly.

"What year is it?"

I had no idea. I took a stab at it, "Twenty ten?"

"I want you to count backward from one hundred by seven."

"Buddy," I explained groggily. "I couldn't do that on a good day."

"Try," he insisted, still blinding me with his penlight.

"One hundred. Ninety-three. Okay, wait . . . subtract ten and add three. Uh, eighty-six? Is that how it works? Seventy-nine? Is that right? Do I pass?"

"Close enough," Salt-and-Pepper Beard said kindly. Then, to a nurse with a mask over her face and one of those paper shower things covering her hair, bearded guy explained that I'd need X-rays and some other stuff I didn't really understand but that sounded quite official. He used words like *stat* that made me nervous, but he confirmed what I'd already suspected. Larkin had slipped me the date-rape drug, Rohypnol.

"We'll need to do a rape kit," the doctor said.

My eyes were wide. "But . . . but . . . wouldn't I know?"

He shook his head sadly and I felt my heart seize.

"They wouldn't have," I insisted, though I hated the idea that I couldn't know for sure and my pulse pounded in my ears as tears came to my eyes. Worse, they had taken my clothes off, though I still had my swimsuit on, didn't I? Lilith slithered along my belly protectively.

"We need to be sure," the doctor informed me.

I didn't want to think about it. "Where's Hero?" I asked suddenly. Trying to sit up, I realized I was quite strapped down. Panic seeped into my voice, "Where's the cat?"

The nurse patted my shoulder. Her touch sent a wave of dizziness through me, and I briefly saw the face of the hawk-headed Horus. "We'll find your kitty for you, honey," she said in that way that made me certain I'd never see Hero again. I tried to relax and not miss my brave feline companion as they rolled me down the hall.

I cried through the rape kit and the HIV blood test and the entire time the admissions nurse asked me all sorts of questions about my insurance. She handed me a Kleenex

and gave me one of those annoying plastic hospital brace-
lets that she fit loosely around the bandages on my wrists
that made me look like I'd attempted suicide. At least the
bandages kept her fingers from touching my skin. I made
her promise six times that she would call Sebastian for me.
I wrote down his cell and explained we were staying at the
Saint Paul Hotel.

Then I was wheeled to a white-walled room that I shared
with a middle-aged black woman who had a horrible cough.
She had the radio tuned to some soft rock station. "Does the
music bother you?"

I'd learned not to shake my head too much, so I simply
smiled and told her that it didn't. My tears had worn wet
tracks on my face, and I could see she wanted to ask questions
but thought better of it. We settled into our own silences.

The room was small and brightly dingy in the way of hospitals. Brackets high up on the wall held a huge box TV—
one for each of us. We both had nightstands. My roommate's
was filled with Styrofoam cups half full of ice water and a
tissue box that hung off the back edge.

I stared out the window. I couldn't really see much between the dusty, plastic venetian blinds and the frost that
thickly sheeted the glass. It was a lonely, ugly place.

I hoped Sebastian got my message.

The doctor with the trim beard poked his head in the
door and, seeing me awake, came in purposefully. I sat up
straighter when he pulled the curtain around the bed. "The
test came back negative," he informed me.

I let go of a breath I didn't even know I was holding.

"The toxicology lab had a lot to say, however." He rattled off a list of chemicals with crazy-long names, and I waited patiently for something in English. Finally, he said, "With all that in your system, I'd say you're lucky to be alive. Thank God you got to the hospital when you did and we were able to initiate a detox regime."

Thank Goddess, you mean.

Closing my eyes, I sent a silent "thank you" to the Goddess Bast, the Egyptian patron of cats, and to my dear Hero, who I prayed found a nice, fat, juicy mouse somewhere to fill that skinny stomach of his.

"Try to rest," the doctor said. "But, you understand, in cases like this I have to inform the police."

As if waiting for that introduction before making her entrance, a Hmong woman in police uniform strolled into the room. The doctor patted my blanket-covered leg and told me everything was going to be okay. I thanked him. My roommate shot me a nervous look and suddenly found a book to read.

"Garnet Lacey?"

Why was it that most of my conversations lately started this way? Just once I'd like a "Good afternoon" or "Hey, how's it going?" With a sigh, I grudgingly agreed to my identity. "I wish I wasn't."

Police officers rarely find my sense of humor to their taste. She just scrunched her thin lips into a deeper frown and nodded like that would have to do. "Do you want to tell me about what happened today?"

Despite the question, I knew there was no avoiding answering, whether I wanted to or not.

"I guess I was kidnapped." I thought about adding the part where I figured that the boys who had me were part of an organization that believed my husband masterminded the course of human history, but I've also learned that when dealing with the law, the smarter course of action was to say as little as possible.

"Kidnapped?" The cop repeated somewhat skeptically. Over the bridge of her small, pug nose, she observed me critically. "I thought this was a case of . . . didn't the doctor say you had the Rohypnol in your system? Usually that involves someone you might have met at a bar or possibly someone you know?"

"Larkin," I said. "Larkin"—oh, crap, what was his last name?—"Eshleman?"

I gave her a description then, too, a damn fine accurate one, because I was mad at Larkin for scaring me with this whole date-rape thing.

"Do you have any idea why someone would try to kidnap you?"

"Ransom. My husband has a lot of money," I said, again sticking with the simple and leaving out the conspiracy theories and vampirism. "We're from out of town. Here for our honeymoon."

For the first time, the cop took a notebook from the pocket of her jacket. She wrote something down, nodding to herself. "What's your husband's name?"

"Sebastian Von Traum," I said, and then spelled his last name at her request.

She looked at me a little disappointed, as though perhaps she'd been hoping I'd say a name she'd recognize as famous. I fought the urge to explain that there were a lot of people of influence she'd probably never heard of out there, and, anyway, that was no reason to get that dismissive look in her eyes.

"If this really is a kidnapping, it's a matter for the FBI." She tucked her notebook away, like she'd already solved the case.

"Oh, good," I said mostly to myself, since she'd started to leave. "I'd feel better with Dominguez on things."

She stopped midturn. "Are you referring to Special Agent Gabriel Dominguez? How do you know him? Are you friends?"

I couldn't exactly say he was a friend and had no desire to tell her I'd been investigated before, but . . . "Yeah."

She nodded and gave me a sincere smile. "He's a good guy. I'll tell him you're here."

"Thank you," I said and really meant it.

A curt nod and she was gone.

The rest of the night I spent intermittently snoozing
and staring at the frost-laced window and wondering exactly

how one got rid of a Goddess that didn't want to leave. And could I even do it? After Coyote tried to steal Lilith, She'd bonded to me in a new and powerful way. Would having another Goddess waiting in the wings be enough to break that bond?

After an hour or two, my roommate got wheeled out for tests and I had the place to myself. I briefly switched on the TV, but I found it more disturbing than restful. Between the drugs and not having owned a television for several years, I found myself much more sensitive to the jerky, fast motion of the whole experience. When I started to feel dizzy, I switched it off.

At some point I must have fallen asleep because I dreamed of the bogeyman.

6.

Justice

❦

It was spring; the birds chirped as I watered my collec-tion of potted herbs. I sat on the front porch of my old duplex. A darkness prowled just beyond my sight, in a deep, coniferous forest that suddenly sprung up in my front yard in that way of things in dreams. At first, I thought it was a wolf stalking me, but then I caught sight of a tattered black trench coat and a down-swept, wide-brimmed hat. A feral, sawtooth smile materialized, Cheshire cat–like, from the inky gloom.

"Oh, hi, Mátyás," I said with a happy wave.

The bogeyman waved back. "Hey, Garnet."

Sebastian's son is not only a half-vampire, slowly aging teenager, but he's also a dream-walker. His Romany relatives call him something in their language that translates roughly to "moon thief." Anyway, since most people's subconscious registers his presence as a threat, he appears as that guy you're always running from in your dreams—the bogeyman.

Mátyás leaned on the porch railing. Closer, he was no less frightening. Considering he was sort of an average-looking kid in the real world, his dream persona was deeply disturbing. His teeth were like uneven blades and his eyes were dark, empty pits. Under the hat, his hair flowed wildly, as if constantly tangled by an unseen wind.

"It's sweet of you to check up on me," I teased. A glass of lemonade appeared in my hand and I offered it to him.

When he took it, the liquid changed black and viscous. He sniffed it and recoiled. "Childhood trauma involving poison, Dr. Freud?" he asked, setting the cup down on the nightstand of the hospital bed.

I lay in a coffin that was propped up against the wall. "Uh, sorry," I said stepping out of it and brushing the spiderwebs from my shroud. "I must be more freaked about being in the hospital than I realized."

"Hospital?"

"Yeah, after the kidnapping."

Mátyás opened his mouth to say something more, but a shake of my shoulder fragmented his image, until it fell like shattered glass into wakefulness.

"Garnet?"

Sebastian had arrived with a huge bouquet of red roses. Blinking away the sleep, I accepted the flowers and a kiss gratefully.

"I just saw Mátyás," I said between yawns.

He nodded but didn't seem terribly surprised. Mátyás was especially drawn to haunt friends and family. "I would have brought some coffee but the doctors told me it might upset your stomach," he said, pulling up a metal chair with a beige vinyl seat. Finding my hand, he took it. His thumb caressed my knuckles. "I'm just glad you're okay. I'm so sorry we fought."

"Me too."

My roommate never returned, I noticed. She must have requested a room in the non-fugitive-from-justice wing. He glanced around the room with the look of someone who loathed spending time in hospitals. I couldn't agree more. Maybe now that he was here, I could be discharged.

"I can't believe you're in the hospital. How did this happen? Where was Lilith?"

So now he wanted Her in my life?

I could sense real concern in his expression, like it suddenly occurred to him that he might have to worry about me a lot more if I somehow had lost Lilith. "Lilith isn't everything, you know," I said. I didn't want to admit how much this whole thing with Larkin scared me too. "I could take care of myself."

Sebastian snorted a little oh-sure-you-can laugh. "I'm just as glad you have a Goddess at your beck and call, what with all the trouble you seem to find or, perhaps more accurately, *make*." His smile broadened. Before I could get defensive, he added, "Do you know what Courtney told me? She said you're the reason people get lost in the Lake of the Isles neighborhood. It's not drunken Irishmen—it's the entire troop of faerie folk you accidentally loosed in a park one Imbolc."

Oh, that.

"Haven't they caught them all yet?"

"Apparently not," Sebastian said with a note of deep amusement.

I rubbed my head, trying to hide my embarrassment. Look, I was a young witch. How was I supposed to know faerie magic wasn't just happy pixies and such? "I didn't have Lilith then," I pointed out. "And I got along just fine."

Now Sebastian laughed in earnest. "That's one way of putting it."

I frowned at the bouquet of roses in my hands, my shoulders slumping against the hard back of the hospital bed. "I'm not like that anymore." I stopped myself when I caught Sebastian's eye. He looked more than ready to make a list of all the various magical mishaps we'd had over the years, as though all the zombies and trolls and monkeys were my fault. I quickly added, "And anyway, I could change my ways. I could be, you know, more responsible."

"Yes, and what would be the fun in that," Sebastian said.

"Hello? Weren't you the one complaining about what Lilith did to the room?"

"Oh, this is about Lilith. I thought we were talking about you. I mean if you're trying to make a point about how well you can take care of yourself without Lilith, you should never have left me alone with Courtney. She had a lot of tales to tell about you—including the one about the genie."

It was my turn to be the annoying know-it-all. "Singular is *djinn*, and that was not entirely my fault."

I pouted for a moment and Sebastian just smiled at me. But after a moment his grin faded.

"I still don't know how you ended up here," he said. "What happened?"

"Didn't the doctor tell you? Larkin slipped me that date-rape drug—what's it called?"

The color drained from Sebastian's already pale face. "Rohypnol."

"Yeah, that's it. Although the doctor said the toxicology test came back with a whole bunch of other stuff and he figured I nearly OD'd because I completely passed out, which isn't supposed to happen quite like that or something, I don't know." I smiled in that grim sort of if-I-didn't-laugh-I'd-have-to-cry way.

Sebastian stood up slowly, deliberately. His face looked hard as stone. "Did he . . . ?"

I put up a hand to reassure him. "Oh! Oh no, nothing like that. I guess they just wanted to kidnap me, you know, for a ransom."

"Did the doctors do a test? I mean, do you know for sure?"

"Yes, they did. I'm okay."

"Okay? Jesus Christ, Garnet," Sebastian exploded. "Why didn't you tell me this right away? Why didn't the doctors tell me? Or the cops? Although that explains that 'poor bastard' look they were giving me. My God, all this time I had no idea. And who the hell is Larkin?"

I didn't take much stock in Sebastian's rant. I totally understood where it came from. I was scared too when I first heard. But in my experience guys don't really like it when you point out that they're afraid of something, so I said, "Larkin is the guy who invited us to the full-moon ritual today or, I mean, last night." Hospitals always messed with my sense of time. "The guy I stole from his girlfriend. When I was dating someone else," I added that last part quietly.

Sebastian either didn't care or didn't notice my confession. "That guy? He came to the hotel? Where was I?"

"Upstairs dealing with the room," I explained. "I went down to swim, remember?"

As if all the air had been knocked out of him, Sebastian sat down in the chair. "So this is my fault."

My hand went to his shoulder. "No, of course not, honey," I said.

He looked up at my unusual term of endearment; it had slipped out, but it felt right.

"If anything had happened to you—" he started.

I put my finger on his lips to stop him. "But it didn't," I reminded him. "Anyway, if I hadn't trashed the room—"

"Lilith trashed the room," Sebastian interrupted. "And She never would have done if Homeland Security hadn't taken me away, which I suspect is all the fault of James Something and his goddamn Illuminati Watchers."

"Because someone had to tip off Homeland Security, right?"

"Right. My cover is airtight. Austria makes certain of that. Only the conspiracy freaks think differently. I think James lied to you about his affiliations. He's no knight, except in his mind."

"Do you think Larkin is working with them? If the plan was to kidnap me, could it be part of whatever they want to do to discredit you?"

"I don't know," Sebastian said grimly, but I got the sense he was well motivated to find out.

"Just don't . . . you know. I used to like Larkin."

Sebastian's mouth opened, and he had a kind of horrified look on his face. "You can't be serious. That bastard could have raped you."

"I put a love spell on him to get him into bed. I'm fairly certain I never undid it before I left town. Maybe he's still under the spell."

"That is no excuse," Sebastian said firmly.

"But he didn't do anything, and we don't know that he was ever intending anything like that. All I heard from those guys was ransom this and their master that."

"Guys?"

Oops. Had I neglected to tell Sebastian there had been more than one of them?

"Well, I thought they might be the same ones that tried to jump me in the parking lot."

"I thought this happened at the pool."

"The bar, actually, but, um—"

That's when a nurse came in to check on me. Sebastian introduced himself as my husband and quizzed her on all sorts of technical bits that had the nurse asking him if he was a doctor. He mumbled something about having studied medicine in Europe, but if she could just check on such and such. She promised to do all that and told me that I should be able to leave once the medicine had a chance to work.

I thanked her profusely. I wanted to be out of this place so badly it almost hurt.

"I was talking to the manager about our room when the cops came in to inform me you were at the hospital. The hotel decided to drop everything out of kindness, I guess."

Kindness? That seemed unlikely. I looked at Sebastian who was concealing a small smile. "You used your glamour, didn't you?"

"Totally," he said, breaking into a broad grin. "I convinced them it was a break-in. Their insurance covers criminal acts."

"But not crazy Goddess guests, I imagine?"

Sebastian shook his head. "No."

The morning rush-hour traffic had begun. Bright dots of neon and fluorescent shone blurrily through the thickly frosted window. The hard, cold whitewash of the room was softened a bit by the track lights over my bed that seemed to be perpetually on. Outside our door, the hospital bustled and beeped with consistency of emergencies, sickness, and death.

Sebastian and I sat in companionable silence for a moment, lost in our respective thoughts. He held my hand lightly, comfortably. I never got vertigo from touching Sebastian. Being a vampire, he apparently didn't have an inner God or Goddess waiting to reveal Him or Herself to me.

I watched him fondly. He stared at the foot of the bed, his thin, dark eyebrows knitted together in thought. He'd tied his hair back into a ponytail. Add the artfully unkempt stubble on his chin, and he looked a bit like a rock star. It was hard for me to believe sometimes that I'd landed such a hottie.

And he seemed to actually love me. Most days, anyway.

Our argument had been foolish, really, hadn't it? Lying in a hospital bed it was hard to deny that I certainly attracted my share of drama—if that was even what the fight had been about.

Of course, as Sebastian pointed out, if Lilith hadn't trashed the room, I would never have ended up at the pool alone. If I wasn't alone at the pool, well, then none of this would have happened. Now more than ever, I felt Athena was right. I needed to get rid of Lilith.

But how?

Perhaps I could do some creative visualization. I decided I needed to meditate. A glance over at Sebastian revealed that my vampire protector had drifted into a light sleep.

How ironic. My darling vampire was probably exhausted from having been up all night.

I knew he wasn't out completely cold, because his body hadn't returned to the position he'd been in when he died. Mostly likely, he'd start to fall out of the chair if he did and wake himself up.

With any luck the doctor would come to discharge me soon. It wasn't even seven o'clock yet, however. I suspected I had some time before people came on shifts and all that jazz.

It seemed a good time to do a little light magic. It's not normally advisable to practice any kind of intense magic when you're sick or injured, but I thought, what the hell. When was I ever cautious about magic? Anyway, I was only thinking about doing a little meditation.

Athena had said—well, demanded, really—that I owed Her a sacrifice. She wanted Lilith out. I mostly still thought that was a good idea, but . . . well, Lilith had been with me for a long time. Certainly, all the time I'd known Sebastian. Despite everything, the positives of having Her had always outweighed the negatives of *not* having Her. Aye, there's the rub. You see, I'd never really had another divine option before. My choice was always have Lilith or have no one.

Athena presented an alternative. I didn't have to go without. I could get rid of the Queen of Hell and still have a Goddess to call on. Better than that, this one definitely fell into the "good" column.

So, really, the biggest obstacle was that I had no idea how

to kick out a Goddess I never really invited in. Did I just chant, "I break with thee, I break with thee" three times?

Somehow I doubted it would be that easy. Especially since Lilith and I were slowly merging into one being if a Native American Trickster God could be believed. Of course, He was the same guy who told me I was now immortal and I bought that one. That was the other thing. What would it mean to separate from Lilith? Would I give up my extended lifetime? Would it kill me?

Maybe if I contacted Lilith on the astral plane, I could just, well, ask Her to leave.

Hmmm. I sucked at good-byes.

Still, I thought it was worth a try.

Since I had no candles or incense to get me in the mood, I focused on a small crack in the wall opposite the bed. It looked a little like a mountain range if I used my imagination to play with shadow and line. I took in a slow, even breath. Concentrating on pushing air in and out of my lungs, I let my shoulders relax. Slowly moving down my body, I released the tension from my neck, arms, legs, and all the way to my toes.

In my mind's eye, I allowed the shadow image of a mountain range to take on form. Perhaps because of the weather outside, I pictured myself standing in a hot, arid place. Lilith had first been a Sumerian Goddess who was adopted and transformed by ancient Jews, so I filled in colors I associated with that part of the world—rusty reds, bright sunlit oranges, and blindingly hot gold. I imagined catching the scent of sea from the nearby Mediterranean. Sand heated the soles of my feet. Wind and sun caressed my naked body.

"Lilith?" I silently called to the mountain.

An eddy of dust swirled in front of me, stinging my skin with bits of sand. It grew larger and larger. I put my hand up to ward off the ripping force of the wind. It howled and screeched like something alive.

Suddenly, a woman stepped out of the whirlwind, as though pushing aside a curtain. The noise and chaos ceased. In its place stood a woman with midnight eyes. Thick, black curls framed a beautiful, sharp-featured face. She wore a simple, long purple robe that dragged on the ground. I could see the hint of a plump breast through the folds of Her dress, and a line of white feathers near Her waist. The feathers of Her owl half. In some images of Lilith, She was depicted as part snowy owl.

She'd donned Her guise as "seductress." Interesting choice, I thought.

I regarded Her for a moment. She'd also chosen to appear approximately my height so I didn't have to look up to Her. If you didn't know Her history, you'd never guess this pleasantly plump, vaguely Israeli-looking woman was the Mother of Demons, Queen of Hell.

She held out her hand. I took it and immediately felt the bond between us strengthen. Her face blurred momentarily, and Her features took on a slightly more Norwegian cast, as though She were physically merging with me. Then, before I could ask any questions, She squeezed my palms so tightly I could feel Her taloned fingernails cut my flesh. After quickly looking behind Her, She pulled me close. Into my ear, She whispered, "Beware, child. Greece is fickle and has a taste for blood worship."

I raised my eyebrows at that pronouncement. Did She know what Athena had planned for Her?

"I think you're projecting," I said to Lilith. "Blood is sort of your gig, isn't it? Haven't I already killed for you?"

"No, darling child," she said. Letting go of my hand, She softly caressed my face with Her palm. "At your request, it is I who killed for you."

She had a point. I preferred not to consider my own culpability in the death of the witch hunters, but She'd done exactly what I'd asked Her to do.

"Yes." She smiled. "You see, I am but your humble servant, and I demand so little from you, really."

I snorted. "Are you kidding me? You're a burden! You're a curse!"

She let go of my hand and retreated from my angry words. Her features began to blur as She was overcome by the whirlwind. "Yet," She said, "I am your Mother and always will be. 'You who seek to know me, know this: Your searching will avail you not, unless you know the mystery. For behold, I was with you at the beginning, and I am that which is attained at the end of desire.'"

Picking up a rock, I threw it into the wind. "Don't be

quoting the Charge of the Goddess at me!" Though it was hardly the first time She had . . .

Just then I felt a sense of disorientation. Everything was upside down. Somehow I stood on my head, or maybe floated, just above the sand.

"Time for breakfast," Lilith said.

"What?" I blinked up into the face of a slightly over-weight, bleached-blond nurse.

"Breakfast," the nurse repeated cheerily. Unfolding a tray arm from some hidden spot in the bed, she expertly swung it in front of me. I pulled myself up on my elbows as she plunked down a plastic serving plate full of bright yellow fluff I assumed were eggs, two strips of brittle bacon, and an unnaturally shiny bagel. A single-serving carton of skim milk and individually wrapped butter, jam, and cream cheese also adorned the platter. None of it looked the least bit appetizing. "I'm a vegetarian," I said.

"Oh," she said, with a tone that implied "not my de-partment."

With a flourish, Sebastian took the bacon from my plate and munched it down in two bites. "Problem solved."

The nurse seemed pleased with his solution, and, after checking over my condition a bit, she left. Sebastian got up to shut the door, as the nurse had left it wide open and the noise and the light from the hallway drifted in. Once he settled back into his chair at my bedside, he said, "Sorry about drifting off there. I guess the excitement of the day caught up to me. Plus I haven't had my morning cuppa."

He frowned at the food. "I guess you're still not authorized for caffeine, eh?"

"There's probably a machine down the hall." There always seemed to be those horrible hot-drink dispensers at places like this. "Or, who knows, maybe Starbucks has a franchise here."

He snorted a laugh. "No doubt."

My meeting with Lilith had left me a sense of unease. Before I'd talked to Her, my resolve to get rid of Her had been strong. Now I wasn't so certain. What had it meant that She quoted the Charge of the Goddess, a prose poem my coven read any time we did a worshiping ritual?

"You're not eating, love," Sebastian noted. "What are you thinking about?"

"The meditation," I said, unwrapping the filmy plastic from around a fork. Was anything in this place natural?

"Meditation?" Pulling the privacy curtain around my bed, Sebastian sounded a little baffled at the idea, like he didn't really picture me the meditating sort. "What about?"

I thought about saying, "Nothing much." I hadn't really kept him abreast of all the strange Goddess comings and goings over the past few days, so it must have seemed sort of awkward when I blurted out, "Lilith, mostly—like whether or not I should get rid of Her."

"Can you do that?" Sebastian sat down in his usual seat beside my bed. He crossed his arms on the metal railing and looked at me with curious eyes.

I shrugged. "What if I could? What if I could trade Her

in for a different model, as it were? What if I could have a new resident Goddess, like, say Athena, should I do it?"

"I'm not a Wiccan, but don't you always say they're all aspects of one whole?"

Maybe that's what Lilith had been saying quoting the Charge like that. She was trying to remind me that She and Athena were really no different. "Except they are. Different, I mean. Even if you think of each Goddess as a different part of one whole, they're still unique expressions. And Lilith is dark. Athena is light."

Sebastian listened intently and considered his answer a moment before speaking. "I know what you're saying, but— well, why fix something that isn't broken?"

"You don't think Lilith is broken? What about the hotel room? What about all the people She—no, really, I—have killed? Don't you think having Her is a disaster?"

"I wouldn't call it that, exactly." Sebastian shrugged. "Besides, Lilith likes me. I'm inclined to return the favor."

It was true that Lilith liked Sebastian, and the one time I asked Athena to help Sebastian, She declined. She wouldn't have helped us at all if Teréza hadn't also needed assistance. I got the sense Athena really preferred to come to the aid of women only.

But wouldn't it still be better to have my inner Goddess be someone like Athena instead of Lilith? Wouldn't that make me a better person? What did it mean that Lilith was not only so attracted to me but also attached?

"I know you're a Catholic, Sebastian, but don't alchemists have a belief in the divine spark being in everything?"

He laughed in surprise. "Of course, the philosopher's stone. Distilling it is my life's work. What made you think of it?"

"Something Apollo told me."

Sebastian opened his mouth, but then stopped. He frowned. "I'm sorry, did you say Apollo?"

I bit my lip. I hadn't meant to, since I'd planned to keep Sebastian far out of all this vision mess. "Uh, the doctors said I might say random things—you know, uh, kind of free-associate and stuff."

Sebastian shot me a skeptical look like he really wasn't comfortable with that idea, even if it were true, which it clearly wasn't. As lamely as I'd lied, I could hardly blame him. "They told *me* that sort of change was a bad sign," he noted, standing up. "I'll get the nurse."

"No, wait," I said, grabbing for his arm and catching it. "I didn't want to tell you. Thing is, I had another vision. Actually," I let out an exasperated, pained sigh. "I've been having a *lot* of them."

Sebastian sat back down, his hand still holding mine. The eyes that searched my face were fraught with concern. "Why wouldn't you tell me a thing like that?"

I put my knuckles on my lip, as though I could hold back what I was about to say. "I didn't want to worry you?"

He lowered his head to the bed and began to bang it

softly against the railing. When he was done, he looked up at me and said simply, "You make me crazy."

Yeah, see, that was the other reason I hadn't wanted to tell him. Scratching my chin, I said, "Well, there's some good news about my visions."

"There's good news?" Sebastian peered up from his awkward facedown position near my elbow. He sat up slowly. "Pray tell, what is it?"

"I might not know *why* I'm having them, but I think I know *what* they are," I said. Seeing Sebastian's encouraging expression, I continued hurriedly. "I think they're, you know, everyone's inner God or Goddess. Like your philosopher's stone or divine spark or whatever it is."

I looked at him hopefully. Most of his face was shrouded in shadows. His long hair fell in loose strands, adding to the forbidding look. The fluorescent light over my bed cast a greenish, unearthly tint to his pale skin.

When he didn't say anything right away, I added, "What do you think?"

He got up and walked over to the window. "I don't know," he said thoughtfully. "But if that's what it is, it seems perfectly harmless. It's just another of your many gifts."

A gift? I'd been thinking of my visions as nauseating inconveniences, but maybe they were flashes of wisdom. And who was the Goddess of Wisdom?

Athena.

I wished I could see Sebastian's divine spark. His arms crossed on the rails of the bed, he stared idly at the roses in my lap. Something about his posture made him seem very young and vaguely disaffected, kind of like his son Mátyás, and a sudden thought struck me: We were going to be married forever—were our inner Gods compatible?

Lilith did like him; he was right about that.

Would Athena? The Greek pantheon was rather famous for its bad marriages. Zeus was always catting around on Hera, and Aphrodite and Hephastus couldn't have been a more unlikely couple. Did those Gods do anything other than have extramarital affairs?

On the flip side, Lilith was supposed to be responsible for men's wet dreams, and in some myths She was Satan's wife, so it's not like She was necessarily a better role model.

I sighed, feeling disheartened.

Misinterpreting my noise, Sebastian patted my hand. "We can't figure anything out stuck here. I'm going to get that doctor so we can get out of this place."

I smiled as he headed off purposefully. I sipped a little milk and wished I'd been okayed for coffee, even if it was just that brown water stuff places like this tended to serve.

Sebastian came back in forty-five with news we would be sprung. He'd brought my suitcase of clothes from the hotel and some good news/bad news.

"The doctor will be coming shortly to get the discharge process started. But the Saint Paul Hotel threw us out," he said, though he didn't sound at all upset.

"What?" I stopped in the middle of pulling on my black, sparkly, spiderweb hose. I'd brought them with milder Vienna temperatures in mind, but now I thought they'd make good insulation under my jeans. According to the radio, the wind chill was an arctic minus thirty-one degrees below zero. The actual temperature was something like minus ten. "What about your glamour?"

"You know it only works in close proximity."

Yeah. They had to smell him. Glamour, as far as I could tell, was some kind of super-vampire pheromone.

Sebastian lounged on my bed. Having kicked off his shoes at the door, he stretched his brown stocking feet over the edge of the metal railing. Today he'd dressed slightly more casually, in faded boot-cut jeans and a Harley Davidson T-shirt that invited us to "Turn Up the Heat." The motto he'd chosen seemed only a bit paradoxical given the temperature outside and the fact that Sebastian had nothing else to cover up with other than a black leather jacket that he'd slung over the nearby chair. Even the nurses kept asking him if he was warm enough.

"The official story is that they couldn't find us a suitable replacement for the Ordway Room, but a hotel like the Saint Paul doesn't really want guests that bring any kind of negative attention. While we were there, they had visits from Homeland Security, the police, and the FBI. Are you really surprised they balked?"

"I thought money talked."

He gave me a little touché nod. "It does, but not this loudly."

I snorted a little gallows-humor laugh. I slipped into my

pants, wishing I'd thought to bring my flannel-lined ones. "So now we're homeless on top of everything else? Could this honeymoon get any worse?"

He pressed a finger to his lips. "Shhh," he hissed. "Don't tempt fate."

Pulling a sweater over my head, I arched an eyebrow at him. Was he looking to start the drama-queen fight again? Instead of pushing the issue, I switched the subject. "So what do you want to do now? Go home to Madison?"

Pinching the bridge of his nose, his expression clouded. "I'll tell you this for nothing," he said, without meeting my gaze. "I'm not exactly getting what you see in this town."

With a heavy sigh, I plunked down on the side of the bed opposite him. I could understand his frustration, but I was disappointed. I really loved Minneapolis/Saint Paul and I desperately wanted to share my memories of it with Sebastian. Though I had to agree, things had not exactly worked out the way I'd planned. Hennepin County Medical Center was not on the must-see tourist destination list usually.

Reaching out, I grabbed his toes lightly. "Hey," I said, waiting for him to raise his eyes before I continued. I had to give his big toe a little squeeze before he did. "Let's give it one more shot, okay?"

He stared at me for a long time without saying a word. I tried to read his mind, because his expression wasn't much help. His chestnut brown eyes had that cold fire I sometimes saw when we faced monsters together. The amber starburst around his pupils seemed to almost glow, despite the muted light of the hospital room.

"As you wish," he said slowly, deliberately, though for a moment I thought I caught the scent of cinnamon and baking bread.

I squinted at him darkly, although there was a bit of teasing in my voice when I asked, "Are you trying to use your glamour on me?"

"I really want to," he admitted. "But that would be a bad way to start our marriage, wouldn't it?"

Hmmm, as opposed to all the secrets I've been keeping? I broke eye contact guiltily.

Misinterpreting my response, he sat up and gave my knee a gentle stroke. "Hey, I'm sorry. How about one more day here?" he offered, and then, pointing to his chest, added, "Then I get to choose our next destination? Fair?"

What could I do when he looked at me with those beautiful, big, pleading brown eyes? Glamour or not, I had to agree. "Fair."

It still took forever to actually leave the damn hospital. There were release forms for me to sign, and, of course, they wouldn't let me just *walk* out. Instead, an orderly arrived with a wheelchair.

"You can't be serious," I muttered.

"Hospital rules," the mop-haired young man in Snoopy-themed scrubs said with a shrug.

Reluctantly, I sat in the chair. After a quick I'll-see-you-in-a-second peck on the cheek, Sebastian went on ahead to fetch the car.

"Your husband seems nice," the orderly said, making conversation as we made our way down the hall. "He's a little younger than you, huh?"

I choked on my response. Sebastian was almost three hundred times my age!

"I'm sorry. I'm probably not supposed to say things like that, but you know, I'm seeing more and more older women like yourself with younger guys."

What was that supposed to mean? Anyway, I thought Sebastian and I looked about the same age these days. What was strange was that Mátyás was starting to look older than Sebastian. I touched my face. Had even considering ditching Lilith aged me?

I was still sputtering over being considered "older" when the orderly cheerfully deposited me next to a plastic potted rubber tree in the lobby. With professional ease, he engaged the brakes, making me feel completely infirm.

Big, full-length windows looked out onto a partially covered, circular drive. Some people sat in square, indestructible-looking couches reading dog-eared, months-old issues of magazines like *Newsweek* and *Sierra Club Watch*. A gray-haired man slumped in his wheelchair also awaiting pickup. The orderlies nodded a greeting. "So how old do you think I am, anyway?" I had to ask.

"Oh, I don't know, thirty-five?"

That was far too close for comfort. Sebastian came to the automatic doors just then, and I tried to see him with the orderly's eyes. The leather jacket, the lean body, the brightness in his eye, the long flowing hair—yeah, Sebastian could easily pass for someone in his early twenties.

So I might be immortal now, but I still looked like I was robbing the cradle?

Just great.

"You look grumpy," Sebastian said as he took my hand to help me up out of the wheelchair.

"I swear you get younger looking all the time."

The orderly nodded in agreement as he released the brake and headed back down the hallway to wherever hospitals keep their seemingly endless supply of wheelchairs.

"It's your love," Sebastian said, kissing the top of my head. "It keeps me spry."

The sun shone brightly, which meant the temperatures were frigid. I could feel all the heat escaping from the top of my head in the three paces it took to get to where the car waited, just under the awning. Sebastian opened the passenger side door for me.

Once he was in the driver's seat, I said, "You know what I want right now? A decent breakfast and a whole lot of caffeine."

Determined to make the sightseeing thing work this time as we drove, I chattered nonstop about the cool things we could do for the day. I suggested all the museums: the Minneapolis Institute of Art, the Walker, the Weisman, the Science Museum, and even the Minnesota History Center. I thought Sebastian might also like the Conservatory and Como Zoo, as well as maybe a trip out to the "big zoo" in Apple Valley. There were tropics trails, indoors, at both zoos, and tons of other indoor exhibits. Besides, I remembered the polar bears at Como got really frisky in weather like this and were fun to watch.

Finally, Sebastian raised his hand for me to stop and said he'd noticed a sign for a coffee shop. Since caffeine had been my first priority, I heartily agreed to circle back.

We ended up back in Saint Paul between Summit and Grand Avenues. The narrow little place was wedged between a dentist's office and a Birkenstocks. When I opened the door, waves of coffee-smelling heat hit my cold-stung face.

"I like this place already," I told Sebastian cheerily.

He flashed me a look that suggested I might be overdoing the happy-to-be-here attitude and headed to the counter to place the orders. Meanwhile, I found a seat among the crowded tables on the wide-plank floors. Black-and-white portraits of chickens hung on the wall intermixed randomly with French nouveau prints. It was an odd combination, but it seemed to work. Each table had a cute little lamp with a primary color shade and beaded fringe. I felt very snug and at home here.

Resting a hand on my belly, I felt around for Lilith. She

was still there, though I sensed Her dormancy, distance. Reaching out with my mind, I tried to connect with Athena. Was She nearby?

Out of the corner of my vision, I could almost see Her. Silver armor encased a muscular body rife with bulging calves and biceps and shoulders. Olive skin and dark hair stood in stark contrast to the pure white of Her toga. Mannish and strong, She stood erect and at attention. Her hand rested lightly on a sword buckled at Her side, and Her ever-present shield was up and ready for action.

Athena was so much *not* like me it was almost funny.

I've never engaged in a single sport in my life, and I couldn't remember the last time I'd been to the gym. Nothing about me was martial or precise; in fact, just the opposite. My clothes couldn't be more girly, from the thong wedging up into my butt to the sparkly hose under my jeans. My shirt was hot pink with sequins and was untucked, and, though I'd tried to make it less so, my hair was a rat's nest of black-dyed spikes. At least I had fabulous makeup on. My lips were ruby red, and dark kohl rimmed my eyes. I'd even added a nice dusting of pale powder.

Somehow I was certain Athena wouldn't approve.

If I gave up Lilith for Athena, would I have to turn into some kind of a sporty jock type? And would I age normally again?

I had to remind myself that at least Athena wasn't known for wrecking hotel rooms. She was a war Goddess, true, but a bit more staid and steady than the Queen of Hell.

Sebastian returned to the table with a tall to-go cup for me and a tiny demitasse for himself. An exploratory sniff told me that mine was a honeyed latte, but I'd never seen Sebastian order anything so dainty in my whole life as the tiny cup he held now. I thought I caught the scent of cardamom, which confused me even more. After watching him lift it to his lips once and smile deeply, my curiosity got the better of me. "What is that you're drinking?"

"Turkish coffee. The young man behind the counter tells me it's a house specialty. I haven't had good Turkish coffee since I was last in Constantinople."

I started singing a half-remembered song from school: "Istanbul is Constantinople, Constantinople, Constantinople . . . many years ago!"

"Yes, so I guess it's been a while." He smiled.

"Was it worth the wait?"

Sebastian's satisfied grin was all the answer I needed. But before I could ask him if he wanted to tackle our itinerary or Alchemy 101 first, his contented expression collapsed. His gaze focused just behind my shoulder, and he snarled, "You again."

I turned and saw James Something pretending to read the sports section of the *Pioneer Press*. "Hey, it's our stalker!" I started to say cheerfully, with a little wave, until I noticed Sebastian getting up out of his chair.

His fists were balled at his sides. In two strides, he moved over to stand in front of James. James hardly had a chance to look up from his paper, when Sebastian grabbed his lapels.

"Wait!" I said, but Sebastian pulled James to his feet.

The coffee shop erupted in hasty commotion. People gasped. Some suddenly found things to do in the back room. One of the baristas shouted at Sebastian, "Cool it!"

But Sebastian banged James hard against the wall and, with a sneer, said, "I should kill you for what happened to my wife. Kidnapping? Ransom? Are you out of your mind?"

James seemed completely caught in Sebastian's menacing stare. Believe me, I'd been there. The vampire evil eye was nothing to sneeze at. However, I would have thought a guy with medieval weaponry in his trunk would be better prepared for—

Thunk!

Holy mackerel! James stuck a sharpened wooden stake right into Sebastian's heart.

7.

Death

❦

ASTROLOGICAL CORRESPONDENCE:
Scorpio

Glancing downward, Sebastian stared at his lower ab-domen where James's fist still curled around the butt end of a wooden stake he'd jammed up under Sebastian's rib cage to pierce his heart.

James looked too. He seemed to be expecting something dramatic to happen next, like maybe a sudden shower of dust, à la a scene from *Buffy the Vampire Slayer*. Then, noticing the fangs that had descended in Sebastian's mouth, James, at least, had the wisdom to appear extremely nervous.

I guess those Illuminati guys knew *jack* about real vampires.

Sebastian placed his hand over James's fist. "You, my friend," he said in a low, dangerous voice, "have made a terrible, terrible mistake."

Meanwhile, at least one person besides me started screaming. I hadn't really meant to shout, but when Sebastian suddenly jerked James's hand and the attached stake out from his gut, blood spewed everywhere.

The barista shouted for someone to call the cops. My only desire was to staunch the wild flow of blood that seemed to pour from the tear in Sebastian's shirt, but a crowd had started to form.

I still stood at our table, gaping openmouthed.

Okay, I thought to myself, this is the moment of truth, girl. Ask yourself: What would Athena do? Athena was a warrior Goddess, strong, powerful, with a shield that had the severed head of a Gorgon that could turn people to stone. She'd start handing people their asses.

I took a steady breath and closed my eyes. All right, Athena, I said to myself. I am your vessel. Commence with the laying out the pain.

But I guess because no women were in peril, I couldn't summon a single iota of butt-whooping. Instead, when I opened my eyes, things had taken a turn for the worse.

Everyone seemed to be yelling now, really helpful things like "Oh my God" and "Jesus Christ" and "What the fuck?"

James Something's face paled as Sebastian's blood continued to spatter across James's tailored, white button-down shirt and average-looking tie.

Sebastian slammed James's hand into the wall repeatedly until James dropped the stake with a clatter. Sebastian kicked it away, but it only clattered against the boot of one of the surrounding gawkers.

I wasn't used to sidelining it; I really needed to do something, even if it was without divine intervention. So many people had crowded around the two combatants that trying to move from my spot by the table was impossible. I got elbowed back to the same place.

Great. I couldn't even make forward progress. I only managed to end up back where I started.

Meanwhile, Sebastian was going to kill James in front of a million witnesses.

"You're bleeding out, man," said a long-haired, blond-bearded guy behind the counter.

Sebastian couldn't really afford to lose a whole lot more blood, it was true. Somehow I managed to catch Sebastian's eye and gave him a look that hopefully said, "Drop the stalker and run for the door," which I indicated with a jerk of my chin.

He seemed to get it, because Sebastian released his hold on James. Taking a step back, he put a hand over the hole in his shirt. As if by magic, which I was sure it was, the bleeding slowed considerably.

The crowd parted for Sebastian as he turned to go. I started to make a move to join him near the door when out of my peripheral vision I saw James raise his hand again. This time I saw the glint of something metallic.

"Look out!" I shouted.

Someone else must have noticed the knife too, because all

of a sudden the bearded guy pushed Sebastian to the ground. Someone else, a middle-aged woman with reddish curly hair, caught James in a wicked, karate-style headlock, which seemed incredibly brave and stupid all at once. In fact, it was sort of the thing I'd hoped Athena would help me do, I thought jealously. I had to say I had no love for the whole standing-around-like-some-kind-of-damsel-in-distress gig. Give me some Queen of Hell magic any day.

Using my own frustration and fear, I managed to elbow my way closer to where Sebastian was pressed to the floor. We were mostly calmed down when the cops came rushing in, brandishing nightsticks, and EMTs followed after with medical kits. The pandemonium that followed was much more suited to a biker bar or the Republican National Convention than a quiet little coffee shop on a Saturday morning.

I tried to protect my head, while trying to kneel next to Sebastian to see if he was all right. Sebastian was hungrily eyeing the bearded guy's exposed neck, as the police helped him to his feet. Sebastian lay in a pool of blood, not moving.

Given how much blood he'd lost, Sebastian had grown so pale that if I didn't know him I'd have thought he was dead.

"What's going on here?" a police officer demanded.

"Damned if I know," muttered the other barista, a dark-haired guy in a short-sleeved bowling shirt. "But this one guy," he said, pointing to Sebastian, "started hassling this other guy"—here he pointed to James—"who like totally stabbed him in the gut!"

With the cops here, people moved away from Sebastian and James like they had the plague. I was able to kneel down next to Sebastian and gingerly put my hand on his shoulder. It, at least, was still warm. "Hey," I said gently. "Are you okay?"

Sebastian leaned heavily on me as I helped him into an upright sitting position. The tear in his shirt was small, and the black fabric of the shirt absorbed the color of the blood. His jeans, however, had that telltale rusty stain. "I've been better," he croaked. "I'm starving."

I'll bet. We had to solve this crisis soon; he needed to drink to regain his full strength.

The cops took one look at James's spattered shirt and the knife still in his hand, and said, "Okay, we'll sort this out downtown."

"No," I said desperately. "We can't go to jail. This is my husband. We're on our honeymoon."

The cop, who had a classically craggy face and streaks of gray in his black hair, said, "I'm sorry, lady. But your husband may need medical attention, and some kind of assault just happened here." With that, he slapped on purple gloves.

Cradling his midsection, Sebastian sat with his knees up. "I'm not pressing any charges," Sebastian said, though his voice sounded very weak.

"Not sure that matters when a weapon is involved," the officer said.

Which was the Minnesota way of saying, "it doesn't" so "forgetaboutit." Sometimes you needed a handbook to understand the sideways, overly politeness of Minnesotan vernacular.

Curly-haired woman handed over James to another purple-gloved cop, who muttered something about how it was safer to let the police handle criminals like this.

I was fairly horrified to hear Sebastian discussed as though he was some kind of degenerate, though of all the days to wear leather and Harley Davidson . . . Compared to suit-and-tie James, Sebastian *did* look like the roughneck.

If only I hadn't stood off to the side like an idiot, I seethed. I wished that Lilith had interceded. It might have been mayhem, but at least I would have done something to help. I hated feeling so helpless. As if waiting for an invitation, Lilith heated my skin.

But even as She started to rise, I smelled cinnamon and baking bread. The scent of Sebastian's glamour instantly calmed the beast within. I felt Lilith settle with a rush that left me a bit woozy.

Though it worked to calm Lilith, I could tell that I wasn't Sebastian's intended target with his glamour. He seemed to be sending out a broad "suggestion" to everyone in the room.

"You don't need to arrest us," he told the lead police officer. I could see the amber star glowing around his pupils.

But Sebastian had been drained of a large quantity of blood. His glamour was weak.

"Yeah, that's what they all say, buddy," the lead cop said.

I placed my hand on Sebastian's shoulder lightly. Into his ear, I whispered, "Try it again." Closing my eyes, I sent a mental, magical call for Lilith's help.

And that's when everything went to hell.

A tremor rumbled from my guts, and my muscles started jerking spasmodically as though I were having a seizure. Somewhere, far outside of myself, I thought I heard someone call for medical assistance, but where I was there was a war going down.

My inner vision swam with images of an owl dive-bombing a hoard of cobras and a warrior woman raising a sword to strike a seductress singing an ancient enchanting desert tune. My brain refused to focus on a single image and instead tumbled randomly through tumultuous pictures. I felt sick to my stomach.

The worst part was that my consciousness seemed unstuck in reality. I shifted in flashes from the present, where a nice, far-too-young-looking ambulance driver flashed a light in my eye, to some alternate reality where I alternatively took swipes at a woman with my short sword and attempted to charm snakes with a song. It was as though I didn't know who or what I was. Was I Garnet? Lilith? Athena?

My stomach churned as I floated in a space that was everywhere and nowhere. Finally, I realized that I could return to the real now, if I just let go of the magic I'd been trying to harness.

I came to in the back of an ambulance. What, I thought. Again? This whole waking-up-in-the-emergency-room thing was getting old, fast.

The far-too-young-but-kind-of-pretty-in-a-super-cleancut-sort-of-way ambulance driver knelt by the gurney I lay on, checking my blood pressure. Oh, Special Agent Francine said I should have that done! Bonus. "How am I, Doc?" I asked groggily. I felt a little sluggish, like I'd had a night full of restless dreams.

"Oh, you're back, then?"

I gave a little, weak wave with the arm that was not currently being squeezed. "I hate to be cliché, but where am I? What's going on? Where's Sebastian?"

"I don't know which guy Sebastian was," he said, "but I can tell you that you're in the back of an ambulance. I'm probably going to ask that you come with me to the hospital to be checked out. You seem to have suffered a seizure. Does your family have a history of epilepsy?"

I shook my head. My vision still blurred between here and the astral plane. From the looks of things, it seemed my body was still up for grabs. I held up my free arm and examined it with magical sight. Armor sheathed my forearm one minute and the next it wore a purple, silken robe.

The ambulance driver gave me a strange look. "Everything okay there?" he asked with a glance at the way I held my hand in front of my face. "Got all your digits?"

"Uh, yeah," I said, though really I seemed to be carrying a few extra sets these days, metaphysically speaking.

The ambulance driver undid the blood pressure cuff with an abrupt rip of Velcro.

With his assistance, I managed to sit upright. "Sebastian was the long-haired guy in the Harley shirt who got stabbed. Did you see if they arrested him or sent him to the hospital?"

"Sorry," he said, tucking the blood pressure kit into a storage unit under the gurney. "I lost track of everything in all the chaos. The police will know. And I'm sure they'll be talking to you." At my look of sudden fear, he added, "They're talking to everyone. We should get you to the hospital."

"You know, I think I'm okay," I said with a hopeful smile. Just then a wave rippled through me, as something happened on the magical plane. The air escaped my lungs as an invisible sucker punch landed in my gut. I grabbed protectively at my abdomen and clenched my teeth.

When I got ahold of myself, the ambulance driver looked mighty skeptical. "I'd feel better if you went to the hospital," he insisted.

I'd just escaped the hospital. There was no way I was going back!

"No," I said, swinging my feet around to stand up. For the moment, the Goddesses warring inside my body had quieted enough that I could make an attempt at looking in control.

The ambulance driver did not, however, seem impressed.

So I went for the pity factor. "I need to find Sebastian. You know, this was supposed to be our honeymoon."

The ambulance driver gave me a you-poor-thing look. "You came to Saint Paul to honeymoon? Where are you from?"

"Wisconsin," I said, then realized how lame I sounded. "But we were actually headed to Austria. Our flight got canceled."

"And you were kidnapped," a male voice added from the doorway of the ambulance. A police officer poked his head around the edge of the door which had been left propped open. Cold air came in along with him as he pulled himself up into the small space.

The ambulance driver looked at me in surprise.

"Yep," I said, smiling feebly. "I guess that's me."

The police officer took off his hat, and closed the ambulance door to keep in the warmth. "I just need to ask you a couple of questions," he said.

On cue, the ambulance guy found other things to do that involved being elsewhere. Once he'd extracted himself, the officer perched on the gurney opposite mine. The cop looked like someone's dad—though not mine, since my dad was an aging, hippie, organic chicken farmer. He had steel gray hair and a face that had clearly seen its share of hard times and cold weather. Though not super-buff, you could tell this guy hit the gym more than the proverbial donut shop.

"Ask away," I offered cheerily, though frankly I'd really

had my fill of law-enforcement types too. If I never saw a police officer or FBI agent again, I'd die happy.

While he asked, I answered as honestly as I could in between bouts of "slippage," when I'd suddenly feel the bruises sustained from invisible blows or a disorienting light-headedness. Somehow, despite a steady stream of astral interruptions, I mostly managed to keep track of the conversation. Luckily, the officer had that TV cop tendency to recap before going on with the next question.

"So what you're saying is this guy, James Something, has been stalking you and your husband for days? And the altercation started because your husband got sick of it."

I nodded. He had a few more questions, but none of the and-why-didn't-Sebastian-die-when-jabbed-through-the-heart variety, so I got through them okay.

All at once, I had a sudden, overwhelming feeling of falling and had to reach out and catch myself on one of the officer's knees. I held on for dear life. Even though my waking mind knew I wasn't really plummeting through an endless abyss, I couldn't quite allow myself to let go. The cop's tone strained in a joking-but-you're-really-hurting-me tone. "You've got quite the grip there, little lady."

Then the sensation faded. A presence settled over me that was strong and confident. I sat up straighter, with almost military precision. "Our apologies," I said, my voice overlaid with another's.

The officer gave me a long measured look and then shook his head like he didn't want to know. "Okay. Well," he said finally. "I think that's all I really needed to know. Thank you for your cooperation. I'll, uh, get that medic back here, eh?"

"No, no, I'm fine," I said. "My husband, Sebastian . . . is he okay? Can we go home?"

"I'm afraid he got a little belligerent with one of my colleagues—he tried to bite him."

Poor Sebastian! He must have been starving to lose control like that!

"He's downtown. I'd be happy to take you."

And that's how I found myself in the back of a police car for the second time in so many days. At least this time I was conscious.

From my vantage point in the cruiser, I listened in on the radio chatter and inspected all the gadgets my officer had in his car. I had no idea, for instance, they had laptops and cell phones these days. If it had been under better circumstances the whole ride would have been kind of cool. As it was, I learned all about Officer Hamilton's family, how long he'd been on the job, and the scariest thing he'd ever encountered (think pit bulls and drug lords with guns). By the time we reached the station, I had him promising to come by the store if he was ever in Madison.

During the ride, I also came to another, perhaps more obvious, conclusion. Sebastian was right: James was a liar. He'd said he was Sebastian's protector, but clearly that wasn't true. I hated when I got played like that. Worse, I wondered if it was all part of some plan to get me to trust him. Maybe he was the "master" the Illuminati boys were referring to when they thought I might die.

Officer Hamilton showed me into a waiting area in the police station. Like my own father, I got the sense he thought I was a little kooky, but he cordially offered me coffee while I paced the scuffed linoleum floor waiting for news about Sebastian's situation.

The coffee was burnt and bitter, but I sipped it, anyway. Before he disappeared back behind the official doors, Officer Hamilton suggested it might be a while until bail was set.

Bail? What a nightmare.

Worse, the longer Sebastian went without feeding, the more crazed he'd become. The waiting area was a shabby, low-ceilinged room. Orange plastic scoop seats circa 1973 were bolted to the floor around the perimeter and in a double row down the center. The beige-painted cinder-block walls were decorated with safety glass–fronted trophy cases filled with curios of Saint Paul police history. A male receptionist or dispatcher in a police uniform sat behind a glass wall that looked like those bulletproof shields some restaurants had in the rattier parts of town, complete with speakers and a kind of transfer box. I guessed he must be an officer, since he wore a uniform. It seemed like a pretty crappy assignment to basically be the receptionist, which might explain why he looked so incredibly grumpy.

A bit nervously, I made my way over to stand in front

of the desk. The officer appeared busy shuffling papers and didn't look up at my approach. I cleared my throat. He still ignored me. Finally, I said, "May I ask you a quick question, please?"

The look he shot me clearly said "no," as did his tone when he replied, "What is it?"

"My husband is being, I don't know, detained? Booked?" I had no idea what the official police term was. "Is there any way I can see him?"

As though disinterested, the officer returned to his paperwork. "What's your husband's name?"

"Sebastian Von Traum," I said.

"Oh," he said with a wry grin, "the vampire."

My heart pounded in my chest, and I felt the blood drain out of my face when the receptionist called Sebastian a vampire. How could he possibly know?

"He likes to bite, huh?" The officer said with what could only be described as a leer. Was this behavior becoming of an officer? I didn't think so. With a little rude snicker, he continued, "I guess they had to find him his own cell. He kept chewing on anyone who came near him."

He must be near starvation! "I need to get him out of there."

"Yeah, well, I hear he's already lawyered up, lady. You don't have to worry about him. Your vampire will be out before the sun sets." He gave me a gross wink and then began sorting his papers in earnest. To make it crystal clear he was done talking to me, he picked up one of the folders and, turning his back to me, filed it.

What a world-class jerk. If I were a cartoon character, steam would have coiled out of my ears. I really wanted to pound the guy in the head, bulletproof glass barrier or not. This was normally the point at which Lilith would have turned up the heat, but instead I felt a now-familiar rush of vertigo.

My Goddesses must still be fighting.

At least they didn't seem to be involving me quite as much, because for the most part I felt fairly rooted in reality.

I couldn't go on like this. My body wasn't big enough for these two. More to the point, I was really, really annoyed with the constant sick-to-my-stomach feeling. One of them would have to go. I needed to make a decision. Was I a devotee of Lilith or Athena?

Time to think this through.

Even though everyone had clearly suggested I should find somewhere else to be, I strode over to the plastic seats. Sinking into one, I put my head in my hands.

I felt like I should make a list of pros and cons or something, but I had no pen or paper. At times like this, I really wished I carried a purse. Or even, Goddess forbid, a BlackBerry.

The atmosphere of the cop shop was hardly conducive to heavy thinking. A woman I hadn't noticed before, sitting in a chair on the opposite side of the room, started swearing into her cell phone. It was cringe-worthy stuff about the "fucking cops." When she saw me, she gave me the classic line, "What you looking at, bitch?"

Lilith grumbled, as She always did, at that word. I don't know if my eyes flashed lava red, but it was obvious the woman sensed Lilith's presence because she was the one to break eye contact first.

I smiled. One for Lilith under "pro."

Okay, it wasn't nice of me, but I did enjoy the way Lilith could make people back down like that.

Of course, as soon as Lilith asserted Herself inside me, Athena went on the attack. The universe undulated like an ocean wave. My knuckles whitened as I clutched the armrests with the effort not to lurch face-first onto the floor.

The woman on the cell phone gave me the you're-a-crazy-lady eye bulge and turned her back to me. Into her phone she loudly complained about the kind of people she had to put up with.

Once my stomach had settled, I wondered if Athena would have the same kind of sass? Somehow, I doubted it. She seemed so upstanding; not the sort to stick out the magical tongue at anyone. But I didn't really know, did I? I mean, Athena had never lived inside me.

That was a strike against, in my opinion.

Lilith and I had been together a long time. My meditation at the hospital seemed to imply that Lilith changed because we'd bonded, thus Her features blurred until we could almost pass as sisters. She knew me. We'd had years to come to various agreements about things.

Sebastian, for instance.

I was never a straight-A classics major, but weren't Athena's priestesses virgins? A lot of those Greek Goddesses seemed to demand celibacy—or whoring, but that was another story. My memory of my first contact with Athena really led me to believe She wasn't all that into men.

Lilith liked sex.

Score two for the evil seductress.

What about the whole "evil" thing? Okay, so Lilith was an evil I was used to, but did that make it right?

It was a tangled mess. I'd pray for guidance, but I hardly even knew who to talk to these days.

What about some positives for Athena? To be fair, I needed to consider what She had to offer.

I glanced around the dingy waiting area, and thought, Maybe a few less visits to places like this?

But what kind of major personality transplant would *that* take? I mean, what had the reversal spell taught me? My normal was fairly messed up. That certainly had its downside, witness this crappy place. But it was in this screwed-up reality that I met Sebastian and ended up at Mercury Crossing in Madison with William and Izzy and . . . yes, even Mátyás.

In a lot of ways, I'd have to become someone completely brand new if I really wanted to have less of the hospitals and cops and monkeys.

That was the other thing—the visions. Were they Hers? And, if they came along with having Athena as a patron, did I really need to know that my waitress was the Norse Goddess Freya or that the teller at the bank had the spark of Shiva in him?

I sighed heavily. I kind of missed Bast, in Her form as my Hero. I wondered where that puss was. I hoped he was okay.

I felt someone take the seat next to me. I was ready to unleash my lava eyes and a nasty "Can't you find somewhere else to sit, jerk?" when I recognized Special Agent Dominguez. My expression instantly shifted from anger to relief, and, without warning, I embraced him in a heartfelt bear hug.

Awkwardly, he returned my affection with a man-pat on the shoulders, so I let him go.

"I'm sorry," I said, "I'm just so grateful to see you."

Dominguez gave a little return wave to a female police officer coming out of the locked double doors, and then said to me, "How are you holding up?"

It wasn't a question I was expecting. Suddenly, everything came tumbling out. I told Dominguez about the Illuminati, Larkin and the "Eat the Rich" kidnapping, and how I figure I must have been fooled by "Green Garter" James since he stabbed Sebastian. I expounded on my visions of monkeys and trolls, my theories about what they really were, and how my Goddesses seemed to be quarreling because all I was getting lately from them was a barf-inducing dial tone.

I even told him about Hero.

Through it all Dominguez nodded thoughtfully and listened intently. When I finally wound down he said, "Wow. What does Sebastian think of it all?"

I sat back and blinked rapidly. "Uh, I haven't told him. Not all of it, anyway."

"Well," he said simply, "maybe you should."

Standing up, he stretched his arms. I sat in my seat feeling like a world-class idiot. Why had I kept everything from Sebastian? I shouldn't have held back anything out of some perverse sense of "saving him worry." After all, he was meant to be my partner, help carry the burdens. To Dominguez, I said, "I just blew the whole marriage thing, didn't I?"

He laughed. "Luckily, it's not over yet." Glancing at the guy behind the glass who'd been watching us intently, Dominguez said, "I'm going to try to persuade the locals into letting me talk to Sebastian."

I stood up and caught the sleeve of his coat before he could head over. "You've got to let me see him."

"I doubt they'll go for it. Why are you so desperate?" Dominguez asked.

I gestured for him to let me whisper in his ear. When he lowered his head, I quietly said, "He's really, really hungry. I'd better go, unless you want to feed him yourself, if you know what I mean."

Dominguez pulled away with a nervous, but knowing look. "Got you," he said. "Stay here," he indicated the seats. "I'll see what I can arrange."

* * *

While Dominguez negotiated with two uniforms the
officer called down, my phone rang. "Hello?" I answered and
quickly pushed through the glass doors to step outside. All
the signs inside said No Cell Phones, and, anyway, I needed
to get better reception.

"Where are you?" It was William. "We stopped by the
hotel, but they said you left."

"'Stopped by'?" I repeated stupidly. "Are you saying
you're in Saint Paul? And who's 'we'?"

"Mátyás and me," William responded.

"Why are you here?"

"The dream," he reminded me. "Mátyás and I hopped in
the car instantly. The last thing you said to him was that you
were kidnapped. We were, you know, coming to rescue you."

"That is so sweet."

"Oh, yeah," William continued, "and we thought we
might need backup, so Parrish will probably come up tonight. You know, after sunset."

As if I'd forgotten that Parrish was a traditional vampire who couldn't stand daylight. That reminded me that
Dominguez warned me that Parrish was supposed to stay
dead. "He can't do that!" I said, turning to hide my face
from Dominguez, as though I thought he might overhear
me. The guy was psychic, after all. In a low whisper, I added,
"The FBI is looking for him."

"Again?" William took that in stride. "Well, I can probably talk him out of it if you're okay. *Are* you okay?"

"I'm fine. I'm at the police station."

"Wait, I thought you said you were fine," William said. "How can you be fine at a police station?"

He had an excellent point. However, it was all kind of the "new normal." I squinted up at the sun. "I'm fine. Really."

And I almost believed myself.

Lilith and I had gotten out of much worse places than this, I reminded myself.

"Hey! If you're here, who's minding my store?" I wanted to know.

"Slow Bob. But don't worry about that, I've got it all covered," William said impatiently. "Where can we meet you? Should we come to the station?"

I looked at Dominguez through the glass; he and the officers seemed to be waiting for me. "I've got to go right now, but I'll call you as soon as I can," I promised. "With any luck Sebastian and I can meet you guys somewhere for lunch."

"Promise?"

It was such a little-kid thing to ask, and I loved William for it. "I promise," I said. "Oh, and William, would you do me a favor?"

"Anything," he said quickly.

"Can you see if you can find a good spell or ritual or something that could banish a Goddess?" Although which I hadn't quite decided.

What I loved about William was that he never even asked why. "Of course," he said.

With a good-bye, I snapped off the phone and hurried inside to where Dominguez waited.

In a word, Sebastian looked like crap.

Or like a seriously strung-out junkie, which in his own weird way, I guess he was. Even so, I hardly recognized my usually debonair, handsome lover.

Hugging his knees against his chest, Sebastian huddled in the shadows of a corner of the cell. Without blood, his body began consuming itself to survive. The shirt that had fit him perfectly only a few hours ago, now hung from taut, rib-thin flesh. His face was drawn, gaunt. Hungry eyes darted anxiously under a curtain of straggly hair. Dried blood spotted his chin. His fangs had protruded so far that he could barely keep his mouth closed.

The moment we entered the cell, his gaze locked on us like a predator spotting fresh meat. The police officers that had escorted Dominguez and me stayed on the opposite side of the bars and then retreated as quickly as they could without losing face with a fellow officer.

I started toward him, but Dominguez put a hand on my chest stopping me. "Are you sure about this?"

I'd seen Sebastian like this once before, when a Vatican witch hunter transfixed him to my living room wall with an arrow. He was so starved that he would have killed William's then girlfriend if Lilith hadn't used Her strength to stop him.

And I couldn't count on Lilith this time.

"One of us has to feed him," I said. "You might have a chance of pulling him off me," I lied. Dominguez was no match for a starving vampire. That whole strength-of-ten-men thing was one aspect of vampirism that Hollywood *had* gotten right.

Dominguez could tell I hadn't told the truth, I knew. But the other option was volunteering for the job and it was easier for him just to pretend he believed me. He let his hand drop with a sigh that sounded defeated and a bit embarrassed. "All right," he said, with a barely detectable blush. "Shout if you need me."

"It'll be okay." I patted him on the shoulder. I didn't think him less manly, after all—merely sane.

Slowly, like I was approaching a wild wolf, I inched closer to Sebastian. I put my hands out in front of me, as though to ward off any sudden moves from him. "It's okay, Sebastian," I said, with the clear implication dinner was imminent. "I'm here now."

When less than a foot separated us, he growled deep in his throat. Only the black pupils of otherwise hooded eyes dully reflected the light. Sebastian's lips curled into a grin more sinister than anyone's had a right to be. No doubt that quick flash of a smile was meant to defuse the growing tension between us, but in the semidarkness the shadows distorted his innocent intent.

I stopped and deliberately began lowering myself down onto my knees.

"This is a bad idea," Dominguez said suddenly, stepping forward. "I'm getting you out of here, Garnet."

Sebastian's eyes jealously trailed Dominguez's movement. "Mine," he whispered just before he pounced.

Luckily, I was ready for the impact and had braced my arms. Sebastian too, despite the desperation of his hunger, seemed almost tender as he cradled my head to cushion the impact when we hit the floor.

Momentarily, I had hope that a man still lurked behind the guise of an animal.

Then he bit into my neck. Hard.

8.

The Moon

❦

ASTROLOGICAL CORRESPONDENCE:

Pisces

All those movies where vampires bite people in the neck neglect one very important fact. If you even nick someone's jugular, they bleed out so fast and with such pressure it's a waste of tasty bodily fluids. A nice meaty shoulder does the trick much better if you want to enjoy your meal. Also? This idea that all you get from the ordeal is two tiny dots where the fangs delicately punctured the skin is 100 percent bull. Even when Sebastian was careful, he left a full set of dental prints on my body.

I held back my scream. I had a lot of practice riding the agony until it became almost like pleasure. This was just a titch more than I was used to, but I breathed through it as best I could.

Restraining my Goddesses?

That was another matter entirely.

Already in response to the searing ache, I could hear the snarling hiss of the snakes on the head attached to Athena's shield. An icy coldness seeped into my muscles then, and they began to grow heavy, almost like stone. To protect me, I suspected Athena had turned the power of Her aegis against me. Like those that gazed upon Medusa, I was gradually solidifying into rock.

Sebastian, unaware, continued to lap at my blood like some wild beast.

Somewhere beyond the haze, I could hear protests from the guarding police officers. Dominguez's voice rose in sharp argument. Words like *security cam* and *breach of trust* rose out of the confusion.

I couldn't muster any alarm about the situation. Everything distanced itself from me as heaviness descended on me. My slowing blood flow seemed to enrage Sebastian even more. Athena was not helping matters at all, actually.

Didn't She understand I wanted this? In fact, if it wouldn't kill me, I'd happily give Sebastian every last bit of blood in my body.

Though I didn't hear the words as such, the response I sensed from Athena was that a woman should never sacrifice so much for a man.

My arms grew sluggish. While part of me agreed with Athena's sentiment, I didn't have time to argue the nuances of my personal feminism with a Goddess who would clearly have me dead rather than help Sebastian live.

Fighting against the spell Athena cast on me, I desperately grasped for Lilith. I'd caught a wisp of Her power, but then was forced to let go as my world went all wobbly again. Worse, my limbs began to stiffen, and I could feel my heartbeat slow with each breath.

I shouted, "Stop! Stop, damn it!" but it wasn't Sebastian I chastised. It was Athena I spoke to when I said, "I don't want you here!"

I wanted Lilith more than anything. She was the Goddess I trusted, I understood, who had, I realized, always been a part of me in a way that no other had. She would help Sebastian; She had always come when I needed Her most.

She was *my* inner Goddess.

Dark or light, it didn't matter. The Goddess was one whole, and Lilith was my reflection. Her face and mine were the same. Even the ugly bits.

At that moment of realization, something shattered. It sounded like an avalanche of stone. The hissing vanished, and a familiar warmth quickly spread through my veins. The strength I knew so well returned to me. I gave Sebastian a quick push just as Dominguez grabbed him by the collar and heaved him off me.

"Get the hell off her, you animal," Dominguez was shouting, his gun drawn and pointed at Sebastian's head. Two officers flanked him, their weapons ready.

Kneeling at Dominguez's feet, Sebastian seemed to come to. His face had gained back some of its substance, and even his hair regained its former luster. He blinked, looking at me holding my hand to the gaping wound on the back of my neck. Sebastian's expression faltered, and he reached out to me. "Oh my God, Garnet. Are you all right?"

Lilith's power sizzled through me. Somehow I knew Her magic staunched the flow of blood and had immediately begun knitting muscle and patching skin. I nodded and gave my stomach a happy pat at Her return. "Honestly, I've never felt better."

Tension broke, and Dominguez's finger left the trigger. He pointed the barrel at the ground. "Santa Maria," he swore.

He told the others to holster their guns and ushered them out. When he returned, Dominguez watched us carefully. Sebastian and I embraced tentatively. Sebastian kept saying how sorry he was, and I kept reminding him that I'd volunteered. "Hey," I said, when I noticed our conversation had been on a loop for some time. "There's still some blood to clean up."

Pulling back to look me in the eye, Sebastian seemed confused as to my meaning.

I pointed to my neck and wagged my eyebrows suggestively. "You could use your tongue."

"Oh, I am so out of here," Dominguez said. "I'm never going to understand the appeal of vampires. All this blood and licking and sucking. It's disgusting."

"I think the boy doth protest too much," Sebastian whispered huskily in my ear before bending down to lap at my wound.

"Aw, Jesus!" I heard Dominguez say through the haze of ecstasy that came over me the second Sebastian's tongue began exploring the edges of my torn flesh. This was another thing Hollywood had totally nailed; there was definitely a lot of pleasure with the pain of the vampire bite.

A lot.

So much, in fact, I couldn't help but make yummy noises and get all aroused. My nipples peaked and a delicious rush inflamed my private parts. I was ready to have sex right there.

"Could you guys cut it out? I'm completely weirded out over here," Dominguez was beginning to sound desperate, so I took pity on him.

With a little tug on Sebastian's hair, I was able to disengage him, albeit somewhat reluctantly. "Oh, sorry, this is our kiss-and-make-up time."

"Yeah, well, after that little show, I don't know if you need more notoriety. You've already been recorded for posterity." He pointed to the cameras overhead.

So much for not being blog-worthy. I gave Sebastian an anxious look.

"My lawyers will take care of it. They can make anything disappear."

"Good for you. We should probably get Garnet out of

here. But . . ." Dominguez's jaw flexed uncomfortably, as he pointed to his chin. "You've got a little, uh . . ."

Sebastian wiped his face on his shirt hem, smearing the blood into a red streak. "Better?"

Dominguez rubbed his face and shook his head, like he just couldn't take it anymore. I used a bit of spit and my sweater sleeve to clean Sebastian.

"You look great," I said, and he really was starting to. Most of the deep lines in his face had filled and his skin had lost its sickly pastiness. He'd be perfect with a couple more pints, but somehow I doubted we could talk Dominguez into donating anytime soon.

Still, he could go for hours without another drink now, I was certain. "How long until bail is set?" I wanted to know.

"Where are these lawyers of yours, Von Traum?" Dominguez asked.

"I was told she's on her way," Sebastian said. Taking my hand, he helped us both to our feet. To me, he explained, "I have a retainer with an international firm. They're sending a representative, a Ms. Yendoni."

"I hope she's a fast talker," Dominguez said. "You didn't help your case biting cops."

"She's an expert in these matters," Sebastian said confidently. Still holding hands, Sebastian led me over to the nearby bunk. We sat together, our knees touching.

"So it's going to be okay?" I asked. My neck throbbed dully, but Lilith's fierce, fiery presence steadied me.

"I think so. My lawyers understand my 'special needs.'"

I wondered if that included providing for Sebastian's, shall we say, particular diet. I shook my head lightly. Some things were better not known. "What can I do?"

Squeezing my hand, Sebastian gave me a peck on the cheek. "You've done a lot already. Thank God you came when you did, I would have been beyond feral soon."

Given how he had been, I could hardly even imagine that. I nodded, feeling the jagged edges of skin catch painfully on my collar.

"There's still those kidnappers to catch—Larkin Eshleman and his gang." I was startled to hear Dominguez refer to Larkin like some kind of hardened criminal. Not noticing my reaction, he continued. "I have a plan to smoke them out, and I need your help."

"No," Sebastian said before I could open my mouth to agree enthusiastically. "Garnet is not to be put in the line of danger."

"Don't take me for an idiot, Von Traum," Dominguez said. The testosterone level in the room suddenly skyrocketed. I coughed.

"How about I decide for myself, boys," I suggested; Lilith hummed pleasantly at my show of force. Sebastian and Dominguez sensed the Goddess's presence and had the decency to look chagrined.

"Of course," Sebastian mumbled by way of apology.

Dominguez just grinned, like, despite my show of feminism, he'd won something over on the other alpha male. "Good," he said, nearly gloating. "Let's go, Garnet."

I gave Sebastian one last kiss and he promised I'd see him soon.

Dominguez made a detour on our way out to stop in front of the communal holding area where they'd put James. Ironically, he was easy to pick out. Not only was he pacing back and forth nervously, he was the most dapperly dressed guy—well, if you looked past the blood spatters. The crisp blackness of his trench coat stood out in the dreary gray of the concrete block room, and his silvery tie with its rich mahogany stains was positively the most colorful thing in the place.

Even the other two men in the room seemed drab and lifeless compared to James. On a bench along the wall, one guy slumped nearly lifeless, though I thought he must be asleep. The other leaned against the far wall tracking James's back-and-forth movement with tremulous, bulging eyes. Apparently, the usual customers on a Saturday morning were pretty hard cases.

"Smythe," Dominguez said, "I want to talk to you."

Apparently, that was James Something's real last name, because at Dominguez's words he slowly came to a halt. He glared at Dominguez and me for a moment and then spat on the ground. "You!"

Dominguez shook his head sadly. "Whoever told you that

it was possible to kill a vampire with a stake was a complete idiot, pal," Dominguez said.

The freaked-out guy leaning against the wall sputtered wordlessly.

James studied Dominguez as if trying to discern any trace of trickery. Frankly, I was giving Dominguez a similar sort of look although mine was more akin to astonishment, since it was kind of against the unspoken rules of the Veil to go blathering the truth about vampirism. I felt like nudging Dominguez in the ribs in the classic "Hey, don't tell" gesture. With some effort, I held back the impulse.

Instead, I shrugged my sweater up to cover the scabbed-over wound on the back of my neck.

James noticed my movement and took a step closer, trying to get a better look. I turned that side of my body away. "You fed him," he said, sounding disappointed.

Dominguez shook his head as though disgusted at James's ineptitude. "Of course! Do you have any idea how dangerous a hungry vampire is? What the hell were you trying to do at the coffee shop, Smythe? Get yourself killed?"

"Hardly." He sniffed. "I struck a blow for the Van Helsings."

Wait, the whats? The whos? Wasn't Van Helsing that vampire hunter in *Dracula*? This didn't sound very Marxist or anti-Illuminati. In fact, it sounded like something altogether different.

"A blow? Well, you botched it, friend," Dominguez taunted. "You hardly even gave him a scratch."

"I could have killed him if I wanted to."

"Sure, buddy. Instead, you were trying to what? Out him as a vamp? I've got some news for you, Smythe. No one noticed. Your little operation failed."

Freaked-out guy's eyes bugged out wider as he listened intently to every word.

Older guy on the nod just kept on snoozing.

Smythe, meanwhile, looked angrier. "There's still time," he said through clenched teeth. "This isn't over yet."

"Oh, I think it is," Dominguez said. "You're in jail. You're going to go down for assault with a deadly weapon. You might even face extradition. Word is you've had some run-ins with the law in Great Britain."

James paled slightly, but his jaw remained clenched. "It's all for a good cause."

"What the heck cause is that, exactly?" I muttered to myself.

Everyone looked at me, even freaked-out guy. Dominguez gave me the way-to-blow-my-whole-shtick glare. Freaked-out guy seemed interested in the answer because he kept flicking his gaze over to where Smythe fumed.

"I'll tell you what cause it is," he said, in that tone that implied a well-rehearsed rant was about to follow. "It's truth. The truth *they* keep hidden from us. If people only knew what kind of monsters really ran the world they'd revolt, I tell you."

It was now quite clear James wasn't talking about the Illuminati at all, but about all the things that go bump in the night that people aren't supposed to see.

I snuck a glance at Dominguez to see if he caught the difference, but he kept his eyes locked on James.

"Demons," James said. "Devil spawn walking around, running the world. It's worse in Europe, you know. They hardly even disguise it."

Freaked-out guy nodded his head like he couldn't agree more. Dominguez nodded too, though clearly trying to encourage James and draw more out of him. "It's disgusting, isn't it?" Dominguez offered.

James snapped to attention, and I sensed Dominguez had pushed things too far with that. "You wouldn't understand," he said. "You're one of their dupes."

"And you and Larkin Eshleman orchestrated this whole thing?"

"Who?" Smythe sneered.

"Eshleman, the one you helped to organize Garnet's abduction."

Smythe looked at me. "Why would I do that? I don't give a rat's ass about the ghouls, just the vampire."

"I'm not a ghoulfriend, I'm his wife."

"More's the pity."

Even I could tell we weren't going to get much more out of James.

"We'll see, Smythe," Dominguez said in perfect cop-ese. "Despite what you say, I plan on catching your cohorts and putting them where they belong."

"Have fun, but they're not with me. I work alone," I heard Smythe mutter as we walked away.

I hated leaving Sebastian in the jail cell, but at least people were on their way to help him. For myself, I was glad that I seemed to have solved the Goddess war for the moment. I had a niggling sense that Athena hadn't had Her last word yet, but I felt fairly confident that Lilith secured the first real victory.

After I returned my visitor's badge to the dispatcher at the desk, Dominguez showed me to his car. I thought James drove the most ubiquitous, unexceptional car, but I couldn't have been more wrong. Dominguez had a silver Ford Taurus, arguably the single most popular and nondescript car in the country. The only stand-out feature was its license plate, which was U.S. government issued. As I walked around to the passenger side, I was pleased to note that it seemed to be flexible fuel capable.

"So," I said once I'd buckled myself into the gray interior. "What's the plan, G-man?"

Dominguez did not seem to appreciate my rhyming skills because he frowned rather sullenly at me before starting up the engine. "I'm thinking sting."

"The musician? Because, honestly, in that genre I prefer Modest Mouse. Although I do like that one song of his about the fields of holly. Do you know that one? It's really kind of pagan."

I would have sung the chorus, except Dominguez was shaking his head slowly and sadly.

We turned up John Ireland Boulevard with the white, Federal-style capitol behind us and the copper-domed Cathedral of Saint Paul to our right. I might not be Christian, but a person couldn't help but be just a tiny bit awed by the sight of the towering church with its ornate stonework and impressive angel statues guarding the doors. Hints of stained glass made me wish I had an excuse to go to Mass.

"I meant," Dominguez said, "a sting, like in the movie with Robert Redford and Paul Newman where they trick those guys out of their money."

"Oh, yeah," I said, though I wasn't sure I'd ever seen it. Any movie made before 1999 was before my time. "So, uh, who are we going to rob?"

Dominguez rubbed his face with his hand. "Maybe I'd be better off on my own. Unfortunately, I need bait to catch the guys who kidnapped you. And you, my dear Garnet, are it."

I nodded. Dominguez might think me an idiot, but I sort of suspected as much when we were talking to Sebastian in the cell.

We made another turn onto Summit Avenue, passing an out-of-place-with-the-upscale-mansions chainsaw carving of a woman in a Victorian-era dress holding what was probably supposed to be a parasol but, thanks to the crude cuts in the tree stump, looked more like an oversized mushroom to me.

"So, are you up for it?" Dominguez asked.

My stomach growled. At first I thought it might be some kind of editorial comment from Lilith, but then I realized I hadn't had anything to eat all morning. "Maybe after lunch," I agreed.

Dominguez laughed a little, but then pursed his lips slightly. "How about we make lunch part of the plan?"

The Ford's suspension bounced unhappily along the pitted street. Between spots of hardpack the plows hadn't removed and potholes caused by thawing and freezing, the ride could hardly be called smooth. I would have complained that the government really needed to send their cars to a good repair shop, but Dominguez was busy filling me in on everything he'd learned since my kidnapping.

Turns out the FBI isn't the completely useless organization that I'd always sort of figured it was. While I'd been dealing with concussions and Goddess wars and arrests, Dominguez and his people had pinpointed an area of town they thought my kidnappers were headquartered.

"Headquartered?" I repeated. "You make them sound a lot more organized than I think they are. Larkin is still living with his mom, I think."

To be truthful, I was having some trouble thinking of Larkin as part of this anti-Illuminati group. After the whole part where he slipped me a Mickey, I shouldn't have so much trouble thinking of him as a villain, but he just didn't fit my own personal profile of a big, bad guy. Larkin and those soft blue eyes and goofy goatee totally had me fooled, I guessed. He was just so darned cute.

When my heart fluttered girlishly, I got suspicious. This guy just drugged and kidnapped me! Maybe there's a bit of that love spell I cast on Larkin so long ago still lingering in the air. Did I ever remember to reverse that? Or had I only done the back-to-my-messed-up-normal spell?

Dominguez interrupted my musings to remind me how foolish I'd been generally.

"You're being naïve. These kids that kidnapped you have an extensive and sophisticated website, which they maintain thanks to thousands of dollars in donations—many of which come from international sources. They might be living with their folks, but that doesn't mean they're not dangerous."

"Hmm, I guess you have a point there." I noticed I still wore the plastic hospital bracelet. I tried to twist it off to no avail. I wondered if Dominguez carried a Swiss Army knife with one of those little scissors attached. He seemed like the Boy Scout type. I'd have to ask him once we got wherever it was he was taking us.

Houses rolled past the window. Someone had built a snow woman in the yard, complete with a fancy Queen Mum—type hat and feather boa.

When we bounced over another ice mound, my body ached dully. Between the drugging and the nasty tear on my neck, no doubt I looked well and truly trashed. At least I didn't feel as bad as all that, thanks to the crazy, vampire-love mojo that kept the back of my neck from screaming with pain.

"I hope this little sting operation of yours doesn't call for a lot of heavy lifting," I said. "I'm not sure there's any place left on my body to bruise."

Dominguez nodded sympathetically. "All you should have to do is sit there and look pretty."

I figured I could handle that. Well, as long as the "pretty" standard wasn't too high.

We passed the governor's mansion, which looked surprisingly sedate compared to the other houses on the same block. One could only guess it was the governor's place because of the large, light blue Minnesota flag flapping in the breeze from atop a tall pole. Surrounded by a forbidding wrought-iron fence, a bronze statue of a stylized man seemed to be pushing a big boulder with arms that had turned into steel girders . . . or something. We drove by so fast, I couldn't really decipher the meaning of that little bit of public art.

On the other side of the street stood another incongruous tree-stump-and-chainsaw creation. This one was a rather forlorn-looking woman in a simple peasant dress holding a water jar. Someone had placed a knitted, deep purple shawl around her shoulders—I guess to keep off the cold.

"Minnesota nice" was legendary, but who knew it extended to inanimate roadside sculpture?

"So where are we going, exactly?" I asked as we continued along the wide parkway. The median dividing the lanes was like a miniature park complete with lilac bushes and the occasional bench. The trees were well-established oaks and there were even some elms that had survived the great Dutch elm disease die-off in the seventies. The bare branches arched over the street like the roof of a cathedral. Adventurous gray squirrels leaped the gaps and built bushy leaf nests near the uppermost tips.

"A greasy spoon on Lake Street called Susan's Cafe. You'll like it."

"Do they have vegetarian options?"

Dominguez took his eyes off the road long enough to lift his eyebrow. "Depends. How picky are you? If you can't have your eggs cooked on the same grill as bacon, you're out of luck."

My stomach gave a hungry little rumble. "I'll cope," I said.

We crossed into Minneapolis on the Marshall Avenue Bridge. I always fondly thought of it as the "hippie bridge" because no matter which party was in office, sometime around rush hour, a small group of protesters would gather with hand-painted signs to yell about the various injustices in the world. When I saw a sign I liked, I reached over and beeped Dominguez's horn. Powering down the window, I gave the woman a two-fingered peace sign. She and her colleagues returned it with much happy cheering.

"Knock it off—this is a government car," Dominguez said snappishly.

"Sorry," I said, though I couldn't suppress a smile.

The street name changed to Lake, and with the switch

came a whole "attitude" shift as well. Most of the time I tended to think of Minneapolis as the funkier, artier city, but here it became more gritty and ugly-urban.

I was happily surprised to see that the creepy old church that had perched on the Minneapolis side of the river with the proclamation "Prepare to Meet Thy God" had been replaced by a spiffy new condo building and a cool-looking restaurant.

But that was the end of the fancy stuff.

Gas stations and billboards proliferated. The traffic picked up, and it wasn't long before someone in a dented old Cadillac cut in front of Dominguez, causing some choice Spanish curses to tumble easily out of Dominguez's mouth.

"Evil ley line," I explained. "Lake Street has bad energy."

"Hmph," he said. "I could almost buy that."

From Mr. Normal Despite Being Psychic that was a ringing endorsement. I nodded.

When I lived in the Cities, a friend had proposed the idea to me, and I thought it made a lot of sense. There was a New Age belief that certain areas had a positive energy flow because they were once part of the routes the faeries used to walk. There was a whole theory out there about religious sites being built at the spots where ley lines crossed.

Lake was the opposite of that, a kind of negative energy draw. People drove crazy here, more garbage filled the street, and businesses had trouble staying afloat. There was even the husk of a burned-out building that had yet to be refurbished.

Dominguez seemed to have found the place we were looking for and pulled into an empty space next to a hole-in-the-wall cafe.

"Is our plan to eat . . . eggs? Is that the sort of thing that's going to flush out the bad guys?" I asked. As we walked through the door, a bell jangled. No one looked up when we came in, but, even so, I felt acutely aware of the skull and crossbones on my jacket and the dried blood on my sweater. I wore black for a reason. It hid those kinds of stains well.

"I should have changed," I said to Dominguez.

"You're fine."

Most of the crowd fell into the average-working-class-Joe variety, though there were a couple of women in pastel hospital scrubs chatting over coffee in a booth. Dominguez looked a little overdressed in his suit coat, but he always carried with him that air of "cop" that made him fit nicely into places like this.

Me, I just looked like a freak.

We took a seat in a narrow, vinyl-covered booth. The tablecloth was plastic and a bit stickier than I usually preferred. A metal ring on a stem held single-sheet menus. From the handwritten notes on the wall it appeared breakfast was the big draw, though we'd missed the early-bird special by several hours. I didn't even know that people ate biscuits and gravy this far north, much less at 6 A.M.

Dominguez displayed a grumpy look—it seemed to be his sort of stock expression so I didn't take it personally. "At first I thought being visible in the right places might do it, but now I'm convinced you need to be"—he waved his hand in an abracadabra motion—"you know, magic."

I looked around at the customers wearing ball caps. "Here?"

"Well, I thought we'd eat first. Then you can do your thing."

"What about my *thing* is so attractive to these guys, anyway?"

"Heh," he said, looking me up and down. "Don't get me started."

A blush crept into my cheeks. "It's not what I meant, and you know it," I admonished, trying to hide my reaction. "I meant, if these guys are all anti–New World Order or whatever, why don't they like magic? Larkin is a witch, or at least a pagan, or was when I knew him, anyway."

Dominguez dropped his voice and, leaning on his elbows, said, "I suspect the Illuminati Watch stuff is just a cover. Like Smythe said, they're vampire hunters."

A strong odor of frying steak filled the tiny restaurant. I nearly choked on the smell. "But . . . but . . ." I sputtered. "Vampires aren't supposed to be real."

Okay, that sounded rich coming from me, but I spent much of my life worrying about whether the Vatican witch hunters would catch up to me again. It never occurred to me that there might be an organization of people bent on killing vampires. People just weren't supposed to know.

"You heard Smythe. He thinks he's some modern-day Van Helsing."

"Smythe totally denied being part of a group."

"Well, he would, wouldn't he?"

The grill sizzled. Condensation dripped in wide rivulets on the window. I fiddled with the menu ring, making it spring and wobble. "Well," I said, "you're the mind reader. I suppose you'd know."

Dominguez grimaced. "I didn't . . . I don't make a habit . . . Look, I don't want to talk about that. I'm just saying that it makes a certain kind of *logical* sense," he accented the word *logical* with a meaningful frown in my direction, as though daring me to bring up his abilities again. When I didn't, Dominguez continued. "Sebastian was the target all along. They kidnapped you to use as bait. I couldn't be certain until Smythe went on his little rant about demons. Their organization uses Marxism and the Illuminati bull as a front to hide their real mission. I only started to suspect—"

"When you read his mind?"

"Before that," Dominguez continued, for once letting one of my references to his psychic abilities slide. "I started to suspect their real focus when I noticed that their website was running a huge campaign to keep certain anti-occult laws on the books in Australia. Knowing what I do about you and your friends, it got me thinking."

"See, all that secret stuff came in handy for once."

He leaned his chin against his knuckles dejectedly. "Yeah, although the funny part is the conspiracy theory stuff plays better at headquarters."

"Even with your partner, the faerie queen? Where is your partner, by the way?"

"My partner the what?"

"Stop acting like you can't hear me. I asked where Francine, Queen of the Faerie Folk, is."

"What? I know she's a tough woman, but she's not gay."

I gave up trying to make him accept the truth.

He removed a fork and a knife from a pebbled plastic cupful of utensils. He lined them up neatly on the table, and he glanced at the grill hopefully. "I'm off the clock. A friend of mine on the force told me you'd been kidnapped, and I promised to always look after you."

It was true, though he'd said so, I'd thought, under the influence of a love spell. Too bad Larkin didn't feel similarly protective. Maybe it had something to do with the fact that I'd managed to break the one with Dominguez, while Larkin's had been festering on for years.

While thinking, I'd been arranging the little plastic containers of jam in their four-slot holder. I looked up to see Dominguez watching me with a thoughtful expression.

"I'd never hold you to a promise like that," I said.

"I know," he replied, but he was still looking at me like he'd take a bullet for me.

Looking into his puppy-dog eyes, I made a solemn vow that I'd never cast another love spell again. And I still had to make right one other mistake. "You know, I should probably tell you that I cast a spell on Larkin. A love spell . . ." I reorganized the jellies again, not willing to meet his eyes.

"I think, you know, maybe more than the vampire thing or the Illuminati, maybe he's motivated by a kind of romantic revenge."

"Revenge?" Dominguez gave a little smile. "That's not what I was feeling."

I glanced up only long enough to see that he had a very wicked smile on his face.

"Yeah, well, I'm a better person now than I was with Larkin." Better now since I had Lilith? Huh, that was an interesting thought. "Oh!" That reminded me. "I need to call William. I promised."

Dominguez didn't seem concerned one way or the other, so I took out my phone. William answered right away. After exchanging the usual hellos and pleasantries, I put my hand over the mouthpiece and asked, "Can they join us here?" At his deep, scowling frown, I quickly added, "They could help with the whole magic thing."

"What magic?" William asked on the line.

"Fine," Dominguez said with a tone that implied he actually thought little of the idea but couldn't think of a good reason to deny me.

"Great!" I said cheerfully, and then explained to William that he and Mátyás could meet Dominguez and me at the cafe.

"No Sebastian?" William asked.

"Not yet," I said, trying to sound chipper. "He'll be okay. He's got people coming."

When I hung up, a waiter had finally appeared. He was

college aged and sandy haired. Tall and athletic, he wore baggy pants and an unbuttoned lumberjack plaid shirt that opened to show off a clean, white undershirt. He smiled at me in a way that made me think he found me kind of cute. "What's your order, hon?"

"Uh, eggs? Over easy and some toast."

"Good choice," he said, showing off deep dimples.

Was he flirting with me? I twiddled my ring finger a bit, hoping the gold band would catch his eye.

Dominguez sensed the flirting too. In fact, he sounded angry about his choice when he said, "I'm having the number six."

I watched the waiter head off to turn in our order. "He's sweet," I told Dominguez.

Leaning in conspiratorially, Dominguez whispered, "And probably sympathetic to your kidnappers. There's a reason we came here."

Were all the vampire hunters/Illuminati/kidnappers vaguely sweet looking? I sighed. When I returned my attention to the table, Dominguez was holding back a smirk. "You don't have to be so pleased about bursting my bubble, you know."

"I do, actually," he said. "It's karma for the love potion."

I blushed all over again, remembering Dominguez half naked in his car, desperate to have sex with me while under the spell. He even asked me to marry him. "Have I apologized for that?"

"Not nearly enough," he said with a sly smile that one could interpret as flirtatious.

"Anything I can do to make up for it?" I said, batting my eyes in mock innocence.

He coughed a bit in discomfort and then said, "Catching the kidnappers would be a good start."

I nodded in agreement. The hospital bracelet caught on the edge of my sleeve when I shifted my arm. As I tried to slip it over my hand, the plastic stretched tightly but refused to break. Dominguez cleared his throat. When I glanced up, he deposited a bright red Swiss Army knife on the table in front of me. It was the deluxe model with the toothpick.

"Somehow I knew you'd have one of these." I found the scissors and used my fingernail to pry it out. One snip and I was free of the plastic. My full name was printed on the band: Garnet Lynn Lacey. "They had to check to see if I'd been raped," I said quietly, turning the plastic over and over in my hand. "It was really scary. How could someone you thought you knew be so different?"

"I'm not sure you can ever really know someone," Dominguez said after a moment. "Everybody has a dark side. Some just keep theirs better hidden."

My first impulse was to deny it, but not only had Larkin's willingness to drug and abduct me gone against my desire to want to think the best of everyone, I'd also been made aware of all the skeletons in my *own* closet.

The big one, of course, was the Vatican witch hunters I'd had Lilith kill in self-defense. Just being in this town brought back that horrible night, and its ghosts lingered in every familiar landmark.

But in a strange way, I felt much, much worse about how I'd treated Larkin. I stole him from his longtime girlfriend, and then, when he didn't turn out to be all I'd hoped for, I kicked him to the curb without so much as a backward glance.

Then I didn't even remember to release him from the love spell. Or the name of my boyfriend at the time.

At least with the witch hunters, if I did enough mental gymnastics, I could see how my actions had been justified. It was kill or be killed. But Larkin? I had no excuse for that behavior.

And, at the time, it didn't even faze me, you know? Until I saw him again, he probably wouldn't have even crossed my mind.

"But just because we have demons, doesn't mean we have to act like one, does it?" I asked, though in my mind the answer was clear.

"No," Dominguez said as he folded the edges of his napkin. "We have to rise to our better angels."

The question was, could I do that when I was merged with Lilith? Or had I made the wrong choice, after all?

The bell on the door clanged, and in walked William followed by Mátyás. Their presence instantly doubled the weird in the room; I no longer was the oddest person out.

A more unlikely pair you could hardly imagine. William's short, spiky blond hair stuck up artfully, and round Radar O'Reilly glasses perched on the tip of his nose. William had trouble picking a pantheon in his various attempts to find the One True Path, and currently he was Pictish with a touch of the Fellowship of Isis. Under a lined leather jacket, I could see a silver chain with an ankh.

Standing next to him, looking a little baffled and a bit disgusted by the greasiness of the greasy spoon, was Mátyás. Thanks to an infusion of Sebastian's blood, once Mátyás hit puberty he'd aged incredibly slowly. He'd been stuck as a kind of perpetual teenager, which didn't make him particularly happy, so, as a bonus, he'd had more than a century to get that sullen thing down pat. He wore his black hair long and stylishly mussed. Ethnically, he was part Romany, and, possibly as a nod to that, he tended toward Euro-trash fashion. Slacks, shiny, snow-covered shoes, a heavy black knit sweater, and secondhand opera coat. It was a look that this place had never seen, I'd bet.

The waiter was eyeing them both suspiciously just as I waved them over. He exchanged a look with Dominguez that seemed to say, "Okay, but they're your responsibility," and then went back to reading the textbook he had laid out on the empty counter.

I stood up and accepted an enthusiastic hug from William and an awkward maybe-we-should-shake-hands-no-how-about-we-just-acknowledge-each-other-with-a-nod from Mátyás.

Dominguez then offered his hand to shake. "This is Special Agent Gabriel Dominguez of the FBI," I said. William smiled and took his hand just as eagerly as he had hugged me.

Mátyás did so a bit more reluctantly and with a glance at me. "FBI?"

"Don't you watch TV?" William asked Mátyás, scooting in next to a briefly flustered Dominguez, who quickly moved his coat to make room. "The Feds always handle kidnapping cases."

Mátyás settled next to me somewhat gingerly, like he didn't want to risk staining the opera coat. To me, he said, "Your love bite is showing, dear Stepmother."

My hand flew to where Sebastian had nipped indelicately on me. I should really get a bandage. Every once in a while an edge of torn skin would catch on the tag of my sweater and sting.

William squinted, as if struggling to see between my fingers. "Did Sebastian do that?"

"He didn't mean to," I said, and then stopped, feeling a blush heat up my cheeks. Whenever I defended Sebastian's occasional animal violence, I ended up sounding like some kind of battered wife. I hated that. So I diverted the conversation quickly. "He lost a lot of blood after he got staked in the heart."

"Staked?" Mátyás was horrified.

"That doesn't kill him," William reminded everyone. "It just transfixes him."

"I know what kills a vampire, William," Mátyás sneered.

Dominguez raised his hands to stop the fight that clearly seemed to be brewing between the two boys. "Just so you know, everyone in this restaurant is listening right now. We should talk about something normal."

"How about them Packers?" I offered. It was a standard joke among my Wisconsin friends to blurt out that phrase whenever things got strained or awkward.

But no one laughed nor really knew what to say next. Luckily, the waiter delivered some biscuits and gravy for Dominguez and eggs and toast for me. The boys declined to order until they'd had a chance to read the menu.

The silence stretched on until William finally broke it. "You know Mátyás and Izzy broke up."

"What?" I was really shocked. Mátyás and my friend Izzy had been dating for months now. Last time I talked to Izzy everything was going great. She told me with far too much enthusiasm how much fun they had in bed together. Of course, all that had been before my wedding, and I hadn't really checked in with her since. "What happened?"

Mátyás shot me a dark look. With an imploring glance at Dominguez, he asked, "Can we go back to vampires now?"

"No," Dominguez said forcefully.

"They had a big fight just before we left," William said. "He told me all about it on the drive up. I guess, you know, Izzy has some problems with . . . well, no offense, man, but you do sometimes look sixteen. Ow!" William rubbed his leg where Mátyás had kicked it under the table.

"Can I visit Papa in jail? Will they let me?" Mátyás asked Dominguez.

"I don't see why not," he said.

"I guess it had been brewing for a while," William continued to me. "They get a lot of hassle in the clubs. He's always getting carded, aren't you, dude?"

"Is it physically impossible for you to keep a secret, William?" Mátyás asked. The booth echoed hollowly with another kick. William had apparently tucked his feet up.

"She's going to hear it from Izzy. Don't you want to have a preemptive strike?"

"I don't really want to deal with it at all, okay?" Mátyás admitted, and now I knew he was really crushed by the breakup because he wasn't snotty or flippant at all. Even though it was weird for my now stepson to be dating my best friend, I did think they were a cute couple. I'd had no idea Mátyás got so hassled about his apparent age, but, when I thought about it, Izzy did look like she was dating jailbait sometimes.

"Oh, Mátyás," I said sympathetically. Momentarily forgetting what might happen, I patted him on the back. He cringed; I flinched.

And then I saw that the bogeyman had a beautiful, if treacherous, soul.

His face blossomed into a thousand flowers, shoots growing and twisting until they became the soft features of a woman. Her lips were truly rosebuds, and her skin bright white lilies. A dark cascade of woodland violets and so-purple-they-were-almost-black pansies formed the curly locks that flowed past her shoulders. I remembered the story of Blodewedd, whom Irish druids formed out of flowers and magicked to life in order to wed her to a chieftain cursed to never be king because he couldn't take a human wife. After their wedding, Blodewedd eventually betrayed the king with another man, Guinevere-style, and then successfully plotted to kill him.

That last part was maybe a little troubling given Mátyás's penchant for taking sides against his father and me.

I wondered if I should warn Sebastian about this, or if I should follow my own advice. After all, I'd told Dominguez not two minutes ago that we didn't have to be the demon we had inside.

When I blinked, Mátyás was himself again and everyone was staring at me. I cleared my throat. "So, uh, I've got something that will distract you from your heartache," I said. "Dominguez needs me to do some magic, and I know just the thing."

"Yeah," said William. "I read up on Goddess banishing for you."

"Oh, great!" I'd actually been thinking about reversing the love spell on Larkin, but I wasn't sure I wanted to get into the history of all that with William and Mátyás. I mean, I didn't want them to necessarily know what a cad I'd been. William might think less of me and I couldn't bear that. And, well, honestly, Mátyás would just use it against me next time we fought.

So I changed the subject. "How've things been at the store, William?"

Though I think Dominguez and Mátyás were deeply

bored by the whole thing, I easily filled the rest of the lunch conversation by asking after clerks, customers, and inventory. After we got the bill, Dominguez motioned me close.

"You should probably fill us in on the details of your plan before we leave." He gave a knowing nod in the direction of hottie waiter. I surmised that the idea was to make sure the kidnappers and their cohorts knew where to find us, so the trap would be set.

"Sure," I said, trying to be overt in broadcasting the information by overenunciating and projecting my voice in hottie's direction. "Okay, so here's my thought," I said, as we all stood around by the door, putting on jackets and hats and mittens. "There's a huge cemetery just up the road called Lakewood. It's where Hennepin Avenue ends," I told William who was already getting out his phone to use the GPS app. "We're going to do a ritual there."

"What are we planning to do? Raise the dead in broad daylight?" Mátyás said with a slight sneer. I understood his objections. He'd practiced the Old Religion his whole life and knew that all the Halloween stereotypes of spooky witches conjuring skeletons and whatnot were a load of bunk. But I wanted to choose the kind of place the Illuminati boys/vampire hunters expected, or maybe even feared, that we'd be up to something powerful. That way they'd be more inclined to check out our activity.

"Something like that," I said.

William looked positively horrified. Even Dominguez raised an eyebrow in concern.

As soon as Dominguez and I drove through the front gate, I realized I was returning to the scene of the crime, albeit the lesser one. Parrish had helped me hide the bodies of six Vatican priests in the lake in the middle of this very cemetery.

Lakewood wasn't your typical garden of stones. The rich and famous had been buried here since before Minnesota became a state, and it had funerary art to rival some of the more famous cemeteries of Europe, à la Père Lachaise in Paris or Highgate in London. There were Art Deco pyramids as large as houses, as well as modern brushed-steel sculptures. Weeping angels perched on top of obelisks well over twenty feet tall and Celtic crosses stood as tall as nearby maple trees. Even the plain headstones tended to be large, as if trying to compete for attention.

Roads wound around numbered, hilly sections, where trimmed cedar bushes stood sentry over markers, and oaks, elms, and pines sheltered noisy flocks of starlings. Passing a bronze, life-size statue of an elk, we made our way closer to the lake in the interior of the cemetery.

Despite the morbidity, there was a stately peace about Lakewood that attracted regular visitors who used it like one of the many parks that stretched between Lakes Harriet and

Calhoun. In the summer, people could be seen picnicking near the lakeside with binoculars, on the lookout for passing wood ducks and gaggles of Canada geese. I'd even heard that foxes and deer lived inside Lakewood's fenced confines, undeterred by the headstones and graves.

Dominguez pulled to a stop alongside the lake. It had changed a bit since I was last here. When Parrish and I had stashed the bodies under the cover of darkness, you could walk right up to the water's edge. That was no longer possible.

Poking through the snow, I could see thick matted masses of prairie grasses. A bit of orange flexible fencing was also visible. I wondered if they'd made the changes after the drought that had unearthed the grisly corpses of Lilith's adversaries.

Lilith stirred warmly under my skin as though pleased with the memory.

When Dominguez coughed, I wondered if he'd sensed Her. I put my hand over my stomach to hide my shame. Snakes hissed in my subconscious. Athena reminded me that I still had other options.

"Uh, so . . ." Dominguez said, with an uncustomary lack of words. He scratched at the short hairs at the back of his neck. "Here we are."

Could this be more awkward? Especially given that he was probably the guy they'd called when the bodies surfaced.

I could still picture Parrish carrying the plastic-wrapped bodies one at a time into the water. His head would disappear under the water as he made his way to the center of the shallow lake while I sat on the shoreline, tears streaming from my eyes.

Not the best night of my life.

Though, without Lilith, I'd be the one dead and buried.

The cloth upholstery creaked as Dominguez shifted in his seat.

"I wonder where the boys are," I said, anxiously looking for something, anything else to talk about. I was seriously regretting my decision to come here, of all places. "Did they get lost or something?" Given the size of Lakewood, it was a real possibility.

Just then William pulled into the space behind us on the narrow road. I all but jumped out of the car to get away from Dominguez.

"Wow," William said. "Did you see this place? It's awesome!"

"How is it I always end up in a cemetery with you?" Mátyás grumbled. "At least this time we didn't have to bring shovels."

A nervous glance confirmed that Dominguez was staring at me very disapprovingly after that remark. "Heh. Heh," I said unconvincingly. "Good joke."

"I'd still rather do this in the parkway or the rose garden," William said, still mostly to himself. "This place is cool and all, but it doesn't seem very kosher to hold a ritual in a cemetery. There's, like, all the dead spirits and stuff."

"Nothing says 'evil witches' like a ritual in a cemetery,"

said Dominguez. "Let's just hope it's worrisome enough to spark the concern of the vampire hunters."

"Wait, vampire hunters?" Mátyás interrupted. "No one told me anything about vampire hunters."

"Oh, yeah, those guys Sebastian thinks are in the Illuminati Watch? Well, Dominguez thinks they're actually vampire hunters."

"Illuminati?" William asked. "Who's in the Illuminati?"

"How did they find out about Sebastian?" Mátyás asked. "He's a day-walker, not exactly your usual suspect."

Dominguez, who had wandered off apparently to do a little reconnaissance, piped up, "That is the question I plan to ask when I catch them."

The wind had picked up a little and murmured pleasantly through the trees. We stepped off the road and into the snow pack. Mátyás complained quietly about his shoes getting ruined. After we came to a good spot, we stopped and stood in a loose circle around a crumbling gravestone that pictured a relief of an upside-down torch. Our breath came in white puffs.

"It's my fault," Mátyás said suddenly. "I'm sure of it."

"What? Why?" I asked.

"I didn't always get along with dear Papa, you know. I could have given something away, especially if I thought they were simply Illuminati Watchers. I know how much those people irritate my father."

Sadly, we all recognized that it was very much like Mátyás to give over some secret of Sebastian's to a blogger simply out of spite.

"Let's not worry about blaming anyone right now," Dominguez said. "I'm freezing. Let's do this thing if we're going to do it."

The plan was for Dominguez to hide in the bushes and keep an eye out for the approach of the Illuminati Watchers/ vampire hunters. William, Mátyás, and I would do our best to make the ritual as flamboyant as possible, even though my real purpose was nothing more than to cement my relationship with Lilith and thank and release Athena from Her service to me.

William, I knew, always traveled with what he called his "magical gym bag," and I asked him to retrieve it from his car. He pulled out an ordinary, navy and maroon nylon duffel from the trunk and brought it over to the spot we'd chosen near the banks of the small lake.

Frost fogged William's glasses as he knelt in the snow in the midst of the graves to unzip the bag. From inside, he pulled out four thick pillar candles, a box of matches in plastic Baggie, and a smudge stick of bundled sage and sweet grass tied with a green string. He found a Boy Scout compass after digging to the bottom. After determining the approximate size of the circle we wanted by marching in the snow, we placed the white candles at the compass points.

Mátyás rubbed his quickly reddening nose. I watched him out of the corner of my eye with concern. Only a few weeks ago, Mátyás suffered a pretty serious case of hypothermia after having been buried in snow during a blizzard. Frowning at his light coat and thin, cotton mittens, I wished he'd dressed more sensibly.

Dominguez watched all of our silent proceedings with his usual disapproving expression, his hands jammed into the pockets of his respectable wool trench coat. He couldn't look more out of place with his precise crew cut and sedate, serious suit and tie, leaning against the smooth trunk of a willow tree—a G-man among witches.

"It's too bad the rest of the coven can't be here," William said, after we had gathered everything. The three of us stood facing each other around the edges of our snow-tracked circle. "Maybe I could get some of the others on a conference call," he suggested.

"Talk about 'phoning in' your performance," Mátyás said with a shake of his head. The sun shone on his back, but he rubbed his shoulders briskly.

"I think we're okay," I said more kindly. "This isn't going to be that big of a thing," I reminded them. "Just an affirmation to Lilith that She's the Goddess I want in my life.

We'd decided that William would cleanse the area with his smudge stick first, walking counterclockwise around the spot we'd marked to banish the negative energy, and then I'd cast the circle. As he moved, William blew on the embers of the incense, sending billows of scent into the frosty air. He paused at each of the candles as though to give the cardinal points extra attention.

House sparrows chatted happily in the nearby branches, despite the chill in the air. The edges of everything seemed crisp and sharp in that way of winter light. The gravestones on the nearby hill slumbered silently under a thick blanket of snow.

Once William had made his way back to the east, he stuck the unlit end of the smudge stick in the snow just inside the circle. Now it was my turn. I used William's athame—his was a black-handled, steel knife with the head of a stag on the pommel (I recognized it from our spring catalog; it was very popular with men). Taking a moment, I attuned myself to the energy in the blade.

His was a very mellow, thoughtful vibe, almost Zen-like. The aura imprint was a deep, rich indigo. After taking three deep breaths to ground myself, I imagined the energy of the earth moving into me and flowing into the athame.

I visualized a bluish beam of light tracing along beside me as I walked the same path William had, only in the opposite direction.

A beat-up white compact car of some variety drove along the road on the other side of the lake. Though it might have been someone just on a tour or searching for a relative, my eyes followed its slow progress until it turned out of sight.

My feet crunched in the snow. After making one full pass around our circle, I stopped in the spot where I'd started. Facing away from the circle, I addressed the east. "Powers of the east and air, be with us and add your abilities of communication and the swiftness of thought." The breeze tugged at my hair, and the image of a woman dressed in a cloak of snow white feathers that shifted in a constant wind came into my mind. Her eyes were clear and bright with youth. She held a bright sword, and her long, blond hair fell past her shoulders.

I moved to the south. There I called upon the element of fire. "Add your enthusiasm and passion to our workings tonight," I ended. Here, I visualized a column of smoke forming itself into the shape of a woman holding a staff. She had embers for eyes and hair the color of fire.

In the west, I invited water to join us and bring with it love and insight from the unconscious. I pictured a waterfall becoming the Lady of the Lake with raven-colored hair and robe that wavered and blurred as though underwater. She held a chalice in her hands. Her belly swelled slightly, as though in pregnancy.

Once I stood in the north, I repeated my invitation, this time calling to earth and wisdom. I imagined an old, black woman with tired eyes and steely gray frizz covering her head. Her body bent with age, but with muscles still strong as stone. In the cup of her withered hands, she held a single gold coin.

When I'd returned to where I'd begun, I turned and faced William and Mátyás. William's eyes were closed, and from the furrow in his brow I knew he'd been adding his energy to my workings. Mátyás had his hands shoved into the pockets of his coat, and he shifted from foot to foot miserably. I scanned for Dominguez but couldn't immediately see him.

A jogger passed, giving us a curious glance as she huffed her way around the bend of the lake.

Now, it was time to invoke the Goddess. My thought was that I'd call to both Lilith and Athena, so I could explain my choice to them both.

Spreading my feet slightly, I lifted the knife over my head, holding it with both hands. Normally, I didn't feel the need to be quite so dramatic, but I tried to keep in mind our dual purpose of attracting the attention of the vampire hunters.

Mátyás snickered a little. William opened his eyes to see what the fuss was about and even his lips twitched in a little smile, though I knew from experience that William enjoyed the more dramatic aspects of witchcraft.

Ignoring them both, I concentrated on drawing forth the Goddesses. Lilith, as usual, lay coiled in my abdomen. Carefully, I conjured the picture of Her awakening separate from me. Mentally, I crafted Her image: a desert woman with brown, sun-kissed skin dressed in rich, silken robes. Her feet, I knew, She'd keep hidden, as in many myths they were those of an owl. Her breasts and hips were full and sultry, and Her eyes held a siren's spell to seduce unwary souls to their destruction.

I knew I'd called Her when I heard Mátyás take in a breath. Again, William cracked an eye open but frowned— apparently he wasn't as able to see Lilith as well as Mátyás.

For William's benefit, I said, "Welcome, Lilith, Mother of Demons."

A weird noise, like the sound of someone moaning, drifted through the breeze. All of us, even William, turned in the direction of the sound. The wind picked up and snow scattered around the edges of the circle. I sensed something that looked to my magical eye like a wisp of smoke curl around the bubble that surrounded us. The guardians of the quarters seemed more alert, as though ready to defend us.

In my head I heard Lilith's voice. "Dark spirits are drawn to me. Do not fear them."

Easy for Her to say, I thought, now clearly seeing the hollows of eyes and an open, screaming mouth in the smoky thing that swirled desperately around the circle. It suddenly dawned on me that it was a ghost.

William must have had the same realization because he asked, "Could we hurry it up?"

Mátyás, meanwhile, suddenly seemed to be enjoying himself. His eyes traced the movement of the ghost with a kind of delight. Lilith smiled at him. Sensing Her attention, Mátyás looked at Her and they briefly shared a glance. He paled and dropped his eyes almost instantly, however.

Wow, Lilith scared the bogeyman. I'd have to ask him about that later. Meanwhile, I had another Goddess to call.

My arms were getting tired so I shifted position. I pulled my legs together and opened my arms, like a cup. Now I created the appearance of Athena in my head.

Broad shoulders and a strong, straight back, Athena stood with Her legs slightly apart as though ready for action. Her silvery helmet glinted in the sunlight, as did the sharp edges of the lance She grasped in a muscular arm. She held Her shield off to the side, though I could see the hint of twisty snakes, coiling this way and that over the rim.

Though regally beautiful, Her face, what could be seen of it under the nose plate, could only be described as fierce. Her expression was stern and forbidding, as dark as the coiled locks that spilled from beneath Her helmet. Seeing the hard look in Her storm gray eyes, I began to wonder if I might have miscalculated how easy it would be to bid Her "hale and farewell."

Again, for William, I said, "Welcome, Athena."

Once Athena had fully materialized, Lilith hissed, clearly unhappy to be sharing the stage with Her.

Mátyás shot me a look as if to say, "This is your other Goddess? Are you insane?" I just shrugged.

William, meanwhile, kept a fretful watch on the churning wisps of ghosts that encircled us. There were more of them now, and their pace increased, dancing around us like oily reflections on a soap bubble.

Everyone waited for me to speak, and I sort of wished I'd prepared something more than "Hey, thanks for your efforts, but Lilith is my one and only gal pal." As usual, I was forced to fake it.

"Mighty Athena, Goddess of War and Wisdom," I said, bowing slightly as I addressed Her. "No one could ask for a better protector. You saved Teréza from the snow and me from my enemies. I'm deeply grateful."

"But it isn't enough," the wind, or maybe the ghosts, whispered in my ear.

Clearing my throat, I continued, "Please accept my humble thanks."

"No."

This time the voice was much clearer. Even William's attention was pulled from the ghosts by the sound of it. I looked at the two images of the Goddesses. Athena's knuckles whitened as She gripped the spear tighter. One foot had moved forward, as if She might be preparing to strike me dead.

Lilith fairly twinkled with an I-told-you-so smile.

I had no idea what to do next. Gods and Goddesses were always supposed to go when you asked them nicely. Of course, I didn't exactly have the greatest track record when it came to getting rid of the ones I'd called.

"Breaking our contract demands sacrifice," the voice said again. It was weird how Athena's lips didn't move, but I now knew the words came from Her.

"What sacrifice?" I asked.

"What is a Goddess worth to you, mortal?"

That's when Lilith kicked Athena in the shin. Goddess, I loved that . . . er, Goddess.

"No blood shall spill today," Lilith said. "Except yours."

It didn't seem like a fair fight, a short, stocky woman with owl legs versus a fully armored warrior. Yet when Athena turned to face Her attacker, Lilith clocked Her with an undercut that snapped Her head back with an audible crack. It was satisfying to see the taller woman sent reeling.

Athena recovered swiftly, though, and swiped at Lilith with Her lance. Lilith easily leaped over it, Her purple robe fluttering in the wind. I could see talon marks in the snow where She'd stood.

"Uh, we need to chant or something," Mátyás suggested nervously. "Pick a side. Help Lilith out."

I'd been so stunned to actually see my Goddesses fighting I'd totally forgotten that we could aid Lilith in Her battle. We just needed to weave a spell to banish Athena.

I started a slow march in the counterclockwise direction. As for words, I decided to stick with the general rule of "Keep it simple, stupid," so I said, "Lilith will stay; Athena will go."

Even though Mátyás rolled his eyes at my lack of poetry, he started moving in the same direction and at the same pace. Picking up my chorus, he repeated the words, "Lilith will stay; Athena will go."

William, alerted that something new was going on, joined in. Soon, we were slowly circling the battling Goddesses, chanting my simple phrases.

Lilith made another attack. She jumped and tried to give Athena a kick to the head, but Athena brought up Her shield just in time.

At that same moment, Athena lifted Her lance. I thought Lilith might be speared, but She spun out of its reach like some Hong Kong film star on wires.

I might have been mistaken, but I think our words were giving Lilith extra speed and strength. Encouraged, I started stepping faster and spoke the chant a little quicker. William nodded, as though to let me know no matter whatever else he missed, he "got" this part. I smiled back at him. I had no doubt that he understood what we were doing, which was raising energy—a basic step in any working ritual.

The only bad part seemed to be that the ghosts seemed affected by it too. Their soft moans increased to a howl. Wind whipped at my clothes as we continued to tramp around the circle chanting.

Mátyás stomped his feet in rhythm with the chant, but started singing something else entirely, something in Romany. I hated when he went off script like that! The song was beautiful, haunting, and a little sad, but I had no idea what spell he might be casting.

Athena seemed distracted by it as well. Taking advantage, Lilith managed to land another punch. It was supposed to be a sucker punch to the gut. But this time, Her knuckles grazed off Athena's breastplate with a hollow clang. Athena didn't even bother to look wounded. Her eye tracked Mátyás menacingly, but he only seemed to goad Her with whatever it was he sang.

Oh, I was really annoyed now. I hated not knowing what was transpiring. That was it. After alchemy, I'd demand Sebastian teach me Romany.

Lilith kept up the fight, but Athena seemed to have found

another target. I increased the desperation of my chanting, but it didn't seem to be working nearly as well as whatever it was Mátyás was saying to Her.

When our circling brought him close, Athena raised Her spear and struck Mátyás through the heart.

There was a deafening explosion. Bright white light flashed so brilliantly I had to turn my head.

Mátyás stood stock-still, his eyes wide. Stiffly, he fell over backward, breaking the circle. William stopped moving so abruptly I almost crashed into him.

"We are satisfied with the offer," Athena's noncorporal voice said, and then She vanished.

Lilith, meanwhile, appeared at Mátyás's side, at least the part of him that still lay within the circle—his feet. "Noble, foolish boy," She said softly. She lay a hand on his boot. "But you are still my creature."

All the while, I scrambled to hastily uncast the circle. Lilith lifted her hand to stop me as I passed by Her.

"Allow me," She said. With a wave of Her hand the guardians disappeared.

The ghosts broke through the remains of the weakened sphere and darted around Lilith, like moths to a flame. They reached out and stroked Her hair and face, and tugged at the hem of Her gown. She kissed each as it passed, and so doing, dismissed it.

I suppose I should have been afraid or horrified or both, but the intention of my ritual stayed with me. As I watched Her lovingly embrace the dead, I felt a strange sort of pride.

She was the Goddess who had chosen me, and now, I freely chose Her.

William rushed past me to check on Mátyás.

I should do the same, but first I opened my arms and welcomed my Mother.

She stepped up to me and placed Her palms against mine. We stared eye to eye, and I realized we were the same height. She wasn't perfect, but She was perfect for me.

As though that thought were a signal, Lilith took a step forward and melted into me. I felt Her instantly settle "home" in my abdomen.

I quickly joined William at Mátyás's side. He was already sitting up, shaking the snow out of his long stringy hair. "I hope that worked," he was saying.

"What did you do?" I demanded.

He coughed and patted his chest in the spot where the divine spear had pierced him. Once he cleared his throat, Mátyás said, "I gave Her what She wanted, a sacrifice."

"What who wanted? Lilith or Athena?" William asked. "Were those ghosts I was seeing?"

"What did you sacrifice?" I asked, ignoring William for the moment.

Mátyás gave me a weak grin, as William and I helped him to his feet. He brushed the snow off his butt and said, "My immortality. I told Athena she could have the damn 'gift.' Maybe now I can be a real boy, Geppetto."

I was about to tell him how stupid he'd been when a gunshot rang out.

9.

The Star

Like the urban guerrillas we were not, we all stood around stupidly looking for where the shot had come from. It never occurred to any of us to duck or drop to the ground for cover. Instead, we scanned the hills and the rows of stone markers. Luckily, the sound of shouting helped pinpoint the activity to just beyond the street on the other side of the large willow tree.

"Stop!" someone masculine yelled, quickly identifying himself by adding, "FBI!"

Dominguez crouched behind the thick trunk of a tree and peered out in the space between it and a six-foot-square gravestone with the name Harper. I followed his gaze to where he seemed to be staring and finally spotted three boys crouched behind a row of graves marked with Chinese characters. I strained to recognize them, but my only response was, "Who the hell are those guys?"

I'd been expecting to see the guys who attacked me in the parking lot, perhaps decked out in their shapeless parkas, but instead there were two dudes I didn't know. Though I thought maybe one of them might be the cute waiter from Susan's. I did notice, however, that one of them had a gun in his fist. And he was turning it in our direction.

Finally, it occurred to me to duck.

Grabbing Mátyás and William, I pushed us all to the ground just as something whizzed past my ear.

"Death to vampire witches!" one of the men shouted.

We landed in a heap. We'd been standing in a slight depression, but I still felt horribly exposed. Worse, my leg sprawled over my stepson's butt and my breasts pressed against the ribs of my best guy friend, but I didn't dare move. My heart beat double time. We were all breathing heavily as we waited for another bullet to sail past.

"Garnet," William whispered, "your ear is bleeding."

I reached up to touch the ear he stared at, and sure enough my fingers came away bloody.

"Too bad Papa isn't here. He could clean that up for you," Mátyás muttered, edging out from under my body. I clutched at his coat. Even though it made no sense, I didn't want him to stray too far away from us. It was like in a horror film: If you separate, you die. He seemed to understand my desire and huddled close, though not near enough to touch.

"Fine time to give up your immortality," I muttered. The cold seeped into the front of my coat. "We could really use a little vampire invulnerability right now, all of us."

"No shit," William agreed, with his chin pressed into the snow. "Or projectile magic."

That gave me an idea. I couldn't exactly throw magic at the kidnappers, but what about a few ghosts?

Maybe a few specters could act as a distraction to the gunman until Dominguez could reach him and take him down or whatever it is that brawny FBI guys did in situations like this. Thank Goddess Dominguez was psychic, I thought in his general direction, so he'd know what the plan was!

"You're doing something, aren't you?" William said, apparently noticing my face scrunched up in concentration.

"I'm thinking really hard at Dominguez," I said. "Then I'm going to try to see if I can sic a few ghosts on the kidnappers."

"We might as well help," Mátyás said, offering me his hand and, I sensed, his magical energy.

"Yeah," agreed William, taking my other gloved hand in his.

Did I have the best friends, or what?

Ironically, I knew there were restless spirits close by. I mean, the bodies of the Vatican witch hunters may have been relocated after their discovery, but they say traumatic events can trap a soul near where it died.

In my mind's eye, I went back to the night Parrish and I drove his van in through the gate near closing time. It had been autumn, and the trees had looked much like they did now—skeletal, bare, stark and black against a darkening sky. Sitting in the passenger seat, I remember I was in shock, muttering, "Oh God, they're dead. My friends. They're really dead."

Parrish had been like an anchor, holding me steady. He asked no questions, only providing answers and constant reassurances that everything would be okay. We'd stopped the van just over there, on that side of the lake opposite where we were now. He'd taken the bodies we'd wrapped in garbage bags with gravel for weight, and walked them one by one into the cold, black water of the shallow lake—sinking lower and lower until they disappeared forever from sight.

I asked them to rise up now. Haunt me.

William scraped snow up into his gloves and padded it into a ball. Once he had a good-size snowball, he set it aside and began making another. Mátyás gave him a wan smile and started doing the same.

In the center of the lake, I heard something splash—a fish jumping through the ice? I turned to look. Wisps of something like steam roiled over the ice sheet heading in this direction.

Ever sensitive, Mátyás turned to watch the smoky creatures' progress, their tendrils snaking out like probing hands. He shook his head at me, disapproving. "Myself, I'd have picked something a little less angry."

William glanced back, doing a classic double take. "Uh, yikes?"

"We're going to send them after the bad guys with the guns," I told the boys.

"If they'll go," Mátyás muttered.

I jabbed him in the ribs with my elbow. "Think positive, damn it."

Faces had begun to emerge, ghastly open maws stretched into silent screams. Like clouds, the images melted into nothing, then reconstituted into even more frightening visages.

Part of me wanted to panic, but I remembered the way Lilith kindly treated the ghosts that had been attracted to Her before. These were the ghosts I had made. Like Lilith was the Mother of Demons, I had birthed these.

I would and could and *should* control these ghosts. If I accepted the fact that Lilith was the reflection of my inner Goddess, then the full implications of that meant that my core magic happened in places like this: dark alleys, pits of hell, and graveyards.

No fluffy unicorns for me.

Just then, the twisting cloud shapes surrounded us. Swirls of smoke snatched at my face. Wetness slid across my cheek. Cold seeped deep into my skin. The certainty I felt about my plan slithered into the mist. Voices whispered in my ear, "Killer." They moaned. "Murderer."

Each word slid, like a finger, over my flesh, raising goose pimples in its wake. I gritted my teeth, shivering. I *had* murdered these men when Lilith took over my body, but I still hated to hear it. I wanted to scream a denial.

Before I could open my mouth, Mátyás put a hand on my shoulder. Just feeling the pressure of his touch helped focus my mind, which threatened to spin off into guilt. I took a deep breath, swallowing my desire to run screaming, while brushing the ghost hands off me like so many spiders' legs. The spirits continued to churn the air around us making it hard to breathe. We needed to do something soon, or the ghosts would overwhelm us regardless of our intentions.

Mátyás placed a snowball into my gloved hand, like he was handing me a clue. I blinked at it stupidly.

"Let's throw them," Mátyás said when it was clear I didn't get his meaning. "You know, focus a ghost on it, and pelt the bad guys with 'em."

"Dude!" William said cheerfully. "Now you're talking."

I wasn't quite sure that one could "focus a ghost" onto a snowball like the game of pinning a tail on the donkey, but, what the heck, I didn't have any better ideas. And maybe it would stop the infernal moaning in my ears.

I reached up my hand with the intention of just grabbing one of the spirits out of the air and threading it into the snowball. Lilith rose up in me, adding Her power. She was the Mother of all the things that went bump in the night, and so I felt Her love course through me like a wave. "Come, my children," I heard myself say with Her voice.

When I felt I had something, I pulled it down and jabbed it into the center of the ball. Sitting up just enough to take aim, I tossed it.

The ghost looked like a streamer flowing off the back side

of the ball. It spattered to the left of where the kidnappers crouched. Before I hit the ground again, I saw them aiming their gun. But that was when William and Mátyás let loose a barrage of balls. And ghosts. Pretty soon everything around where the Illuminati Watchers/vampire hunters hid was a vortex of white: ice, snow, and spirit bits.

"Help," we heard them shout. "We're being attacked by . . ." and "what the hell is this?"

"Snow ectoplasm!" William suggested helpfully. We laughed.

Suddenly, a whole herd of cars descended on us, brakes screaming, doors slamming, as men and women in trench coats jumped out, brandishing weapons and shouting, "FBI!"

Wow, so this was what the cavalry looked like.

"You've got a little ghost there." Dominguez frowned and hooked a finger through my hair, as though pulling something out. We both stared at the wispy thread of smoke that he dissipated with a shake of his hand.

I shivered. I was going to be feeling their creepy crawliness all over me for a week.

"Ectoplasmic snowballs?" Dominguez said. "This is a new one, even for me."

"You're turning into a regular Fox Mulder," I teased him with a poke of my finger.

"Perish the thought," he said with a grimace.

A group of well-armed FBI agents, including Special Agent Peterson, hauled the surly youths into nearby cars. The waiter I'd found so charming at Susan's spat in my general direction and muttered something about witches and whores that he was lucky I didn't quite catch.

"Who are those guys, anyway?" I asked Dominguez as the door slammed on the waiter's face.

Dominguez looked at me as if to ask if I was kidding around. "Your kidnappers, right?"

"Um, wrong," I said. "My kidnappers were nerds with positive political message shirts and curly hair. Kind of cute in their own gawky way, but not ruggedly handsome like that guy."

"Are you sure?"

Well, actually, I wasn't. "Okay, actually, I never saw my kidnappers. I had my eyes closed. But I assume they were the same guys that jumped me in the parking lot, although, honestly, other than their shirts, I didn't really get a good look at them either."

"So what you're saying is that these could be the guys."

I looked over to where William and Mátyás sat in William's car, and sighed. "I don't know. It doesn't feel right."

"Don't give me that mumbo-jumbo. These are the guys I've been after," Dominguez said matter-of-factly. "These are the people running the vampire-hunter front that are working with James Smythe. You're not going to have any trouble from that quarter anymore."

He sounded so convincing that I didn't have the heart to disagree. I shrugged. "Okay."

"Oh, I almost forgot to tell you. Sebastian is out on bail. He's waiting for you."

We met Sebastian at a Jewish deli across the street from a Catholic women's university.

The restaurant was at the back of the store. A husky guy took us to a seat in a narrow room. The tabletops were Formica and the chairs could have been taken from a cafe in the 1950s. On the walls were oversized pictures of someone's family, presumably the owner's, in various professionally done photos.

Sebastian looked a little rough around the edges—a bit too thin, with dark circles under his eyes—but his expression brightened when he saw us. Mátyás, William, and I wrapped him in a giant bear hug.

Over several cups of coffee, we caught up on everything. Turns out Sebastian's lawyers convinced James to confess. Between that and the concealed weapon and the antistalking laws in Minnesota, he'd been extradited to the U.K.

He was a little shocked at what we'd been up to, though.

"Shot at you?" he repeated, and then he said something in Romany that made Mátyás chuckle.

I shook my finger at Sebastian. "You're teaching me that language as soon as possible."

"Yeah," said William. "It would have been nice to have a heads-up before Mátyás sacrificed his immortality."

Sebastian, who had been sharing a secret smile with Mátyás, blanched. "You what?"

Mátyás shrugged it off with a casual lift of his shoulder. "Oh, Papa, please. Living forever has been such a hassle. I'm glad to be rid of it. Now I can finally grow older—"

"And die," Sebastian finished, grief heavy in his tone, as if he'd lost Mátyás already.

Weirdly, I don't think any of us at the table outside of Sebastian had really considered the implications of that particular cost of Mátyás's sacrifice. William's eyes were wide. My hand covered my mouth in horror. Mátyás tried to act nonchalant, but the hand that held his coffee mug trembled.

"Everyone dies," he said with a sniff. "It's natural, Papa."

"What's natural is for a father to die before his son, not live on long after."

"Oh, Sebastian," I said. "I'm so sorry."

But Sebastian wouldn't be consoled. He got up and walked away from the table, leaving William and I to stare at Mátyás.

"Are you really ready to die?" William asked.

"Of course not, stupid," Mátyás said a bit harshly. "I'm not doing it anytime soon either, so you can all stop burying me already."

So we left it at that and talked about the weather and what their plans were now that the excitement was over until Sebastian came back from wherever it was he'd gone off to.

He gave Mátyás's shoulder a brief squeeze before sitting down but otherwise didn't mention it again.

William and Mátyás explained that they'd had enough adventure and were ready to head back to Madison. They offered to caravan with Sebastian and me, but Sebastian had another idea. From his coat pocket, he pulled out two airline tickets.

"Paris," I read. "Are you sure?"

"We need a vacation from our honeymoon," Sebastian said with a tired smile. "It was what I could get on short notice. Unless you think we'll be haunted by Gods and Goddesses . . . ?"

I was pretty sure I wouldn't be having double vision now that my second Goddess had gone, but I'd also embraced the fact that "normal" life for me was anything but. "We're always going to be haunted," I said. "So we might as well do it in style."

Speaking of style, I was a little dismayed at Sebastian's choice of replacement hotel. The place was called the Thunderbird and the entire building seemed to be decked out in what could only be called Native American–inspired, politically incorrect tackiness. There were totem poles in the reception area, for crying out loud.

"This is a little different from the Saint Paul," I muttered quietly. While the concierge printed our receipt and key cards, we leaned our elbows on the desk.

"Kind of cool, huh?" Sebastian smiled broadly enough to show off the pointed tips of his canines. "We should have come here in the first place, don't you think?"

"Sure," I said somewhat wanly, not being nearly as fond of kitsch as he was. "Well, it's only until we can get a cab in the morning for our flight to Paris." Now that I *was* excited about.

Our room was a sight to behold. A ginormous throw rug decorated in faux Indian designs covered a large section of the floor. The light fixture was a rustic-looking wagon wheel, and over the bed hung an overly romanticized Western-style picture of a Native warrior on horseback.

"Is this place for real?" I asked as I set my suitcase on the floor near the TV.

"This is one of those it's-so-wrong-it's-right places," Sebastian assured me. He flung open the window blinds to let in a view of Highway 494. We could see the airport's Humphrey Terminal and the large stretch of Fort Snelling military cemetery's precisely spaced white headstones.

"Great view," I said, coming up beside him. Cars and trucks stood in bumper-to-bumper traffic. I sighed. At least it wasn't snowing. The day had stayed cold, which meant the sky was crystal clear—not a cloud in sight. The sun shone so brightly it hurt my eyes.

"I don't care what you think." Sebastian sat down on the bed with a happy bounce. "This place is cool."

"I wonder what Micah would think of it." Micah was a sometime friend who was Dakota Indian and, as it happened, the embodiment of the Trickster God Coyote.

Sebastian lay back and tucked his arms under his head. Apparently noticing the wagon-wheel light fixture for the first time, he snorted. "Are you kidding? Who could take this seriously?"

Seeing Sebastian stretched out on the bed—the lean lines of his body outlined against taut fabric—caused Lilith to quiver along my nerves. I think I must have growled seductively, because he looked up quizzically at me.

Well, it was our honeymoon, wasn't it?

He must have understood the look on my face, because a slow smile spread across his.

"Do you want to watch some cable?" I teased, as I lowered myself onto the bed and proceeded to crawl up the length of his body.

"Or how about some sightseeing?" A broad smile spread across his face.

I kissed his chest chastely. "Great idea. I mean, it's worked out so well."

"Honestly, I am a little sad we never got to the theater or that park with the giant cherry in it," he murmured in between the soft pecks on his lips that I gave him. Reaching his arms up, he caressed my shoulders.

"Too cold," I said, nibbling lightly on his lower lip.

"Still, the Guthrie is supposed to be pretty good," he said, pretending disinterest.

"We can come back," I said, deepening the kiss. "Or see something in Paris."

"I don't know. I think we should really go—ah!"

His suggestion was cut off by a well-placed squeeze. I straddled Sebastian and put my hands on his chest as though to hold him down. Lilith purred deep inside, combining Her strength and mine. Sebastian's eyes widened in surprise, but his smile was wolfish.

Leaning down, I kissed his lips. He opened his mouth to mine, and I felt the sharpness of his fangs against my tongue. The sensation excited Lilith. At Her prompting, I slid my hands down Sebastian's body until I caught his wrists. I pulled them up over his head and pinned them there with all of Lilith's strength.

"Oh my," Sebastian said, his body clearly responding to his enjoyment of our turnabout position. His cock strained against the fabric of his jeans and pressed into my mound. I ground against it slightly, making Sebastian struggle against his bondage. His resistance only served to arouse me.

I felt the tips of my nipples stiffen. I kissed him again, deeply, and let my body leisurely stretch across his, teasing my own sensitive breasts. Sebastian arched his back urgently. Our bodies pressed together hotly.

And we hadn't even taken our clothes off yet.

That needed to change, fast.

Letting go of Sebastian's wrists, I pulled my shirt over my

head and tossed it aside. I allowed Lilith's strength to tear my bra off with a snap. Sebastian's hands instantly cupped them, his thumbs stroking the sensitive areolas. Shivers ran down my spine, deep into my core. I threw my head back and rocked against him with the rhythm of each caress. He groaned.

Taking pity on him, I lifted myself up just enough to unzip his pants and free his cock.

I gripped his shaft in my hand, and Lilith flashed him a toothy, possessive grin. Sebastian actually looked a bit nervous, if also hopeful. I don't think he was disappointed when I took him into my mouth or with the fierceness of my . . . er, Her . . . or was it Our skill?

The disorientation I felt wasn't the ground-swaying sort of having two Goddesses fighting over bodily possession of me, but it was more than a little disconcerting to be awake at the same time as Lilith. It had happened before, but rarely have we been quite so integrated, and, shall we say, in tune.

Lilith and I were having fun.

Quickly shimmying off him, I tossed off my pants and underwear.

But Sebastian was ready for me. Taking hold of my wrists this time, he flipped me onto my back. The bed bounced on squeaky springs as we switched positions. I felt Lilith retreat slightly, as he pressed his lips into mine hungrily. It was my turn to play.

Arching my back, I returned his probing, strong kiss. My nipples tickled against the fabric of his shirt. My legs stretched to receive him. We met each other in a pounding, heated rush. I gasped, but he held on tightly.

His head bent to nip lightly at my neck, but he only taunted me with each soft bite. He drew no blood, but his intense rhythm took my breath away.

It didn't take long at all until I came and he followed shortly after.

"Wow," I heard him say under his breath as I fell into a deep, satisfied sleep.

We had an easy morning filled with a complimentary continental breakfast and a lot of sheepish grins at each other over the breakfast table. "You know," Sebastian said finally. "We could do that again anytime . . . the three of us."

Lilith purred deliciously at the idea, but I couldn't help but shake my head with a little laugh. How lucky was Sebastian? He could have a ménage à trois anytime he wanted. Of course, it had been nice to have Lilith there. It felt strangely complete, like more of me had participated.

"Yeah," I finally said into his smiling face, which was beginning to show a trace of anxiety over my slowness in responding. "We'd like that."

In fact, Lilith was already imagining all sorts of scenarios involving Sebastian-Lilith shows of strength. My cheeks burned deep crimson even as I leaned over to whisper some of Her more tantalizing ideas into his ear.

We got so excited by the possibilities that we managed to miss the shuttle to the airport. Miraculously, an unhired yellow taxi waited just outside the door.

I was so pleased that we weren't going to have any more airport mishaps that it wasn't until we we'd missed the turn into the terminal that I noticed our cabbie was a troll. Not just any troll either. He was the mossy-haired bus-driving troll I'd seen earlier.

"Um, sir?" Sebastian was saying, pointing to the rapidly retreating International Terminal. "I think you missed our exit."

"It's a troll, Sebastian," I explained, my voice nearly cracking with frustration. "We're going to miss our flight. He's probably going to eat us or whatever it is trolls do."

The car slowed into a steep turn as we headed for the Mendota Bridge. It was a huge, ornate stone bridge that spanned the Mississippi.

"I demand a toll," said the troll in a voice that sounded like gravel. The car continued to slow, and we veered onto the shoulder. He hit the emergency blinkers as we came to a stop in the middle of the bridge.

Sebastian was frowning and seemed to be gauging whether or not troll blood was poisonous to vampires. At least, that's what I figured, anyway, when I saw his fangs descend.

"What do you want?" I asked.

The troll turned to face us. His skin was the color of slate, and his eyes glittered darkly, like obsidian. Large ears drooped from a deeply wrinkled face. "I want your other Goddess. Where is She?"

His eyes seemed to search my whole body, as though I might be hiding Athena in my jacket pocket.

"Um, Greece?" I had no idea where She went after She stole Mátyás's immortality.

"Bring Her back," the troll demanded.

I didn't really want to.

Beside me, Sebastian's head swiveled suddenly, like a predator tracking prey. My eyes followed his gaze and I saw three young men clambering up over the railing of the bridge. They had on matching navy hoodies, but I could see the curl of a goatee on one sharp chin.

Larkin and my kidnappers!

"They work for you!" I said with sudden realization. Had Fonn been in on it too? After all, she had been at the ritual when Larkin conveniently hadn't been and gave up chasing us the second we'd headed toward the hotel.

Sebastian snarled. "Who are these guys? The billy goats gruff?"

I would have snickered, except at that same moment I got an idea. Wrenching the car door open, I stepped out onto the shoulder of the road. Cars whizzed by, tires singing on the metal grating of the bridge's surface. The troll quickly scrambled out after me. Sebastian, on the passenger side, leaped out and headed straight for the approaching boys.

Leaving me and the troll.

Standing up, he was massive. He had square, broad shoulders and the kind of slender waist I'd find very appealing, except for the whole knuckle-dragging thing he had going on. The troll lifted two bruising, hammer-shaped fists; I raised Lilith.

With a familiar surrender, I closed my eyes. Lilith's lava-hot spirit coursed along my veins, filling my body. I expected to happily sink into that no-place bliss and wake up to the aftermath, but when I opened my eyes I saw a rather surprised-looking troll.

He'd been bringing down his fists, Incredible Hulk–style, to smash me into the pavement. I stopped them easily with one hand, which I held over my head. My other hand slapped, open palmed, hard into his chest. He flew back about ten feet and stumbled back onto his butt.

Cars careened out of the way to avoid hitting him where he'd landed near the center aisle.

Out of the corner of my eye, I saw Sebastian laying down a little vampire smack down on the little billy goats. Even though there were three of them, they had no chance against his preternatural speed. One would only just be recovering from a smack upside the head when Sebastian appeared behind another to rip deeply into fleece and down with sharp fangs.

Feathers fairly flew.

Honks alerted me that the troll struggled back to his feet and had begun to charge me like some kind of faerie rhinoceros. I felt Lilith smile wickedly. My heart pounded in my chest but, for once, not with fear. Adrenaline coursed through me with each beat like an aphrodisiac. He was nearly on me. I took in a deep, exhilarated breath. Then, in a flash, I grabbed him by the coat and swung him in an arch, à la some World Wrestling Entertainment star. One part of me registered that he was far too heavy for my normal muscles, while another reveled in the ease at which I hefted his weight. Once I had good momentum going, I let go. He sailed over the railing and off the bridge. His screams echoed in the river valley followed by a deep-sounding splash.

Meanwhile, over by Sebastian, Larkin was the only one left standing. He caught my eye and shouted, "I'll always love you!" Rushing over to the railing, he paused for a moment. Then, with a bob of his Adam's apple, hoisted himself over the barrier and jumped after the troll. As soon as they could pick themselves up, the other two followed suit.

Sebastian and I leaned over the edge. Where the current bubbled, there was an open spot in the river, but I couldn't see any trace of the troll, Larkin, or the others.

"Oh my God." I could tell I was upset because I reverted to my pre-pagan swearing. "Do you think they're okay?"

"This is how the fairy tale ends, isn't it?" Sebastian asked. "That's how you defeat the troll, right?"

I nodded. "But do you think they're alive?"

"I don't think they're dead," he said. "That seemed more like an escape than a suicide."

"So they could come back."

"Maybe," Sebastian admitted.

"Okay. There's one more thing I need to do for it to really be all over."

"What's that?"

"I have to break a really old love spell."

Lilith's heat retreated, leaving me suddenly chilled. I shivered, feeling the soreness creeping into my muscles. An airplane roared overhead. Sebastian and I tracked its progress as it came in for a landing.

"Do you think we can still make our flight?" I asked.

"We're sure as hell going to try," Sebastian said, making a dash for the driver's door. I hopped into the front seat beside him. "What about your spell?"

"I'll do it while we drive."

"And then you'll explain why you needed to do it, right?"

"Right," I said without hesitation. My new life with Sebastian was going to be all about full disclosure.

Sebastian nodded as his eyes watched for a break in the bridge traffic. The muffler sputtered loudly as he revved the engine.

I buckled my seat belt and tried to remember what exactly I had done when I first ensnared Larkin in the spell. Had I made a sachet or a pouch? Did I sprinkle him with herbs?

I couldn't remember!

It just hadn't been that important to me at the time. I'd probably recorded it in my Book of Shadows, but on the night I'd fled from this town I'd left my journal behind along with everything else—except my cat.

Maybe what mattered more than the details was the intent. What I wanted with Larkin was closure. I wanted to break the spell to free him from his memories of me. I needed to make this right.

In my lap I cupped my hands into the shape of a bowl. I imagined filling my hands with bluish light. The car jerked as Sebastian swerved across lanes, but I concentrated on filling my hands with the energy of release. As I poured into it my regret, I also added forgiveness—for what Larkin had done to me but also for past callousness. I had better angels to answer to these days, even if one of them was the Queen of Hell.

In my mind's eye, a blue ball sparkled between my palms. Flashes of color representing my emotions flickered and danced in the light like fireflies. Once I got the impression I'd put in all the healing energy I could, I brought the ball to my lips and I mimed kissing it. After sealing the spell, I blew it in Larkin's direction.

I took a moment to release any excess energy into the floorboards of the taxi and then through the tires into the earth. Slowly, I came back to myself. The heater smelled of dust and stone.

"We're kind of stealing this cab, you know," I said to Sebastian, who was busy passing a semitruck that slowed as the road inclined.

"We'll find a bridge to leave it under. The troll will find it there."

I was satisfied with that. I gripped the dash as Sebastian hightailed it, New York cabbie-style, the rest of the way to the terminal.

In the airport parking lot we found a spot underneath a bridgelike pedestrian walk. Leaving the doors of the troll's cab unlocked, Sebastian tucked the keys into the glove compartment. If the troll was alive, he'd find it here. I grabbed our bags from the trunk. We needed to hurry if we were going to make it this time.

We were dashing across the street to the ticketing area's doors when I saw Fonn. She was standing at one of those electronic check-in spots, wearing a Delta Airlines uniform. Our eyes met as I crossed onto the curb. She started for me, and I felt an icy wind tug at my hair.

"What now?" I heard Sebastian snarl.

There was no way I was going to stand for another delay. Lilith roared up into me like a wildfire. I dropped my bags and ran toward Fonn. As we met, I slammed my fist into her gut with every ounce of Goddess I had in me. She went sailing across the crowded sidewalk, knocking down a bunch of people, crashing two cart stands, and bowling over a traffic cop.

When I turned to pick up my bags, I saw that Sebastian held the door for me. "That might work for the troll," he reminded me as I started to pass under his arm, "but I'm not sure it will with Fonn."

I was about to protest when I felt something soft bump up against my leg. I looked down and saw Hero rubbing against me. "Look who's back!" I squealed joyfully. Despite my awkward position halfway in the door, I was about to kneel down to pick up Hero when he hissed. I pivoted just in time to see Fonn leaping through the air to pounce on us. I had no time to react. Sebastian still held the door. I figured we were doomed, but, with a yowl and extended claws, Hero sprang at Fonn.

The two of them went rolling down the sidewalk.

"I love that cat," I told Sebastian. "He's going to come live with us in Madison, okay?"

Sebastian's eyes were wide as he watched the cat versus ice-giant battle. "Okay. Sure."

I tugged Sebastian's sleeve. "Come on. We're going to miss our plane."

"Are you sure?" he pointed vaguely in the direction of the commotion of spitting hisses and gale-force winds.

"Hero's got it. Trust me."

Somehow we made it to our gate just as they were calling for stragglers. At the scent of cinnamon and baking bread, security waved us through. The flight attendant smiled warmly when she saw our first-class tickets, and she showed us to plush, comfortable seats in the front of the plane. I let out the breath I was holding.

Sebastian still looked concerned, and he scanned the view outside the window. I, meanwhile, lay my head back with a deep sigh. I felt Lilith humming along my skin, and I knew, even if somehow Fonn got on this plane, I could totally kick her ass.

Sebastian and I sat in a cafe in the fifth arrondisse-ment gazing out at the rain-drenched streets surrounding the Panthéon. Our waitress, it turned out, was Kali, but I planned to give Her a nice tip, anyway, because She let us sit here for the last two hours just people watching and enjoying each other's company.

I'd heard from William and Mátyás, who called to let me know they'd made it home all right and that a skinny black cat showed up on my doorstep a few days later. Mátyás reported Hero was a bit scratched and hungry but had walked right into the house like he owned the place. Barney, apparently, disagreed, but they were working it out.

I held Sebastian's hand and smiled as the rain streamed down the window.

So were we.

Printed in the United States
by Baker & Taylor Publisher Services